FEAR OF FLAMES

ALEATHA ROMIG

NEW YORK TIMES BESTSELLING AUTHOR

A romantic thriller novel

By New York Times bestselling author Aleatha Romig

COPYRIGHT AND LICENSE INFORMATION

ALEATHA ROMIG'S MOST RECENT AND UPCOMING RELEASES

Visit Aleatha's store to purchase e-books, signed books, and store exclusive items.

COMING SOON

NAUGHTY AND NICE - A Brutal Vows Holiday Novella

Marriage of convenience, Mafia/cartel romance, romantic suspense, friends to lovers, he falls first, strong heroine, possessive hero, dangerous romance

RECENT RELEASES

DEFENDING LOVE - Standalone Novel

A steamy, high-stakes, romantic suspense with body-guard vibes, second chances, and all the feels—set in the same world as the Sinclair Duet

TO HAVE AND TO HOLD - Brutal Vows, book five - March 2025

Arranged marriage, Mafia/cartel, enemies to lovers, age-gap, he falls first, protective hero, Romeo and Juliet vibes, dangerous romance

QUEENS AND MONSTERS - Brutal Vows, book four - January 2025

Arranged marriage, Mafia/cartel, alpha hero, virgin heroine, touch her and die, family saga, he falls first, possessive hero, sheltered heroine, dangerous romance

BOUND BY A PROMISE – Brutal Vows, book three - October 2024

Arranged marriage, age-gap, forbidden, Mafia/cartel dangerous stand-alone romance

ONE STRING – July 2024

Aleatha's Lighter Ones - Second-chance, enemies-to-lovers, fake-date, little-sister's-best-friend, forbidden, stand-alone contemporary romance

TILL DEATH DO US PART- Brutal Vows, book two - June 2024

Arranged marriage, enemies to lovers, Mafia/cartel, he falls first, stand-alone, dangerous romance

NOW AND FOREVER – Brutal Vows, book one - May 2024

Arranged marriage, age-gap, Mafia/cartel stand-alone romance

LIGHT DARK – April 2024
Cult, psychological thriller, forced proximity, romantic suspense stand-alone
*Previously published through Thomas and Mercer as INTO THE LIGHT and AWAY FROM THE DARK

REMEMBERING PASSION – Sinclair Duet book one – September 2023
Scorching hot, second-chance romance filled with the suspense and intrigue

REKINDLING DESIRE – Sinclair Duet, book two – October 2023
Scorching hot, second-chance romance filled with the suspense and intrigue

For a complete list of all Aleatha Romig's works, turn to BOOKS BY ALEATHA at the end of this novel.

SYNOPSIS:

She writes thrillers for a living, but nothing could prepare her for the one she's living now.

By day, Michelle Holdcraft is the quiet woman-next-door in small-town Indiana. But by night, she's *D. Valentine*, a bestselling thriller author with a mind for murder and secrets.

Her real life?

Completely ordinary. Until one unplanned trip to visit her estranged father in Iron Falls, Massachusetts, flips everything upside down.

She wakes to a gunshot only to find her father's body in a pool of blood on the first floor and flames engulfing the walls.

She barely escapes the burning house. Fleeing barefoot into the snow, Michelle becomes the only witness to a crime that no one in Iron Falls wants solved. Especially the sheriff.

Hiding in the snowy pines as she watches her father's home burn, Michelle doesn't know what to do, until a mysterious man appears, offering to help her—to save her life.

Michelle has never met Fletch—surely, she would remember this handsome and dangerous man if she had. However, Fletch knew her father and knows a lot about her, including her alter ego and her mother's mysterious death.

With limited options, Michelle accepts Fletch's help. It isn't until she sees the large tattoo across his wide shoulder blades that she is shaken to the core. Michelle has seen that exact tattoo before—on her father.

Fletch might be her only ally... but he is hiding something. Somehow, her life has become one of her thrillers.

This time, the heroine doesn't get to write the final page. The story's out of her hands—and the ending might just kill her.

Have you been Aleatha'd?

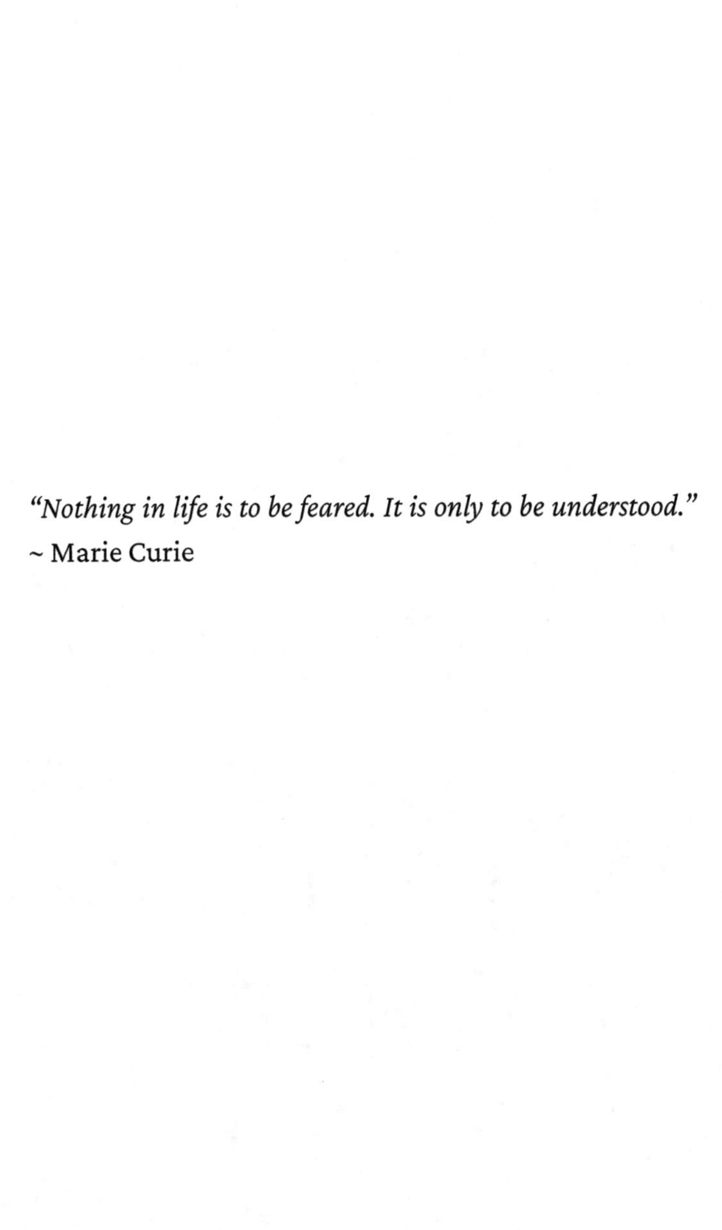

"Nothing in life is to be feared. It is only to be understood."
~ Marie Curie

PROLOGUE~

Shelly Holdcraft woke from her sleep. With the alert eyes of a seven-year-old, she peered around her bedroom, searching the shadows for movements. Colorful circles of light danced on the carpeting from her butterfly nightlight.

Getting out of bed was the scary part. Her mind filled with the same questions. What if someone was under her bed? What if there was a monster in the closet? Shelly wasn't sure where those questions came from. Her parents said she had an overactive imagination.

The thoughts probably came from her camping trip last summer with her Girl Scout troop. They sat around a roaring campfire while the older girls told ghost stories. As Shelly shrieked and shivered with her friends, she wondered what scared her more, the stories about ghosts and monsters or the crackling of the campfire.

On the way home from the camping trip, Shelly asked her mom about ghosts and monsters. Tracy, her mom, assured her that ghosts, Frankenstein reincarnations, and zombies weren't real.

Out of her room, as Shelly started for her parents' bedroom, a light from downstairs caught her attention. Quietly, she went down the staircase and through the dark hallway and living room. Light came from the slightly opened door to the basement.

Normally, Shelly didn't mind the unfinished basement. She often went down there to help her mom with the laundry or search through boxes of treasures. It was when darkness came that she recalled the stories around the campfire. Maybe it was the flickering flames of the old gas furnace. Or perhaps the shadows that lurked in the corners, the pipes that made strange noises, or the coolness of the cement floor beneath her bare feet.

She stood at the door, debating if she should descend the old wooden staircase. Curiosity was a strange motivation. The sound of her dad's voice propelled her to move forward and downward. She stopped on the landing where the staircase changed directions. Dad sounded different. There was an edge to his voice that she didn't recognize. His words didn't make sense.

"Roger."

The one word floated through the damp basement air as Shelly turned the corner at the bottom of the old steps and spotted her father's back. He wasn't wearing his police uniform. He was seated on a tall stool near his workbench, wearing a white t-shirt and pajama pants.

Shelly noticed his tense shoulders and straight neck. In front of him was the old hand radio he'd been fiddling with over the last few years. He explained it was like the CB radios the truckers used. Last she recalled, he hadn't gotten it to work.

The sound of a scratchy voice replying let her know it was now working. Or maybe it wasn't. The reply didn't make sense. Her dad hurriedly scribbled on a notepad as the voice spoke in odd words arranged in an unfamiliar pattern.

"Copy. Male. Mike, Alfa, Lima, Echo." Pause. "Ten-year-old. Tango, Echo, November." Pause. "Yankee Echo Alfa Romeo." Pause. "Oscar Lima Delta. Over."

"Copy," Dad replied. "Last seen. Lima, Alfa, Sierra, Tango." Pause. "Sierra, Echo, Echo, November. Over."

"Hammond. Hotel, Alfa, Mike, Mike, Oscar, November, Delta. Over."

Her dad was so focused on the conversation, he didn't notice Shelly watching with amazement. For as long as she could remember, she'd been told not to interrupt adults; however, she wanted to go closer. The curiosity was overwhelming.

What did these strange words mean?

It was as if her father knew a foreign language. Except it wasn't foreign—not like the Spanish or French she'd heard. These words were English. What made them unusual was that they were spoken in such a strange pattern. A shiver scurried over her skin.

As quietly as Shelly went down the stairs, she returned up, keeping a careful eye on the basement shadows. Her feet warmed as she made her way up to the second story and the soft carpeting.

Shelly's mom met her at the top of the stairs to the second floor. "Are you okay, honey? Why aren't you in bed?"

Shelly leaned into her mother and wrapped her arms around her mother's waist. "I woke up and was scared. I saw a light." She looked up with her blue eyes as round as saucers. "Dad's talking funny in the basement."

"Funny?"

Tracy squatted down to Shelly's height and widened her smile. "Silly, you're not supposed to be down in the basement in the middle of the night."

"Dad fixed that funny radio."

"He did?"

Shelly nodded. "Do you think he'll show it to me later?"

"I'm sure he will if you ask. Now, let me get you a drink and tuck you back in bed."

Back in her bedroom before getting in bed, Shelly bent down and lifted the eyelet bed skirt. Her heart jumped in her chest when her black cat, Ebony, came out and stretched, rubbing his head against Shelly's leg.

"The basement at night is scary," Shelly told her mom when Tracy returned with a glass of water.

Sitting on the edge of Shelly's bed, her mom handed her the cool glass. "The basement can be frightening, especially to someone with as good of an imagination as you." Her smile made Shelly feel better. "Just remember what it's like down there in the light and hopefully, that will help you remember that it's safe."

Shelly took a sip of the water, then handed her mother back the glass. With her eyelids growing heavy, she asked, "Are you sure there aren't monsters?"

Tracy tipped her forehead to her daughter's. "Not the kind your friends talked about. Those came from stories and legends. They're like the books in the library. Ideas that people made up."

"Okay."

Tracy kissed Shelly's forehead. "Goodnight, sweetheart."

It would be years later, but eventually, Shelly would learn that not only did monsters exist, but there was reason to fear the flames.

CHAPTER

ONE

Twenty-one years later

Michelle's body trembled as she hunched down, hidden among a row of pine trees, her bare feet buried deep in the snow and her body wedged between the heavy branches. It wasn't only the temperature or her lack of clothes causing her to shake—she'd run from the house in only her nightclothes and panties—the trembling came with the growing terror that someone nefarious was out there, the same someone who struck the match and sparked the flames now engulfing the house where she'd been sleeping.

"Michelle. Shelly."

The deep voice carried by the cold wind confirmed

her fear, taunting and stretching her nerves. Her breath caught, filling her lungs with chilled, smoke-filled air as the person walking around the perimeter of the remains of her father's house came into view. While she hadn't recognized the voice, there was no mistaking the person calling out to her.

In the orange illumination from the flames, she watched the man's boots stepping in and out of the melting snow, the rifle in his hand, and most importantly the badge on his heavy coat.

Closing her eyes, she wished for invisibility. It was a childish wish for a grown woman, but there was something about losing your last remaining parent that had a way of sending your thoughts into childish dreams.

"Shelly, honey, I know you're out here. I saw your car in the garage. Come on, honey. Denny wouldn't want you to freeze."

A lump of emotion caught in her throat. Denny, or Dennis Holdcraft—her father—would never again be concerned with Michelle or anyone. That was undeniable. The other fact that solidified in her chest with steely determination was the realization that Sheriff Perkins didn't want to save Michelle from freezing.

His quest to find her was due to what she'd witnessed.

If Michelle made it to morning alive, she would have a story to tell, one that, no doubt, the sheriff wanted silenced.

When she opened her eyes against the harsh blaze, the silhouette of a second man came into view. He was standing with and speaking to Sheriff Perkins. With the crackling fire only yards away and the rustling of the branches above, Michelle couldn't make out what the two men were saying, nor did she recognize the second man.

It wasn't that she knew every person in this godforsaken town. Her father moved to Iron Falls in the middle-of-nowhere Massachusetts eight years ago after the passing of Michelle's mom.

Michelle rarely visited, yet she and her father spoke often via phone or video calls.

Trying to ignore the pins and needles in her freezing extremities, Michelle kept watch on the two men. Every now and then, they would turn a full circle, their heavy boots trampling the slush and mud near the burning structure.

Michelle's thoughts circled back to fleeing the fire.

Could those men track her footprints in the snow?

She hoped that the heat of the blaze melted away the evidence of her escape.

Escape?

She was trapped between the sheriff she feared and a frozen wilderness.

As the two men spoke, the sheriff maintained his grip of the long gun, the heel butting against his shoulder. It was the second man who seemed more animated, his head shaking and his hands gesturing.

If only she could hear their words.

Michelle fought the urge to fall apart. She couldn't, not after what she'd seen. She knew why the sheriff wanted to find her. She was the last person to see Dennis Holdcraft, her father...

Michelle would have liked to have finished that thought with the word *alive*.

That wasn't her. It didn't take a great detective to surmise that one of the two men before her was the last person to see him alive.

Less than an hour earlier, the blast of the gunshot awakened Michelle from a sound sleep. In her tired state, she thought the sound was the blowing of a transformer due to the heavy snow. The blast shook the house with the bang of a firework. Never in her wildest dreams had she imagined that the sound was a gunshot.

When Michelle descended the stairs, she stopped, transfixed. On the floor of his living room, her father lay, his body contorted, and a dark pool of blood growing around his head.

It was almost too much for her mind to comprehend.

Michelle wasn't supposed to be in Iron Falls tonight.

Her surprise trip to visit her father was supposed to last one day—come and go.

It was Mother Nature who changed her plans.

Despite the blizzard warning, her dad encouraged

her to leave while there was still daylight.

Michelle assumed it was because he didn't want to spend time with her. Whenever they were together in person, he always remarked at how much Michelle looked like her mother, Tracy, the love of his life and the woman he couldn't get over.

The snowfall grew dangerous. She had to spend the night. Her plan was to take off Monday morning if the roads were clear.

As the roaring blaze destroyed the evidence of her father's murder, Michelle reasoned that maybe it wasn't that her dad didn't want her close—maybe, instead, he was trying to protect her.

She wanted to believe that.

He'd always been her protector.

And now he was gone.

The sudden movement of the second man grasping the sheriff's elbow drew Michelle's attention. The second man led him away from view, moving toward the front of the house.

Realization hit almost simultaneously.

Sheriff Perkins mentioned seeing Michelle's car. That meant he'd been inside the garage before the blaze. Of course he assumed a car with the Indiana license plate would belong to Denny's daughter.

She swallowed as she stared out of her hiding place. The roof of her father's house crashed, sending sparks and flames into the icy night sky.

Her suitcase

Her car.

Her laptop.

Her keys.

All were inside the burning house, the last two probably nothing more than melted blobs of plastic. Her mind scrambled with possibilities. Without a vehicle or shoes, where could she go? Who could help?

The sheriff wasn't a possibility.

Was there anyone she could trust?

Why would anyone want her father dead?

The questions continued piling up with no answers to follow.

A brief flash of headlights signaled the leaving of a vehicle. Michelle hoped the other man convinced Sheriff Perkins to leave. That reality filled her with both relief and also alarm.

Here she was—all alone—watching her father's home burn to the ground, knowing his dead body was inside.

Crouching down, she wrapped her arms around her shoulders, remembering the dinner they'd shared only hours ago. The stories they'd told about her mom and about Michelle's childhood. Dad was a retired policeman who could talk for hours. He had enough stories to fill volumes of tomes.

Michelle couldn't possibly comprehend why anyone—much less a fellow law enforcement officer —would want him dead.

Lost in the cyclone of her thoughts as second-story

beams continued to crash to the ground, the sense of isolation consumed Michelle's being. No mother. No father. No transportation. No way to retreat to her life.

That loneliness enveloped her, muting the world around her.

She didn't hear or sense another person, not until a gloved large hand grasped her arm in a vise grip and lifted her to standing.

Her nearly frozen muscles protested as Michelle gasped, stood, and turned, meeting the dark stare of a stranger. Even with her height of five feet, seven inches, this man towered over her. His intense gaze brought back the surging circulation the cold had waned. She wanted to protest his breach of her personal space. However, as she took him in, from his hair covered by a stocking cap to the heavy coat over his massive body, any words she could think to form were muted.

"You're coming with me." His harsh baritone command came in vaper-filled clouds and echoed through her consciousness.

Michelle tried to wrench her arm loose as her words returned. "No. Let go of me. I don't know you. I'll scream for help." As soon as the last sentence left her lips, she knew it was an empty threat. Assuming the sheriff and other man were gone, there was no one who would hear.

The man lowered his mouth to her ear. "You have about twenty minutes before Sheriff Perkins and

Deputy Skiles return with the firefighters and more deputies. It won't take him long to determine you're the one who set Denny's house on fire."

Michelle shook her head. That's impossible. She'd never do such a thing. "I didn't." Emotion and memories bubbled in her throat as she gave up the fight to retrieve her arm from this giant of a man. Instead, she went slack, confessing what she'd seen. "He's dead. Dad. I saw him. Someone shot him."

The man leaned even closer, his warm breath scurrying over her exposed flesh. "And you're next if you don't come with me."

Michelle lifted her face, studying the unfamiliar man before her. "Who are you?"

"Right now, I'm your only hope. You're on your own now, and Daddy's not around to make these charges go away."

Michelle's lips opened in a gasp. How could this man know her history? "He never made—"

The grip of her arm grew tighter and his words more forceful. "Save your story. The priority right now is to get out of here."

Michelle looked down at her nightgown—actually, one of her father's old shirts and significantly insufficient for covering her body. "I can't leave like this."

Letting go of her arm, the man tugged on the front of his coat, unsnapping button after button and revealing a dark hoodie beneath. In a fluid motion, he pulled the coat from his arms and shoulders and wrapped it around Michelle's body. The sudden burst of warmth and masculine scent was a heavenly escape until her blood's circulation sped faster, bringing life and pain to temporarily frozen nerve endings.

Pulling her long copper-colored braid out from beneath the coat, she asked again, "Who are you?"

CHAPTER

TWO

Wordlessly, the man led Michelle away from the fire. In what direction she didn't know. Everything was mixed up in her mind. Iron Falls was the nearby town, small and seemingly friendly. Her father's property was on the outskirts, still considered Iron Falls yet miles from human neighbors. Elk, bears, wolves, and foxes roamed these wooded acres and open fields.

As her circulation hastened, the pain in her feet intensified to the point that each step was agony. "Please, my feet."

The man looked down, seeing her bare feet in the snow. With a shake of his head, he scooped Michelle from the ground, cradling her against his chest as if she weighed nothing when she knew that wasn't the case.

Those childish thoughts she'd entertained back at

the site of the blaze returned. No longer a woman in her late twenties, Michelle was a child, cradled by her dad. Trauma seized her thoughts. She rested her face against the stranger's soft hoodie as heat radiated from his chest, and the scent of burning wood filled her senses.

There was no reason to trust this man.

Were there reasons not to trust him?

In his embrace, as if in the eye of a storm, a sense of security soothed the recent trauma.

In his arms, she was carried.

How far did they travel?

How long had they been trekking through the snow?

While in her trance, once again, large snowflakes began to fall, landing on her eyelashes and cheeks. Michelle was on the verge of being lulled to sleep, an escape perhaps, when in the distance, the sound of sirens rang through the cold night air.

"Fuck," the man growled.

She lifted her head attempting to determine the direction from which the loud wailing came. "Are those fire trucks?" she asked, the first question she'd posed since asking the identity of the man holding her.

"Probably. Sheriff's cars and ambulances too."

Michelle shook her head. "My dad doesn't need an amb…" Her words trailed away. With tears teetering on her lower lids, she looked at the man's face. Even in the dark, she could make out his chiseled jawline with a dark stubble, prominent cheekbones, and strong, pursed lips—the latter filled with determination. His strength, demonstrated by his ability to continue to carry her, was evident. Still, she wondered who he was. "Why are you helping me?"

"I won't be helping you if they follow us." He stopped walking.

Michelle followed his gaze with hers, soon realizing they were at the shore of Iron Reservoir, the large body of water created by the Iron waterfalls. This time of year, the falls and reservoir were frozen solid. Despite the continued snowfall, with the sun now teetering on the horizon, she could make out shadows on the ice. She'd seen them before, dozens of small huts—fishing houses—out on the vast reservoir surface.

"This wasn't my plan," he confessed as he stepped toward the frozen water.

"I need warmth," Michelle admitted. "I can't have that on ice."

"You'd be surprised."

The strength Michelle had mustered to flee the scene of her father's murder was depleted. Currently, to her displeasure, her future was in the hands of this stranger. Michelle was stubborn about her independence. Nevertheless, whether she stayed on the shore and froze or was found by Sheriff Perkins or one of his deputies, she was afraid there would be no future.

The man carried her from the shore to the snow-covered ice. As they approached one of the buildings, Michelle assessed that the wooden hut was too small to hold both Michelle and the man. However, after he wedged the door open enough for their entry, the dimly illuminated inside was roomier than she'd imagined.

With a tentative gentleness, the man set Michelle on a wooden bench perched on top of a wooden platform and closed the door. Simply being out of the wind made the temperature within the hut seem downright comfortable.

As the man lit a Coleman lantern, the flame flickered within, bringing both illumination to the interior of the hut and the memory of her father's home ablaze. Without a word, she took in the surroundings.

There was a small section where there wasn't flooring. It was opened to the ice, with a round hole drilled nearly a foot into the depths. The hole was refrozen over, giving it a clear dark look. The walls of the hut contained shelves filled with provisions including blankets.

The man reached for one of the heavy blankets and handed it to Michelle. "I want to look at your feet. There could be frostbite. First, get warm while I make us some coffee."

In the light of the lantern, she could more clearly see his face. Her attention was pulled to the depths of his dark eyes. She looked down and thought about what he said.

Coffee.

Really?

Like a date?

She snickered under her breath. Right. Instead of Starbucks, let's have coffee in a fishing hut on a frozen reservoir. Michelle pushed that thought away. A man like him wouldn't ask someone like Michelle on a date.

"Do you have a coffee maker I don't see?" she asked.

He pointed to a small hotplate, one with an attached gas canister.

As the man pulled the stocking cap from his head, he revealed a dark-brown mop of messy hair. The next to go were his gloves, exposing strong hands with tattoos gracing his fingers. Each piece of clothing found a peg on the wall to hang and dry. He ran his long fingers through his tangled tresses, the length reaching his shoulders.

Staring in his direction within the dimly lit fishing hut, Michelle was certain she'd never met this man before. If she had, she'd remember. He could be on the cover of a romance book or starring in the latest Hallmark movie. He'd be the lumberjack in a small-town who helped the New York executive. The movie would end with her leaving her busy life and them settling in a cabin in the woods.

Michelle's profession of writing fiction had a way of seeping into her everyday thoughts. The coming to life of the nerves in her feet let her know this wasn't a holiday movie, and the ending was unwritten.

Curling her legs beside her, Michelle secured the blanket around her waist and legs. While its texture was scratchy, the added warmth made it worth it. Within minutes, between their body heat and the lantern, the temperature inside the small fishing hut grew. The circulation in her feet and lower legs felt as if something was nipping and biting at her flesh. The jolts were as painful as bee stings. Pushing the blanket away, she began rubbing her skin.

"Let me look at those," the man said, his tone less harsh than earlier.

Michelle pulled her feet back under the blanket and met his gaze. "My name is Michelle. I think you know that."

He nodded as he hunched down near her knees.

"And you are?" she asked for the third or fourth time.

He appeared to consider his answer before replying, "Fletch."

The name bounced through her thoughts, vaguely familiar. "Fletch, why did you help me—are you helping me?"

He lifted his chin. "First, let me see your feet."

Raising the blanket, Michelle slowly pushed her feet from the warm covering. As she did, Fletch lifted his cellphone and hit the flashlight app. The bright illumination put her feet in the spotlight as he tenderly lifted her heel and inspected her reddened skin.

"First-degree frostbite, I'd say."

"Are you a doctor?"

His dark eyes sparkled as he met her stare. "No, I'm not a doctor. I've seen my share of injuries, some man-made, others unintended. You couldn't grab shoes?"

"No," she answered matter-of-factly. When Fletch didn't respond, she went on. "There was the gunshot, and I went downstairs, I saw Dad…" New tears clogged her throat. "The fire was already running up the walls. I was afraid I wouldn't be able to go upstairs and make it down again."

Fletch nodded. "Good decision. I'm not sure what accelerant was used. The house went up fast. I suppose a little frostnip is worth the payoff of saving your life."

Michelle reached for Fletch's hand. Unlike in the snow and wind, there were no longer gloves separating them. For a moment, her gaze lingered on the place they touched. She felt the tingle of energy coming from him. He had the hands of a working man, strong and calloused. Slowly, she looked up, wondering if he was feeling the same electricity.

She cleared her throat. "You saved me. I would have frozen out there."

"If you were lucky." He retrieved his hand. "I was more concerned about what would happen if Ralph found you."

Ralph.

Ralph Perkins.

The sheriff.

"I think he's the one who killed Dad." She shook her head at the gravity and implausibility of her statement. Her gaze met Fletch's. "I didn't see it happen. It's a feeling. He was there so quick." She let out a sigh. "I don't understand. Why did he kill Dad? What does he want with me?"

Fletch handed Michelle his large gloves. "Put these over your toes. Don't rub them. That can cause more damage if the frostbite is severer than I assessed." He exhaled. "The goal is for the skin to warm but not too quickly."

Taking the gloves, she slid her feet inside. While they only covered up to her mid foot, the fur within was still warm from Fletch's hands. Next, she covered her feet again with the blanket. When she looked up, he was lighting the small hotplate.

Another flame.

Closing her eyes, she saw the fire consuming her father's house. With the speed at which the flames climbed the interior walls, incinerating the curtains and furniture, she barely had time to check for her father's pulse. There was none.

Oh God, she hoped there wasn't.

What if she missed it?

It wasn't that she wanted him dead.

She didn't want him to die by fire.

What a horrible death.

A single bullet would be better.

Fletch removed a large cooler hidden under the bench where Michelle was seated. Within were gallon jugs of water. For a moment, she considered asking why they couldn't use snow or ice, but the idea that a cooler kept the water from freezing was enough to fill her scrambled mind.

"Is this fishing hut yours?"

He shook his head.

"Then how do you know where everything is?"

"Because people are predictable. All you need to do is open your eyes and look around." After adding the coffee grounds and water, Fletch turned away from the old-school coffee pot and crossed his arms over his wide chest. "Tell me about Tracy's death."

CHAPTER

THREE

T racy—her mother.

"How do you know about my mom?"

Michelle's thoughts went back to eight years ago. The years warped into seconds of snapshots. A rapid display of images ran through her thoughts, their speed increasing like cards shuffled into a deck. She recalled that night.

Michelle opened the door to their home, the house where she'd lived most of her life with both her parents. Located south of Indianapolis, Indiana, the small city was quiet and uneventful. Michelle went to school in the area from kindergarten all the way through high school, where she was part of the State Championship Band. She made it home more often her first year away. Her sophomore year at Purdue University kept her busier. With her job, classes, and friends, she'd only made it back home one other time. It was already semester and holiday break.

"Mom. Dad," Michelle said loudly as she stepped inside the house. She called out again. Nothing. That wasn't like her parents. Usually, they were waiting for her. They knew she was on her way.

The inclement weather on I-65 and resulting traffic wasn't conducive to a quick drive. What usually took an hour and a half, doubled. Three hours after leaving her apartment, she was finally home.

Michelle dropped her backpack by the front door and called again, her voice echoing throughout the house. A decorated tree in the living room was the only illumination, filling the room with vibrant, colorful lights. A smile curled her lips as she walked toward the tree, drawn by the memories of the ornaments.

Her mom never threw anything away.

Her smile grew as she stared down at the picture of a toothless, childish her pasted to a wooden tree. Flipping the ornament, the year was written on the back. She made it for her parents in the first grade.

The ring of Michelle's phone made her jump.

Pulling it from the pocket of her jeans, she saw the screen said Mom. "Hi, where are you?"

"Oh good, you're home. I wanted to be there before you arrived," Mom replied. "I'm doing some last-minute shopping. And your father got called into work."

Michelle's heart sank. She wasn't expecting a welcome-home party, but she was expecting her parents. Disappointment sounded in her tone. "How long does Dad have to work?"

"Until seven tomorrow morning. There's a convention in town, and they needed more officers on the street."

There was always something. As the daughter of a police officer, Michelle was used to the interruptions caused by his work. "Are you coming home soon?"

"Yes," Mom replied. "I'll bring home a pizza, and we can catch up."

After ending Mom's call, she saw that she'd missed a few text messages. They were from high school friends. Their tight group had scattered to different colleges. Now, everyone was in town for the holiday. They were all asking her to meet them at Misty's house. It was an impromptu get-together, and they wanted Michelle with them.

Michelle wasn't trying to be difficult or rebellious. She was simply young. Instead of staying and waiting alone, she quickly wrote a note to her parents and left. When the party grew late, Michelle sent a text to her mom saying she was spending the night. After all, she still had her suitcase in her trunk.

"We can catch up tomorrow," Michelle texted.

At nearly four in the morning, the house of friends awakened to screaming sirens. Firetrucks and police cars raced past the front window as each friend woke up, drawn to the parade of lights.

"Did you hear something before the sirens?" Misty asked.

"No, I was asleep."

"I did," Taylor, another girl camped in the living room, said. "It was like an explosion or an earthquake."

Indiana rarely had earthquakes.

A cold chill scurried over Michelle's arms as she found her phone and contemplated calling her mother. Surely, Mom was awake with all the activity. Then again, Michelle didn't want to wake her if she wasn't.

Instead, she sent a text. "Mom, something happened in the neighborhood."

MISTY LIVED ONLY *a few blocks from Michelle's house.*

A SECOND TEXT. "If you're awake, let me know what you know."

MICHELLE LOOKED *up at her friends. "Maybe Mom heard something from Dad?"*

FLETCH OPENED a director's chair and set it facing Michelle. "Your mom's death was eventually ruled an accident. Initially, you were blamed."

Michelle's chest ached at the memories, the accusations, and even the questioning by the police. Her dad tried to intervene, but Michelle was nearly twenty years old and, according to the law, an adult. The conspiracy theories ran the gamut. The most believable was that Michelle accidentally, or intentionally, hit a burner on the gas stove. Without a flame to ignite it, the gas accumulated.

"I was cleared," she replied matter-of-factly.

"Your mother died in a house explosion, attributed to an accumulation of methane, yet no construction had occurred in the area. And now your father will be declared deceased due to an unexplained fire."

She sat taller. "My father was already dead. I heard the gunshot. When I went downstairs, he was on the floor. There was blood." She shivered. "The flames... someone started a fire to cover up the crime. You mentioned accelerant." Her eyes opened wide as she scooted closer to the wall. "Was it you?"

"No." Fletch's gaze narrowed. "Why would your parents be targeted?"

She shook her head. "I have no idea. My mom was a librarian—a great mom but as boring as they come. Dad was a policeman, thirty years with IMPD. Sheriff Perkins or that deputy with him killed my father or knows who did." She shook her head. "Dad's house is miles outside of Iron Falls. They were there too fast. I think they know what happened." Her gaze narrowed as she recalled her previous question. "Wait a minute. You were there fast too."

"I didn't hurt Denny."

"Why would anyone target him?"

The percolating coffee exploded in the glass top of the coffee pot, their bubbles interrupting the conversation. As Fletch stood, he pulled the hoodie over his head, further ruffling his hair and revealing a tight black dri-FIT shirt, the kind that hugs each muscle, each indentation and bulge.

She narrowed her eyes, wondering if she'd made the right decision. Maybe she should have trusted Sheriff Perkins instead of Fletch. Without conscious thought, Michelle scanned from his messy hair to his boots. The way his shirt hugged his toned abdomen and biceps made her realize why he had no problem carrying her through the woods. Either Fletch worked out religiously, or he was simply created to near perfection.

Noticing the obvious rise in temperature from the hotplate and lantern, Michelle unsnapped the large coat she was still wearing. Leaving it draped over her shoulders, she asked, "Am I safe with you?"

"I'm not a threat. Your safety is up for debate."

"You don't by chance see any spare clothes around here, do you?"

Fletch turned her way with a curl to his lips before turning a complete circle. "I don't see any clothes here. After dark, we'll move. He took a step and lifted his eye to a peephole near the door; one she hadn't noticed earlier. "The snow is falling heavier than before. That's

good. Along with the wind, our tracks should be difficult to follow."

"Are you a cop? You don't work with Sheriff
Perkins, do you?"

"I'm not employed by the sheriff's department."

"Private eye? Some kind of survivalist?" she questioned as he handed her the steaming cup of coffee.

"Sorry, no cream or sugar."

Michelle sighed. She liked both in her coffee. "The
warm mug feels great on my fingers." She took
another look around. "Seriously, how do I know I can
trust you?"

Fletch retook his seat across from her. "I'd say
that's up to you, but at the moment, your choices are
rather slim."

"Do you know more about my mom's death?" It
was a question she hadn't broached with anyone since
she was determined not guilty—not guilty, not innocent. Yes, she remembered the state prosecutor
making that distinction.

"The less you know, the better."

The small hairs on Michelle's arms stood to attention. "Less I know about what?"

"Why were you at Denny's house last night?"

"He's my dad."

Fletch nodded. "Why last night?"

"It was a surprise visit. I wasn't planning on staying. Dad is always..." She took a deep breath, deciding
to make a less emotional declaration. "...*was* always

concerned about the roads around here, especially when the weather got bad. I'd been in Boston over the weekend for an event. With a pause between projects, I decided to visit him on my way home. I hadn't seen him since he visited me a few months ago."

"Did he know you were coming?"

Michelle shrugged. "No. Like I said, it was a surprise."

Fletch inhaled and leaned back against the chair. "Did he act in any way unusual?"

She pushed through her memories. "He wanted me to leave—which wasn't unusual—but finally relented, allowing me to stay when the snow got worse." Her eyes opened wide. "Do you think he knew what was going to happen—that there was danger?"

"What do you think?"

Michelle didn't know what to think. Her gaze met Fletch's. "Do you seriously think Sheriff Perkins would have hurt me if he found me?"

"I think that there would be two casualties of the fire, not one. Dead men tell no tales."

Michelle smiled. "You know Disney didn't come up with that quote."

"Are you telling me," he asked with a hint of a grin, "that you're not a *Pirates of the Caribbean* fan?"

"I am. Remember, my mom was a librarian. She was all about research, not taking things at face value. The phrase is originally credited to a man" —Michelle tried to recall— "a religious man, I believe. Thomas Becon who lived in the sixteenth century."

Fletch tilted his face. "You sound like you take after your mom."

She wasn't sure, but that felt like a compliment.

"What else did your mom research?"

"Everything." Before Michelle could answer further, Fletch's phone buzzed, and he read a text message. When his dark eyes met hers, the spark that had been present a moment earlier was gone, leaving them a deeper black—a void.

"We can't wait for nightfall. We need to get out of here now."

"You can't be serious. It's daytime and we're in the middle of Iron Reservoir. We're sitting ducks."

"I've gotten out of worse."

FOUR

Tension rippled through the sheriff's cramped office as beyond the windows, the blizzard continued in the brightening morning sky. "Where the fuck could she have gone?" Ralph Perkins growled.

Deputy Skiles shook his head. "Sheriff, I didn't see a woman run from the house. Are you sure you saw her?"

"The car in the garage had an Indiana license plate. It was Denny's daughter's. I'm sure of that."

Tom Skiles wiped the perspiration from his forehead, leaving an ash mark much like the ones seen around town on Ash Wednesday. Tom's forehead didn't bear a cross, more of a giant smudge. His winter coat was covered with soot and reeked of smoke.

Sheriff Perkins sat in the weathered tall chair behind his cluttered desk. Taking a deep breath, he tried to prioritize his thoughts. First, the fire was mostly out. The investigators identified a body in the rubble. The scene was still too hot to retrieve the body. Once it was retrieved, it would take some time to make a positive ID. And then there was the possibility of a witness. He concentrated on that. "I'm sending Wilcox to Indianapolis. He can learn if Shelly is there or if I'm right and she's here."

Skiles took a seat in the wooden chair across from the sheriff. The lack of comfort was intentional. Ralph wasn't in the business of making his guests comfortable.

Ralph slapped the top of his desk, causing pens and papers to jump. "She's out there. They won't be happy if there's a possible witness." He leaned forward. "Drones. We could send up heat-sensor drones."

"Not in this weather. They'd be tossed around like paper airplanes. The council would shit a brick if we destroyed those drones after they fought you about paying for them."

Ralph hated bureaucracy to the point of obsession.

"What about an APB?" Skiles asked.

"Premature," Sheriff said. "It'd look suspicious." He took a cleansing breath. "Maybe my old eyes were playing tricks." He liked the sound of that, even though he knew what he'd seen. A woman, through the flames and smoke. He hadn't seen her face. The bright red hair was enough to identify Shelly Holdcraft.

"I'll call the chief of police in Indianapolis in a few hours. By then, we should have a possible identification. I'll ask them to give Shelly the news about Denny." His mind was sweeping through scenarios that wouldn't get him punished or dead. "No way she could get from here to there without a car. If they find her…"

Skiles shook his head. "Yeah, that car in the garage blew, blasting out the side of the garage. Shit, no one could make it away from there on foot."

Ralph's sleep-deprived mind was in overdrive. "If I'm right, we need to find her." He met his deputy's stare. "Where would you go? If you ran from Denny's?"

"Depends on what I'm wearing. If I had boots, coat, and all that shit, I might consider walking to town."

"We had cars and trucks up and down the road last night. No one reported a runaway woman." If Ralph were a cartoon character, there would be wisps of smoke coming from his ears.

Skiles exhaled. "Hell, I don't know." His eyes brightened. "The reservoir. It's frozen solid, and there's easily a dozen or more fishing huts out there."

Ralph suddenly stood, sending his chair flying. He bent down rubbing his left knee. "My joints don't like this cold. Look out that window. You're right. She'd search for a way to get out of the storm." He walked to the window and nodded. "If Shelly was in Denny's house and ran, either she's frozen in some snowbank and we won't find her remains until spring, or she sought shelter."

"Sheriff, Pete Morrow's boy trains hunting dogs for the Winston Hunting Lodge. I bet he's got some dogs that could track Denny's girl if she's out there."

Ralph turned back to his deputy. "Dogs need a scent. Anything with her scent went up in smoke or is under layers of ice from the tanks of water the fire department carted out there." He waved toward the closed door. "Go find out what they're saying about the investigation. We need to be prepared that they might be able to determine the COD." A grin curled the tips of his lips, giving him a sinister sneer. "How'd Denny seem the last few weeks?"

Tom, who was now standing, paused and tilted his head. "Same. Same as always."

The sheriff shook his head. "Quieter than usual. Kind of depressed." He nodded. "That's right. Dennis Holdcraft was depressed, possibly suicidal." His voice took on a sympathetic tone. "Real shame. Just pitiful."

No one had ever called Tom Skiles out for his intelligence. In the first grade, his teacher thought he should repeat the year. His father wouldn't hear of it. Despite his lower-than-average intuitiveness, Tom's lips too began to curl. "Right. After I report back what I learn about the investigation, I'll head over to Gloria's and get some coffee and breakfast. I'll let it slip about poor Denny's mental decline." He shook his head. "Sad story."

"Ask if anyone saw his daughter around. You know, she might have visited him because she was also worried about his well-being."

Tom made a salute gesture and opened the heavy door.

"Close that," Ralph barked. He wasn't in the mood for company.

As he retook his seat behind the desk, his private cell phone vibrated in his breast pocket. It was the call he'd been expecting.

"Morning. Ralph here," he said after hitting the green icon.

"That loose end, Dennis Holdcraft, tell me it's tied up."

Ralph sat forward. "He's taken care of, just like you asked."

"Good job, Sheriff. I had my doubts. Tell me what you found. Did we get the right guy?"

The Sheriff's shoulders slumped as he leaned back. "I didn't find anything to suggest that he had the type of operation you described. Shit, I asked around, even spoke to his previous employer. Most everyone said that he was a good ole boy who wanted some privacy after he lost his wife."

Ralph scribbled a note on a small pad of paper: *Wife dead. Never got over it.*

"What did he tell you?"

"I didn't exactly have time to interrogate him."

The man on the other end of the call sighed. "You looked around his house, right?"

"Yes, sir." That wasn't a complete fabrication. Ralph surveyed the garage and first floor. He'd been about to go upstairs when Tom started the fire. Ralph sure as hell wasn't going to get caught in the inferno. The rest was a bit hazy.

"Well, fuck. That might mean our loose end is still out there. Keep your eyes and ears open. Our experts were certain they had the hacker's IP geolocation tracked to the property owned by Dennis Holdcraft."

"The house went up like a tinderbox. If he had that kind of setup, it's gone now. Not much left but smoldering ashes." Ralph debated coming clean about Shelly Holdcraft before he recalled Skiles's thoughts about the fishing huts.

No, first Ralph would set up a search. If he found her, there was nothing to worry about. No sense adding more pressure.

After the call disconnected, Ralph didn't concentrate on the possibility of having killed the wrong man. It didn't matter. If he had shot the wrong person, it wouldn't bring Denny back. Instead, Ralph was focused on locating Denny's girl. He picked up the phone, the old landline on his desk, and pushed the button for his deputy assistant.

She answered right away. "Yes, Sheriff."

"Britney, come in here."

Deputy Britney McBride opened the office door. "What can I get for you?"

Ralph scanned his deputy from her yellow hair to her shiny shoes. She was in her twenties and still wet behind the ears. Britney made a mean pot of coffee, though, and he liked the way she filled out her uniform. He liked the way she looked when she wore civilian clothes even more; they showed off skin that was currently covered. Ralph also knew that in today's world, it was wrong of him to think about an employee the way he was, especially a subordinate.

Old habits die hard.

He might be over sixty, but a man still had desires.

"Call everyone in whether they're on or off duty. We need to set up a search and rescue. Stat."

"Who's after us?" Michelle asked, as the now-familiar serum of fear flowed through her veins.

Without replying, Fletch untied his boots and removed a wool sock from each foot. "Here, put these over your feet."

Michelle didn't argue as the anxiety she'd allowed to lessen in the confines of the small fishing hut returned with a vengeance. Watching this man return his feet to his boots, out of the corner of her eye, she was struck by the efficiency of his movements. Nothing was wasteful. He was a man on a mission.

"A soldier?" she asked as she snapped the front of his coat around her.

"Stop trying to figure me out. Now isn't the time to make up stories."

Making up stories was what Michelle did. Her life

hadn't started out that way, but after an undergrad degree in pre-law led her to courtrooms in central Indiana, Michelle found herself making up stories about the people in the trials. One night she sat down and began to write, bringing to life her pseudonym, D. Valentine. Four bestselling novels later, she didn't finish the law degree and no longer needed the courtroom. Her legal thrillers paid the bills. The settlement she and her father received from the gas company after her mother's death was also helpful.

One million each.

The money was enough for Dad to retire and disappear into the wilderness of Massachusetts and for Michelle to live on advances, royalties, and interest. Her editor was after her for her next big hit. While she'd planned to write it, she didn't plan to live it.

Michelle's eyes widened as Fletch pulled a revolver from the back waistband of his jeans.

How had she not noticed that before?

Fletch turned off the hot plate and lantern. The flames flickered until the only light came from the edges of the door. With Fletch's socks on her feet, his coat hanging to mid-thigh, and the hood over her head, she followed close behind him as he slowly opened the barrier to the outdoors. Gusts of wind, carrying large snowflakes, swirled in cyclones around them and stuck to her unprotected shins.

"Stay close," Fletch commanded.

Unlike when they'd arrived and the sun was rising,

it was now nearly midday. Nevertheless, the falling snow limited visibility to nearly zero. If there were people looking for them, they could be fifty yards away and never be seen.

The freezing air nipped at Michelle's cheeks as the wool socks did little to protect her legs and feet from cold. "How far—?"

Fletch turned, silencing her with a finger to his lips.

Without another word, she followed, step by step, placing her feet in the footprints created by his boots. His strides were much longer than was comfortable.

She gazed up, seeing his wide shoulders braced against the blizzard. He could be leading her anywhere —to safety or her death.

That was the problem with Michelle's chosen profession: she had a vivid imagination. Sometimes that was helpful, other times, it was a handicap. For example, if she chose to let her mind wander, she may run back into the fishing hut and wait for her fate.

Fletch led them to another fishing hut. Through the falling snow, Michelle saw why he'd brought her here—a snowmobile. She wanted to ask who it belonged to and if they could borrow it, but the memory of his intense stare told her to keep her questions to herself, at least for now.

After clearing the snow, Fletch motioned for Michelle to get on the seat. When she hesitated, he moved his hands faster, indicating for her to hurry. He swung his long leg over the seat in front of her. At the first turn of the key, the engine gave a weary groan. "Hold on," Fletch whispered before turning the key again, bringing the engine to life with a reverberating roar.

As they sped away, a voice screamed from the distance. The air around them quivered with the bang from a gun.

Her heart thumped against her breastbone. "Did someone shoot at us?"

Fletch shrugged his shoulders, Michelle's cheek feeling the movement of his sweatshirt. Great, she thought. Now she could add accessory to theft to her list of suspected crimes.

With her arms around Fletch's solid waist, Michelle laid her face against his back. The snowmobile sailed over the ice, plowing through the freshly fallen snow. When she opened her eyes, they were met with the same ferocious snow and wind painfully stinging her exposed legs. With her eyes closed, she could escape this craziness in Fletch's manly scent, the warmth of his coat, and the roar of the engine vibrating beneath them.

Her fingers and toes tingled as she balled her hands into fists within the sleeves of his coat. They both bounced as the snowmobile left the ice. One look at the maze of tall trees was enough for Michelle to know that she didn't want to watch. Their bodies swayed as he wove in and out around trees. When she was certain she would lose all feeling in her extremities, Fletch slowed the engine.

Up ahead through the falling snow was a house, not big and not small. Judging by the lack of tracks, it was either uninhabited, or the inhabitants were squirreled away for the duration of this storm.

Slowing the snowmobile, Fletch turned, craning his neck toward Michelle. Despite the windshield, his face was covered in miniature icicles.

"Oh," Michelle reached out her hand to his cheek. "We need to get you someplace warm." Even with the coolness of her skin, her palm was warm against his chill.

Fletch reached for her hand. "Stay here. I'll see if anyone is inside."

"Where are we?"

"A hunting cabin. It belongs to a rich dude who vacations up here to gather more heads for his walls."

The thought of heads as trophies made her squirm.

Fletch eased himself from the seat. "Move forward. If you hear things go south—"

"South?"

"Gunshots...you know, south."

Michelle shook her head.

"Listen, if things sound bad, I want you to take off as fast as you can. Don't worry about me."

Michelle's eyes widened. "I can't do that."

"You can. You're innocent in this mess. I'm not." He reached for her hands and placed them on the handlebars, giving her quick instructions on acceleration, braking, and steering. "Tell me you have it."

She looked up at him. "I do. But don't make me do this. I don't know who to trust."

"No one." He jutted his chin toward the west. "That direction."

"I can't..."

Without another word, Fletch removed the revolver from his waistband and moved slowly toward the front door. The door didn't budge as he turned the handle. To Michelle's dismay, Fletch pulled something akin to a Swiss Army knife from his pocket and crouched down. After pushing different tools into the keyhole, the door opened.

She held her breath, waiting for the sound of gunshots.

This was unreal.

How had her life taken such a drastic turn?

She couldn't think about her father. Or her mother. Her emotions were too fragile.

What did Fletch mean that he was guilty?

That phrase weaseled its way into her thoughts as she contemplated restarting the snowmobile. Relief filled her circulation as Fletch came out of the cabin, appearing through the still-falling snow. The darkness of his gaze had morphed to a few shades lighter. "It's empty. I'll get you inside and start a fire. Then I need to start the generator and hide the snowmobile."

Michelle took his hand as he helped her from the seat.

"Generator?" she asked. "As in warm water and cooking?"

Fletch nodded. "I saw some food in the pantry and even clothes in the bedroom."

"Clothes." She said the word as if it were a treasure. She could get out of her father's old shirt. A bathroom. And warm water—a shower.

"And I'll be able to charge my phone," Fletch added.

Michelle smiled. The smile she saw in response was enough to warm her from the inside out. They may not be completely safe, but in that instant, she could sense that Fletch was satisfied with this destination.

If she were writing this story, she could think of what would happen next. She'd be able to explore Fletch's toned abdomen. He'd help her with her shower and frostnipped toes. They'd find a stash of wine and sit by the fireplace.

Alas, this wasn't fiction.

She didn't know anything about Fletch.

There was no reason her thoughts should be going in that direction.

CHAPTER

SIX

The rich dude who owned this cabin was a mystery, but drastic times called for drastic measures. Michelle helped herself to the clothes in the closet and dresser. Thankfully, the owner had a woman at his side or at least one he kept clothed. While the jeans were too small, she found a pair of black athletic pants that fit—albeit snugly.

Now, nearly two hours after they'd arrived, Michelle was showered, dressed, and thanks to a blow-dryer beneath the bathroom sink, her long red hair was dried and secured on her head in a messy bun. She'd been exploring the cupboards in search of something more substantial than coffee when the front door opened. A snow-filled gust of wind scattered white flakes on the wood floor seconds before Fletch entered.

He closed the door, careful to engage the locks.

When he turned, he pulled the scarf from around his face.

No icicles.

Michelle grinned.

"No one will see the snowmobile. The way the wind is whipping around, a snowdrift will have it fully buried in an hour or two."

"The water is warm. You should go shower."

After removing his coat, hat, gloves, and boots, Fletch stood in front of the fireplace, lifting his hands to the flames. With his back toward her, he said, "I'm sorry you've been dragged into this." He turned, his jaw clenched. "Denny must have hoped if he gave himself up, you'd be safe."

Michelle moved from the kitchen area to the living room, her forehead furrowed. "What in the world could my dad have done that he would need to give himself up?" When Fletch didn't answer, she stepped closer and placed her hand on his arm. "I'm sorry I was dragged into this too, but I don't know what *this* is, and that's scaring the hell out of me."

Fletch turned, taking her hand in his and looking down into her blue orbs. The coolness of his long fingers surrounded her warmer ones. "You weren't supposed to be here—aren't."

Michelle's pulse quickened, and she took a step back. "Did you...did you kill my father?" It wasn't the first time she'd asked.

"No," he answered immediately.

"But you knew it was going to happen?"

Fletch shrugged his wide shoulders. "There was chatter. There always is. Finding it, hearing it, understanding it...that's the trick."

"Did Dad know? Had he heard the chatter?"

He nodded once.

"I don't understand."

Fletch took a step back. "Shelly." The nickname her father used for her came like a baritone melody from his lips.

Fletch went on, "I wish I could tell you more. You've already been strong, and I know that not understanding magnifies your fear." It was a potent component of the rush of emotions racing through her circulation. "I can tell you that you don't need to be afraid of me. All I need is one thing in return."

"What?"

"Forget me."

Her gaze was glued to his as if somewhere in the black hole of his orbs were the answers she needed. She blinked once, twice, letting his words register. "Forget you?"

"Once I get you back to your house in Indianapolis, forget I exist. Claim amnesia or shock or whatever." His smile curled in a wistful, sexy way. "You're the expert at making up stories. Make one up, one that doesn't include me."

"Why?" she asked, needing more understanding.

"Because" —sadness was obvious in his expression— "I don't exist."

Michelle ran her hands over Fletch's arms. Though he was covered by his hoodie, she could still feel the hard definitions of his muscles beneath. "If you're a figment of my imagination, I deserve a damn award."

His cool palms framed her cheeks. "If I could be real, I would be with you for even a snippet in time."

"Why me? I'm not anyone—"

"You're real, Shelly. I have you here. After all this time, it's more than I ever imagined."

Irrational.

Unexpected.

Michelle waited for the punch line, a comment to ease whatever was happening.

Maybe this wasn't real. Neither of them was. If that was the case, where would her story go?

"Fletch." His name came out in a breath as she leaned closer and pushed up on her tiptoes.

Time stilled.

As if every clock forgot to tick.

Every molecule stood at attention.

His framing of her cheeks tightened. Pulling her face toward his, their lips met. Warm and strong. Solid yet silky. Michelle's soft, curvy body leaned onto his hard planes as his hands dropped, skirting down her arms to her waist, pulling her hips against him.

The heat of the fire burning in the hearth was a flicker in comparison to the flames surging between these two lost souls, strangers in a dangerous, fear-filled world. As time passed, Fletch's interest was increasingly evident against her lower stomach.

Neither one knew who was the first to break away. But once it happened, an awkward silence prevailed until Michelle uttered the words from her heart. "I can't forget you."

"You don't have a choice. This is bigger than both of us." His nostrils flared as he inhaled. "I'll do everything I can to get you home safely. Avoiding the aftershocks of your father's death will be up to you. I hope you have better discernment than I've had." He shook his head. "I'm off to shower." Lifting his chin toward the kitchen, he said, "I saw cans of soup. It's afternoon, and I don't know about you, but running for our lives builds my appetite."

Michelle wanted more information than Fletch was willing to give. Yet her instincts said to wait. Neither one of them would be going anywhere in this blizzard. She nodded. "I saw more than soup. I'll see what I can throw together."

She watched as Fletch walked toward the bedroom. As he made it to the doorway, he tugged his hoodie and dri-FIT shirt over his head, revealing his toned shoulders and back. While those alone were gawk-worthy, it was the tattoo covering his upper back and extending to both of his shoulder blades that held her attention. She'd seen that tattoo on only one other person—her father.

CHAPTER

SEVEN

Despite the cabin being in the middle of nowhere, with the generator running and the fire blazing, the interior was warm and welcoming. The appliances weren't modern, nor were they archaic. Michelle found cans of vegetables, potatoes, and broth. In no time, she had a vegetable stew simmering, a fresh pot of coffee brewing, and she even found a pantry with vacuum-sealed perishables. She put a few slices of homemade bread in the oven, filling the cabin with the delicious aroma.

If it wasn't obvious by Michelle's curvy physique, next to creating heart-pounding stories, cooking and eating were some of her favorite activities.

When Fletch emerged from the bedroom, her pulse quickened as she scanned from his head to his toes. Damp dark hair fell to his shoulders. His stubble was still present beneath his cheeks still pink from the earlier cold. He must be closer in size to the cabin's owner. Fletch donned a gray t-shirt, his long legs were covered with light-gray sweatpants, and his feet covered by wool socks.

"Something smells amazing."

"Not eating for a while makes everything smell delicious."

Fletch made his way to the coffee pot and poured a cup. When he turned, he did the same scan Michelle had just done. Self-consciously, she imagined her wavy hair piled on her head and small unruly curls dangling near her cheeks, her blue eyes faded into no-man's-land without makeup, and her curves accentuated by the tight activewear pants. And yet judging by his expression, Fletch wasn't seeing what was in her mind's eye.

His cheeks rose and his lips curled. "I'm a selfish bastard."

"Why is that?"

"I asked you to forget me, but I don't want that to happen. I know I won't be able to forget you."

His words were like magnets, dragging her closer.

When she was only a few inches away, Michelle looked up. "Where did you get your tattoo, the one on your back?"

Fletch stiffened as if she'd asked for his deepest, darkest secret. "Something I got one drunken night in the service."

"Service? Army? Navy? Marines?"

"Service." He took a step away.

Michelle reached for his hand. "My dad has the same tattoo." She swallowed. "Had. He told me the same story only he said while in the academy."

With his jaw clenched, Fletch nodded.

Michelle's brow furrowed. "Don't you think that's odd that you and my father would have the same tattoo?"

"How many unique tattoos are there? I mean, you walk into a shop and point. 'I want that.'" He lifted the lid from the pot of soup. "Damn, this is better than straight from the can."

"It's straight from a few cans and some added spices I found."

After Fletch took a spoonful of the broth, Michelle asked, "Are you really going to get me home and disappear without any information about what's happening? Will I be safe?" She wondered if these people would follow her back to her home.

"You weren't supposed to be in Iron Falls. My assignment, self-imposed as it may be, is to get you safely home. I suggest we work on some alibis. If we can come up with a story that includes you not visiting Denny this weekend, you can act as if none of this happened."

"Self-imposed?"

"You ask too many questions," Fletch said as he began opening cupboards and removing bowls. Next, he opened the oven and retrieved the warm bread. "Shall we eat?"

"Your assignment wasn't to save me?"

He placed the bowls on the small table.

"Not officially," she said for clarification.

His dark stare lingered on her as they sat. Without a word, he reached for his spoon and stirred the vegetable soup. Steam rippled from the warm broth.

"Are you Secret Service or something?" she asked. "I mean you said you don't exist."

Fletch's lips quirked. "Secret Service agents exist. They're real people with real names and identifications who work to protect entitled people."

Entitled.

Interesting.

"Okay, then what? A spy?"

He looked up through his exceptionally long eyelashes. "You've forgotten witness protection."

Her eyes grew wide. "Oh, that would make sense." She scrunched her nose. "Except why would anyone in witness protection risk their life and new identity to save me? I'm nobody."

After a spoonful of his soup, Fletch laid down the utensil and shook his head. "You're not nobody."

"I am. I've written a few books. If I would have died last night, no one would go without reading. There's always someone else, someone newer, someone better. I don't have siblings or even parents."

That reality threatened her façade. "No one would care if Sheriff Perkins ended me too."

The legs of his chair screeched across the flooring as Fletch stood. "You, Shelly Holdcraft, are not nobody. Your father died last night but never think it happened without him caring about you. You were all he ever spoke about. And maybe there are other people who can write a book, but it's not *your* book—not D. Valentine's addicting novels." He shook his head. "*The Wishing Well* had me confused until the very end. That takes talent."

Michelle couldn't believe he'd read her work or knew so much about her father. "You read *The Wishing Well*?" She shook her head. "And you're saying you and Dad were friends?"

"I've read it, but the answer to your second question is no."

"You spoke with him...about me?" Something occurred to her. "How do you know that I'm D. Valentine? That isn't public knowledge." After what happened with her mother, Michelle chose to keep the two parts of her life separate. That was why she had a pseudonym—a pen name.

Fletch exhaled and walked toward her chair.

With each of his steps, she took in his predatory movement. His actions were fluid. Each step calculated. She sucked in a breath. There was something dangerous and enticing about Fletch that Michelle couldn't pinpoint. It was as if he were another flame capable of destruction, yet she was unable to look away—she was drawn in by his heat.

"Shelly, in a different world and a different time, I'd tell you everything you want to know. Maybe that day will come. Maybe it won't." He offered his hand.

Michelle looked at the size of his palm as she laid her hand in its center and stood.

"I can't tell you why," Fletch said, "but I've been watching you and Denny for years. As for Tracy, what I know is from stories."

"I don't understand."

"Have you ever wanted someone?" he asked.

Had she?

This exact moment would be a prime example.

"Wanted them, knowing you'd never have them?" he questioned.

Michelle looked down and back to his gaze. "I'm not exactly a waif of a model. I think almost anyone I want I won't have."

Fletch reached for her hair, tugging the ponytail holder from her messy bun. Long auburn locks cascaded over her shoulders. After teasing rogue strands away from her face, his hands came to her waist, and he pulled her closer. "You're beautiful."

She felt the warmth as pink infiltrated her cheeks.

Fletch lifted her chin. "And in the fishing hut when you started talking about Thomas Becon, I realized that all I had imagined about you was real. You can't concoct what it's like to watch someone, watch over them, and never talk to them." He tilted his forehead to hers. "To never touch them. To not physically know they're real."

"I'm real, but you said you're not."

"I want to be...for you."

A lump formed in her throat as she nodded, ready to feel the burn of his fire.

CHAPTER

EIGHT

With her hand in Fletch's, Michelle followed him into the bedroom. The loss of proximity to the fireplace caused a scattering of goose bumps over her skin, or maybe it was the realization of what was about to happen.

Did she want Fletch?

Did she want him in the way things were headed?

Yes, without a doubt.

Could she go into a physical relationship knowing that tomorrow they'd say goodbye? While her heart argued with her mind, her body gave in. Michelle was indisputably infatuated. Being in proximity to his sheer bulk dwarfed her in a way she liked. There was something in Fletch's kiss—a spark of wanton desire she'd only written about in her books.

It was in the way his hand possessively wound in her hair at the nape of her neck, the way he directed their movements, and the intimacy of his tongue against hers.

Coffee and spice.

Each nip and nibble of her lips sent jolts of lightning through her nervous system. Synapse after synapse exploded, mini detonations all building toward the promise of more.

Michelle raised her arms as Fletch lifted the hem of her shirt. Instinctively, she crossed her arms over her bare breasts and stomach.

"No," he growled, reaching for her wrists. "I want to see in person what I've only ever imagined."

"I'm not—"

"You are utterly stunning." He cupped one breast and then the other. "I could get lost in your boobs."

Michelle scoffed at his prediction. They were large—triple D to be exact.

She moaned as he lowered his face, sucking one nipple and then the other. Each touch was a direct line of electricity to her core. The kneading of each breast wound her tighter and tighter still. Gathering her wits, Michelle reached for Fletch's shirt, and mimicking his movements, lifted the hem over his head and dropped the shirt to the floor.

The sight before her was as if a Greek god had descended from Mount Olympus. Perhaps one had. That was why Fletch didn't exist. He was a god who escaped the heavens to save her. She ran the pads of her fingers over his toned chest and abdomen. If only his story was written in braille, she would read it in its entirety.

"I hope you like what you see" —his voice held a new, more gravelly tone— "as much as I like what I see."

She did like what she saw. That didn't stop her from tentatively taking a step back. When Fletch tilted his head in question, Michelle spoke her mind. "I like what I see. It's that" —she hesitated— "I'm lost and strangely out of control of, well, everything."

Fletch took a step closer. "Shelly, we don't..." He ran his hand over his hair. "Adrenaline, well, it's real. I want you to know that if we take comfort in one another, it's not because of the high from what we've been through." His gaze stayed on hers. "Or the lows. You don't know me. I know you and fuck" —he exhaled— "I never thought I'd be with you like this. You really are beautiful. You decide."

Would it be wrong to take pleasure where she could?

Michelle stepped closer. "I want memories of the man who doesn't exist."

As if the flames from the fireplace spread to the bedroom, the temperature rose. Their words were as scrambled as their movements as they shed one another's remaining clothes. Fletch flung back the covers exposing the sheet beneath and together they fell onto the cool bed. His dark orbs focused only on Michelle.

Kneeling on the mattress, he moved closer. As their proximity lessened, her breathing shallowed. It was as he spread her knees and buried his face in her core that Michelle cried out. What he was doing was ecstasy and agony all at once. There was no way for her to describe what he did with his mouth, tongue, and fingers. It was too much and at the same time, not enough.

As she grasped the sheet to remain earthbound, her body ignited. Faster than the blaze consuming her father's house, the heat overtook her. Riding the waves of the best orgasm of her life, Michelle was met nose to nose with the man responsible.

His forehead met hers. "You're gorgeous when you come, and you taste like fucking honey."

With his weight over her, Michelle spread her legs, welcoming his long and muscular form between her thighs. Her hands went to his shoulders, feeling his warm skin and assuring herself that without a doubt, this man was, in fact, real.

"If we don't stop now..." he began.

"No." Her head shook. The cascade of recent events was too much. Michelle's emotions were raw. The visceral need to be physically with Fletch overwhelmed her rational thinking. "Don't stop. I want to remember you."

"I don't have a condom."

She shook her head. "I'm on the pill."

He lifted his brow in question.

Michelle nodded.

Fletch's jaw tightened before his eyes closed. Moving back, he lifted her knees and lined himself up with her entrance. "I can't believe I have you like this."

"Please, Fletch. I want you."

Her neck straightened and her back arched as they came together as one.

Moving hard and fast, Fletch seemed as though he was afraid that Michelle would disappear before they could both find bliss. As the day turned to evening and the skies darkened, their lovemaking slowed. They explored one another's bodies, touching, kissing, and licking. Their activities took them from the bed to the rug in front of the fireplace and finally back to bed.

A few times they paused for food and drink.

There were questions to be asked and answers to be sought, yet in this reprieve, they both allowed those to stay silenced. Darkness abounded beyond the windows as they continued their one night of existence. If this was all they would have, neither one of them wanted to stop for something as insignificant as sleep.

Nevertheless, at some point, sleep prevailed.

When Michelle woke, the sky beyond the windows was lighter, and she was alone in the bed.

Sadness and loneliness fell over her like a thick, soaking rain.

Fletch was gone.

He left her. He left her alone.

He didn't do any of the things he'd promised, taking her home or making sure she was safe. Maybe he wasn't real. Maybe she'd imagined everything—hallucinations brought on by stress and grief.

As the tears that had been held at bay at the loss of her father and all that she and Fletch had endured began to overflow onto her cheeks, she heard the front door open. Wiping the tears with the back of her hand, she stood and wrapped the sheet around her breasts. Tentatively, Michelle stepped into the living room.

Fletch's smile wasn't as bright as it had been last night, yet it was there, along with the shimmer in his black eyes. "The goddess awakes."

She tugged the sheet tighter around her form, unsure if she could believe his words. "I thought you left me."

Fletched paused as if he were fighting an internal battle. His dark stare remained on Michelle, something unknown swirling in the black hole of his orbs. She couldn't read his expression, yet at the same time, she didn't want to look away.

Finally, Fletch inhaled. "Not leaving you yet." His answer was honest. "My contact has a truck for us a few miles from here. We can be there in less than fifteen minutes on the snowmobile. I just dug it out of the snow. The storm is over."

"A truck? And then where?"

"Indianapolis, to your home. My contact has been working on alibis." Fletch turned away. His neck and shoulders braced with determination as he paced near the hearth and the lingering embers from last night's fire. "I can get you back to your house, and you can deny any knowledge of what occurred at your father's house."

"My car."

He nodded. "You left your car at Denny's house on your way to Boston. He asked to borrow it."

"But…"

Fletch lifted his hand. "You took a bus to Boston. My contact will have a ticket for you." Before she could question further, he went on. "After the event, you went straight home via airplane. The weather was too unpredictable to go back to Iron Falls. Since then, you've been holed up in your house writing. All your communication was turned off. You had no idea of what was going on."

"And record of my flight from Boston to Indianapolis?"

"You'll have it."

Michelle blinked, trying to make sense of everything. "Who do you work with or for who can magically create a paper trail that doesn't exist?"

Fletch's firm lips pressed tightly together.

Swallowing her emotions, Michelle conceded. This was her fate—their fate. It wasn't as if Fletch had made her promises he wasn't keeping. Inhaling, she nodded. "I need to get dressed."

The thought of a shower occurred to her, but she

wasn't ready to wash Fletch away—not yet. She'd carry their connection until it was fully severed.

"What about the cabin?" she asked, taking one last look around. "Should we clean it, erase that we were here?"

"It will be taken care of."

"By your *contact*." Michelle exaggerated the word.

"Yes. He'll also return the snowmobile."

She dressed in clothes from the closet. Fletch didn't want her to wear the bright orange hunting coat. Instead, he found a brown Carhartt coat a few sizes too large. Her feet were covered with fur-lined boots that fit as snuggly as the yoga pants.

Outside the cabin, they were met with a bright and beautiful frozen world covered by a thick blanket of white. Michelle squinted against the glare, taking in the surroundings that were hidden a day ago. Soon they were back on the snowmobile, her arms wrapped around Fletch's torso and her cheek against his warm, strong back. The world passed by as they sailed through the trees.

The truck Fletch's contact had secured was an old white Chevy, one of thousands on the roads. In the middle of nowhere, the vehicle sat on the shoulder, appearing abandoned. Yet after stowing the snowmobile behind snow-covered brush, Fletch knew where a spare key was hidden.

Michelle swallowed as Fletch opened the passenger door. This was her escape back to reality. As she strapped herself inside with the seat belt, she wondered if reality was where she wanted to be.

Fletch reached into the back seat and brought forward a plain paper bag and handed it to Michelle. Inside, she found a standard burner phone and a small key.

"What's the key to?" she asked.

"P.O. box in your neighborhood post office. In two days, you'll have a new driver's license and all your credit cards."

The question of how was on the tip of her tongue, yet Michelle was confident Fletch wouldn't answer. She set the bag near her feet on the floorboard.

As they traveled the eleven-hour trip from Massachusetts to Indianapolis, neither Michelle nor Fletch discussed any pertinent matters. Instead, as the daylight morphed to darkness, they dined on cheap fast food and gas-station snacks. They spoke of the scenery, literature, movies, and television—polite first-date happenings.

It was as they crossed the state line into Indiana that the proverbial fire beneath her feet was turned up, and Michelle could no longer restrain her questions. She opened the flip phone to see one programmed number. The contact simply said '1.' "Is this number you?"

Fletch nodded. "You can reach me if there's an emergency."

"I need a new phone—a real phone."

"When you're home, order one online through your carrier. You should have it in less than 48 hours."

The back of her eyes stung with the weight of what was ahead of her.

"What if Sheriff Perkins shows up?"

"You give him your alibi. You'll have the receipts to prove it."

"I don't understand any of this. Why have you been watching me? Why was my dad killed?"

Fletch's proficiency at the art of avoidance lasted until they were nearing Michelle's city via back roads. He reached across the seat, his hand landing on her thigh. "You can do this."

She looked over, unsure if Fletch was convincing her or himself. "My father is dead."

"You don't know that yet."

The heaviness in her chest was difficult to ignore. Her eyelids fluttered as she stared out at the dark road, the truck's headlights cutting through the crystalized air. While it was cold in Indiana, there wasn't the quantity of snow that had fallen farther east.

Michelle swallowed. "I'm supposed to forget something like that?"

He shook his head. "Not forget, just act as if you didn't know."

She inhaled, her chest filling with the warm air blowing through the vents. "Okay. I can do this."

The sound of Fletch exhaling filled the cab.

"What if...?" she began, turning from side to side.

"We haven't been followed."

"Sheriff Perkins could have sent someone ahead."

Fletch's jaw clenched as he shook his head. "I've had your house watched."

"By whom?"

"Another contact. Everything is clear. Go inside." He reached over to her thigh. "The bus ticket and airline ticket are on your kitchen counter."

"Someone was in my house?"

"Someone who wants you to stay safe."

Her chin fell to her chest. This was all too much. She wasn't supposed to be a character in her stories... and yet..." She looked up. "None of this is real."

Fletch's eyes opened wide. "Shelly, I'm sorry, but it is real and to keep yourself alive, you need to face that."

"No," she said with new energy. "I can do this if I imagine it's not real. It's my story." She shrugged her shoulders. "Of course, I wouldn't have written my own father's murder, but maybe if I..."

Fletch slowed the truck a few houses away from Michelle's home. "What kind of security do you have?"

"The usual. Camera doorbell, a camera by my back door."

"Inside?"

"Nothing."

He pressed his lips together.

"If you've been watching me, wouldn't you know that?"

Putting the truck in park, Fletch reached for Michelle's hand and brought her knuckles to his lips. "You can do this. You come from incredibly brave parents."

"My dad, yes, but...*parents*...what do you mean?"

He inhaled. "I mean, you can do whatever is necessary to put this behind you, Shelly. Denny never wanted you to be involved in any of this. Go, use the paper trail and continue living your life. Use the keypad on the garage to get inside. I'll stay close for a few days, to be sure Perkins stays away."

"But I won't see you."

He shook his head. "You never have. Remember, I'm not real."

Michelle reached for the door handle and turned back. "Thank you for saving me."

The tension eased from his features. "Thank you for...for being you."

With tears in her eyes, Michelle made her way up the sidewalk to her driveway. After entering the code, her garage door rose.

CHAPTER

NINE

40 hours earlier – Iron Falls

Dennis Holdcraft trudged through the accumulating snow. His destination was veiled by the blowing flakes creating near white-out conditions. He'd purchased the twelve-acre property near Iron Falls, Massachusetts, nearly eight years earlier. While his house was isolated enough, where he was headed was even more hidden. The old shed had been on the property when he bought it. Back then it was filled with hunting and fishing gear.

Today, the old shed was something completely different. There was no way the original builders could have conceived the changes in technology. Built in the early 1900s, the shed didn't have electricity or indoor plumbing. It took Dennis about a year to finish the renovations. He did little to the exterior, other than blacking out the few high windows. Dennis gathered supplies a little here and a little there, not working to raise suspicion.

Dennis's use of off-grid electricity was a combination of hydroelectric and wind integrated with a backup generator. The system kept the shed warm in the winter and cool in the summer. It also supplied the necessary power for his advanced computer setup. The plumbing was rudimental. Thankfully, the water table was accessible for a well. Sewage was less precise. In most cases, he was the only person who used the shed.

Dennis turned back toward his house. It was invisible in the unexpected blizzard. He'd taken the opportunity to step out while his houseguest was busy. A glance toward the ground alleviated his concern. The blowing wind and heavy snowfall quickly covered his tracks. If he hadn't been to the shed hundreds of times, it would have been easy to become lost and disoriented.

The only person who would be looking for him was his unexpected guest—his daughter.

Michelle was Dennis's pride and joy. He wished he could be the father that welcomed her with open arms. The feeling in his gut wouldn't ease. He'd do anything to go back in time and get her back on the road before they became dangerous for travel.

That gnawing feeling began a few weeks ago.

Hannah Jensen, a six-year-old girl from Pennsylvania disappeared while on vacation with her family in New York City. Her parents sought help from law enforcement as well as the public. In no time, the missing girl was a trending story.

Denny's agency focus had always centered on missing and exploited children. It was personal. The photograph the family released threatened his cold heart. Years of watching children disappear without a trace could do that to a person. Each time he believed he could stop it.

He spent hours out in his hidden computer shed, what Tracy would have called his Bat Cave. After years of working on the frontlines for the agency, now Dennis did as his wife had taught him. He followed trails across the hidden corridors of the web. He'd spent years trying to infiltrate different networks that treated human beings as commodities. The monsters had no respect for human life.

Over the years, Denny learned the networks ran deep, involving men and women in all economic brackets and social levels. The wealthy used lowlifes to do their dirty work. Getting the lowlifes was only one goal. Denny wanted to shut it all down. To do that he needed the men and women at the top of the food chain. Sadly, those were the people who were becoming brazen, as if daring anyone to make an accusation or raise suspicion. Not too long ago, he happened upon another name, one that sent chills down his spine.

Congressman Patrick Lehman. Representative to Massachusetts. There was communication that shouldn't have been found. Dennis found it. As soon as he made the connection, alarm bells began to ring.

Literal alarms that indicated his heavily layered server was detected.

Detected by the trafficking network or by the congressman, it didn't matter.

Denny ran a counter program that found and deleted the virus in record time. No more than a minute had passed. However, with his work in cyber security both for IMPD and the agency, Denny knew, with a sinking feeling, that in the world of gigabytes, a minute was an eternity.

He'd had a choice to make. Tell the agency about the mishap or not. There was no telling what the person who planted the virus might have on the agency.

Denny made the call. The fact he was still alive and working for the agency meant the agency wasn't as alarmed as Denny had been. Nevertheless, he couldn't shake the feeling that he'd turned up the heat on himself.

The last thing he wanted was to put Michelle in harm's way.

His thoughts went to Tracy, his wife of over thirty years.

Michelle didn't have the training that he and Tracy had. Throughout Michelle's childhood, they worked diligently to keep her separate from their secret lives.

Her surprise visit was welcomed. Mother Nature's unrelenting snowfall was not. That was why Dennis called this meeting. He wasn't certain what or if anything would happen, but he'd been with the agency too long to ignore the feeling.

The small shed came into view.

Dennis saw a snowmobile wedged on the side of the shed, away from the drifting snow. The tracks were mostly covered. He took a deep breath, knowing the man waiting inside was part of an elite team within the agency. That didn't mean that Dennis enjoyed working with others. When given the chance, he preferred to do his job, report his findings, and keep to himself.

Sometimes the only person a man could trust was himself.

The thermal sensor hidden behind a weathered *No Trespassing* sign turned green, allowing Dennis to open the door. The inside of the shed buzzed with the energy coming from the technology. The man in the far corner turned. His dark eyes scanned Dennis. While he stood over six inches taller than Dennis, Dennis wasn't intimidated. "Arrow."

CHAPTER
TEN

Present day

Outside Shelly Holdcraft's home, Fletch clenched his jaw, placing mounting pressure on his molars as he cut the lights on the truck. Sitting as still as a statue, he watched Michelle make her way up the driveway. If he hadn't been assured by Colton that her house was safe, there would have been no way he could have let her leave like she was doing. It was selfish what he'd done.

Making his presence known to Michelle.

Saving her.

In reality, her death would have saved her from ever learning about the agency.

Fletch could tell himself that he did what he did for Denny, and that wouldn't be a lie. However, after all these years, he could admit if only to himself that he saved Michelle for her and for him.

Fletch included two other operatives on this mission, and he knew he'd get his ass chewed. Leo had been close. Fletch could have taken cleanup duty at Denny's, but not with Shelly at his side. The work needed to be done. The shed had to go. Any evidence that Dennis Holdcraft wasn't simply a retired policeman living in the woods had to be erased.

Leo went above and beyond by providing the pickup truck, returning the snowmobile, and scouring the cabin. When two people faced death together time after time together, and a favor was requested, questioning never occurred.

Yes. Copy. Received.

Without Leo's help in Iron Falls and Colt's help in Indianapolis, the shitstorm Denny found himself in would have been a lot worse.

Fletch turned off the truck and settled in, Shelly's house in his view. He recalled the first time he'd laid eyes on her; she was a recent college graduate. He'd been assigned to a case in Indianapolis. Prior to Denny's move, the case would have been his.

The time had come for jury selection in a high-profile case. The agency had a stake in the verdict. Sometimes the agency took care of the problems themselves. Other times, they allowed the appearance of justice. Allowing a case to go to trial accomplished many things, such as bringing evidence to light that would have been hidden with the alternative.

There in the courtroom was Michelle Holdcraft, sitting in the third row. Fletch was new to the agency, but he knew Denny. He'd heard about Tracy. Seeing Shelly Holdcraft in person was a starstruck moment. Somehow the two agents had pulled off the double life. Not many in the agency could do it. They had and the proof was right in front of him. Shelly Holdcraft was indeed real.

Her light-blue eyes studied each potential juror with the narrow-mindedness she'd acquired in pre-law. The defense wanted impartial, open-minded, and sympathetic candidates. The prosecutor wanted jurors who would follow instructions, consider facts objectively, assess credibility, and base their decisions on evidence.

That was basic jury selection.

It wasn't the way the agency looked at juries. The world was more black-and-white in their eyes. Good versus evil. Right versus wrong. Understanding the sides was more complicated than a simple moral dilemma.

Fletch hadn't been certain which way Michelle was leaning. The case involving the abduction of a young girl had received national attention. There was more at stake than the future of the accused. A network involving abducted children needed to be exposed. The perpetrator, while guilty as sin, needed to be released. Doing so would make him a target to those over him.

The agency wasn't satisfied with putting the man in prison. They wanted those higher up the ladder. Those people would probably kill the defendant in time. That was less expensive to the taxpayers.

It took Fletch's discipline and grounded determination to stay focused on the case at hand. Despite that training, Fletch had the urge to move a few rows up and introduce himself.

Of course, he wouldn't have used his real name.

When they finally met, he did. Fletcher was the name he used to have, when he was alive. In the agency, he was known as Arrow, an agent that found his targets.

Fletch had been mostly right about the jurors to be seated. There was one in particular who would be useful. Fletch couldn't visit the courthouse every day of the trial without calling attention to himself. He didn't return or see Shelly again until the day of the verdict.

He knew the outcome before the announcement. That was why he was shocked at the ending of Michelle's novel *The Wishing Well*. In her story, she changed a few key pieces of evidence. If she only knew how accurate she'd been. In reality, it wasn't the storyteller who altered the evidence. It was the agency.

It took only one juror to cause a hung jury.

Seat the right influential juror and that one person can persuade the entire group. In the actual case, it was a woman—juror number seven. In *The Wishing Well*, the trial ended with a guilty verdict.

While Fletch hadn't expected that, he liked the way it worked on the page. After all, the author didn't know all the layers at work, or that despite the mistrial, the defendant would soon be no more.

Fletch's cellphone buzzed, returning him to the present. The name on the screen was COLT. Fletch answered right away. "She's in the house." He didn't need to say her name.

"Peterson is irate."

The agency didn't have ranks.

It wasn't an official national agency within the military or intelligence community.

However, if it were and if there were ranks, Peterson would be a sergeant major who thought he was a four-star general. He was a blowhard who opened his mouth too often.

"Fuck him," Fletch replied. "Both her parents gave their lives for the agency. That's enough sacrifice for one family."

"He wants you out there tomorrow. You'd better start driving or get yourself a plane ticket."

Fletch had no intention of traveling to the agency's

complex in nowhere Montana tonight or even tomorrow. "Been driving for eleven hours straight. I'm getting some shut-eye, or the agency will be down another agent. Peterson can stew for a while."

"Listen, Arrow," Colt said, his voice lower. "My assignment has me in her area for a few more days. I'll keep an eye on Denny's girl."

The muscles tightened in Fletch's neck and shoulders. *Denny's girl* was a woman who had a name. Fletch had no intention of leaving Shelly's life in the hands of anyone else, even if that was what the powers that be wanted. "Appreciate that," he replied. "Thanks for getting her the paper trail. I owe you."

"You would have done it for me."

Fletch would have done it. No questions. That's what they did.

"I'll contact Peterson. Once she makes it through the next couple days, she will be able to carry on with her life."

"Kind of nice when things work out."

Fletch shrugged. "Not so great for Denny."

"You're right, man. Stay where you are for him."

Fletch disconnected the call.

There were more lights on in Michelle's home now than a few minutes ago. Illumination glowed from behind plantation blinds. The ranch style house sat on less than half an acre. Yet, the neighborhood was one of the upscale ones in the area.

On his phone, Fletch pulled up the app to her

cameras. These weren't the cameras she told him about, but the ones Fletch installed inside her house as a favor for her father.

Denny wanted to keep an eye on his daughter. Of course, he didn't know that Fletch also had the ability to watch. Fletch hit the history on the camera in the kitchen. The recording was activated by movement and sound. What he was seeing occurred minutes ago.

Shelly came on the screen upon entering the house and going directly to the kitchen counter. Lying on the granite surface was a crumpled Greyhound ticket. Fletch couldn't read the paper from the camera, yet he knew it had the appropriate dates. Colt sent him pictures. The American Airline paper ticket had her name, a first-class seat from Boston to Indianapolis, arriving the night before Denny was killed.

Fletch leaned back against the vinyl seat and exhaled.

Every *i* was dotted and every *t* crossed.

Fletch figured he should find a place to sleep for at least a few hours. A nagging pull in his gut told him to stay put. Maybe he didn't want to leave Shelly, not yet. Every fiber of his being told him that ignorance would be Shelly's savior, not him.

Fletch would only bring danger.

From where Fletch had parked, he could see one of her bedroom windows on the side of the house near the back. That room was now lit. He switched to her bedroom camera on his phone. Watching her in her private bedroom and bathroom was undoubtedly crossing an ethical line. The agency didn't answer to a higher entity or even congressional oversight. In other words, they weren't big on ethics. Results were what mattered. Statistically, if someone wanted to harm Shelly, entering her home at night and encountering her in her bedroom was the most probable situation.

That was why he placed the camera there.

Fletch's breathing deepened as Shelly disrobed. Less than twenty-four hours ago, he'd had her in his arms. His lips and fingers roamed over her soft curves. He recalled the sounds she made as she came, the sweet tang of her essence, and the undeniable pleasure of being inside her.

The tendons in his neck pulled tight as she washed him away, the first step in doing as he asked—forget him.

After her shower, Shelly combed her long fiery hair, donning soft shorts and a large shirt. He watched as she walked barefoot from her bedroom and entered her office. Curiosity grew within him as she sat down at her desktop. If Fletch were set up with more than just his phone, he could share her screens, seeing in real time as she researched and typed.

Most of Shelly's books, Fletch read as she wrote. It fascinated him the way she would write and rewrite, as if the voices in her head were too loud and fast to ignore for anything as mundane as adjectives or adverbs. Those came later, adding depth, color, and emotion.

As Fletch considered pulling away from the curb, content with Shelly's safety for the night, a local police car came slowly down the street, its headlights narrowly missing Fletch sitting in the cab of the truck. The cruiser turned, pulling into Michelle's driveway.

ELEVEN

It was nearly midnight.

Michelle's hands became suddenly cold as the sound of the doorbell reverberated through her house. She looked around her office in search of something to take with her to the door. Using a weapon had never been her go-to, but the last twenty-four hours had changed everything.

When she was a girl, her father taught her to shoot a rifle. Clay pigeons flying in an open field. He was a policeman and wanted his daughter to be able to defend herself. If she were prepared and attacked by a flock of clay pigeons, Michelle would be safe. Before he moved to Iron Falls, he'd given her a handgun—a Sig Sauer P238. It was a small gun. He even took her to the shooting range.

The reason that handgun was in a gun safe at the top of her closet was because while she could hit a flying piece of clay and any target at twenty-five yards, the idea of killing was inconceivable to her.

Killing.

Her father.

Someone had done that.

Taking a breath, Michelle reached for her phone. It wasn't there. It was a melted glob of goo back in Iron Falls. Quickly, she activated her doorbell app on her desktop. Two uniformed police officers were on her porch. She studied their attire and body types, determining that they weren't from Iron Falls.

The attire looked correct for the local police department.

"Hello," she said through the doorbell.

The female officer spoke into the camera. "Ms. Holdcraft, we need to speak to you."

"It's late."

"We won't take too much of your time."

"Do you have a warrant?" Michelle asked.

The female officer responded, "Please, ma'am, this is important."

Michelle hurried to her bedroom and pulled a hoodie over her shirt. All the time she mentally repeated the alibi Fletch had provided to her.

Unlocking the door while keeping the chain latched, she peeked through the opening. "May I see your badges?"

Both officers produced their badges.

Officer Darla McCoy and Officer Jamison Andrews.

Michelle closed the door and released the chain lock. Opening the door, she stood in the doorway and looked up and down her street. "Is there a problem? Someone in the neighborhood?"

"Ma'am, we've been trying to reach you since yesterday."

She feigned a smile. "I was working. I turn off all my notifications when I'm working so as not to be disturbed."

"The doorbell?" Officer McCoy asked.

"Earphones." She crossed her arms over her chest with a shiver. Civility was hard to restrain. She motioned into the living room. "Would you like to come in? It's cold out here."

"Thank you," the officers said in unison.

After closing the front door, Michelle turned to face her visitors. "Why have you been trying to reach me?"

Officer Andrews removed his hat. "Ms. Holdcraft, we're sorry to inform you that there has been an accident at your father's home in Iron Falls, Massachusetts."

Michelle knitted her eyebrows together. "An accident? What kind of accident? Is my father okay?" She took a step back. "I need to get to him."

"We're sorry to inform you that your father perished in a fire. Sheriff Ralph Perkins from the Iron Falls Police Department called our department late yesterday. That's why we've been trying to reach you."

"By phone *and* in person," Officer McCoy added.

The sound of Sheriff Perkins's name sent a shiver scattering over Michelle's skin. Tears teetered on her eyelids. "I just saw him a few days ago." She shook her head. "There's some kind of mistake."

Officer McCoy handed Michelle a business card. "Here's my card. On the back, I've written the contact information for Sheriff Perkins. He'd like you to contact him as soon as possible. He has some questions."

Michelle stared down at the card in her grasp, reading the information. "It's late."

"I'm sure he wouldn't mind. He seemed very anxious to speak with you." Officer Andrews's brow furrowed. "When was the last time you saw your father?"

"It was a few days ago—Thursday. I drove out to Boston for an event. I stopped at Dad's and left my car with him."

"You didn't stop to get your car on the way home?" Officer McCoy asked.

Michelle allowed the tears to cascade down her cheeks. "No." She wiped her cheeks with the back of her hand. "I thought there would be time. The forecast was bad out there, so I decided to fly home instead of drive."

"Please contact Sheriff Perkins. He has questions."

Michelle nodded, knowing good and well she had no intention of speaking to the sheriff.

"Your father," Officer Andrews said, "was an esteemed member of IMPD. We've also contacted Chief Bradley. He offered his condolences and said that IMPD would be honored to take part in your father's celebration of life." He handed Michelle another card. "Here's the chief's contact information."

Michelle shook her head. "This is too much."

"If you need anything," Officer McCoy said, "you have my number. Call anytime." She took a step back. "We're sorry."

Michelle looked up, her eyes glassy with tears. "Do you have any information on the fire? How did it start? Was he trapped?"

Officer McCoy pressed her lips together. "I think you should hear the details from the sheriff. We were told the Iron Falls fire investigators have contacted ATF."

Michelle wrinkled her forehead. "They don't suspect arson, do they?"

"Ma'am," Officer Andrews asked, "how was your father when you saw him?" When Michelle didn't respond, he added, "Did he seem depressed or upset?"

Michelle shook her head. "I don't understand." Her eyes opened in alarm. "The sheriff doesn't suspect Dad would set his own home on fire, does he?"

"Right now, everything is under investigation," Officer McCoy said. "I believe the sheriff simply wants to ask you a few questions."

"I can't." She shook her head. "My dad..."

Officer McCoy did a good job of appearing sympathetic. Michelle wasn't sure if she truly was or if it was the role the officer was playing.

"Ms. Holdcraft, you have our sincere condolences. I'll contact the sheriff and let him know we've spoken to you. Understandably, you're not ready to speak to him until tomorrow."

"Thank you," Michelle managed as she walked the two officers to the door, opened it, and stood motionless as they walked back into the cold night. Once they were back to their cruiser, she closed the front door and engaged the locks.

Before she could turn, she heard the vibration of the burner phone coming from the kitchen. It was the one Fletch gave her. It vibrated again by the time she reached it. Opening the flip phone, she saw the numeral one. "Hello."

"You did good. I knew you would."

Michelle turned completely around, wondering how Fletch was up to the second on her visitors. "Are you watching me?"

"Doing my assignment."

"Unofficial assignment."

He went on. "Have you ordered a new phone?"

Her mind was still concentrating on the fact that she was being watched.

"Shelly?"

She inhaled at his use of her dad's nickname for her. "Um" —phone, he'd asked about a new phone—

"I just finished the online order before the police arrived. I paid extra to have shipping expedited. It's supposed to arrive tomorrow."

"Good. It will have the same number as your old one. You can call Perkins after you get it activated."

Holding tightly to the phone, Michelle slid down the wall to the tile floor, pulling her knees beneath the oversized hoodie. "I'm afraid to talk to him."

"His only proof that you could have been there was your car. Stick to your story. You'll be safe."

"He's going to lie to me, tell me that Dad perished in the fire. I know what I saw. I know he was shot." Her words were coming faster. "The fire was the cover-up. The one officer suggested that Perkins is investigating arson as if Dad set the fire himself." Her voice cracked. "He didn't."

"You don't know that, Shelly."

"Does this phone work both ways? Can I call you?"

"I don't exist, remember."

She nodded. "I felt your heartbeat and your warm skin. You can't tell me that you don't exist."

"You can call me. If I don't answer, don't keep calling. I'll call you back as soon as possible."

Michelle swallowed and looked up to where the ceiling and walls met. As she scanned, she noticed small irregularities that she hadn't paid attention to in the past. "Are you watching me now?"

"It's all part of my assignment."

Inhaling, Michelle stood, feigning strength she knew she didn't possess. "I should sleep."

His baritone timbre reverberated through her body. "We didn't get a lot of that last night."

She nibbled on her lip, synapses sparking to life in her nervous system at the memories his comment brought to mind. Their one night was the eye of the hurricane. She needed to prepare for the rest of the storm. "Goodnight, Fletch." Before he could reply, she hit the red button.

Once this was done, once her father was laid to rest, she would do a thorough scan of her entire home. Michelle knew a little about surveillance from research she'd done for her books. The bulky nanny cams of yesteryear were replaced by slim and stealthy options, ones difficult to detect with the naked eye.

If Fletch was going to disappear into the unknown, she knew better than to try to hold on. They had one night filled with fear, flames, and desire. Michelle would call it research and recall the details when they would fit into a story.

TWELVE

The clock read after two in the morning when Michelle finally made her way to bed. Doors were locked and double checked. Her new phone wouldn't arrive until tomorrow, meaning her doorbell apps had no way to notify her if anyone came near. The idea that Sheriff Perkins was trying to call the tragedy in Iron Falls a suicide had Michelle unnerved. For a few minutes, she lay looking up at the familiar ceiling. Her mind raced with uncertainty.

The crackle of flames eating away at her father's home played on the ceiling like a movie. The scent of burning wood filled her nostrils. She knew that these were memories, yet they seemed real enough for her flesh to warm. Finally, Michelle threw back her blankets and went into her closet. Turning on the light, she pulled out a step stool and climbed. The small gun safe was where she remembered. Shocking even herself, she brought it down from the top shelf.

It had been years since her dad's lessons. So, Michelle did what anyone would do. She went back to her office, put her computer in incognito mode, and went to YouTube. Her hands trembled as she laid six cartridges on her desk. Next, she picked up the empty magazine and one by one, she inserted the cartridges into the magazine. More than once, she thought about stopping.

Her brain was telling her that she was being ridiculous. Since her brain was turning to mush from stress, sadness, and lack of sleep, Michelle wasn't sure if it was a reliable source of information.

Once the magazine was filled, she slowed the video and mimicked the movements of inserting the magazine. A click told her it was properly seated. With a firm grip, Michelle pulled the slide backward and released it. The slide sprang forward.

According to the woman on YouTube, that meant a round was in the chamber. After engaging the safety, she exited YouTube and turned off the lights in her office and bedroom. A sense of exhaustion crashed over her as she made her way back to her bed. The Sig Sauer lay on her bedside stand, beside her glass of water and the book she hadn't yet begun to read.

With too many thoughts competing for space in her mind, Michelle found a bit of reassurance in the presence of the gun. Maybe because it reminded her of her dad or she felt proactive.

Being independent was always important to Michelle.

Even she was surprised when sleep finally came. She expected nightmares or a cascade of tears. After all, the Indianapolis police delivered and confirmed the news she already knew—her father was gone.

The tears would come, she knew they would.

Perhaps she was too drained to cry.

Maybe she was still in shock.

Whatever the cause, sleep was a welcome void.

Michelle wasn't certain how much time had passed when she woke with a start. Panic sent her circulation racing. She flung one way and the other, but she barely moved. She was trapped. A pillow covered her eyes and blocked her vision. Pressure from a hand pressed against her lips, muting her scream. The taste and overpowering aroma of cigarettes made her stomach revolt.

This wasn't a nightmare.

It was real.

Someone was in her house—in her bedroom.

The gruff, unfamiliar voice came as putrid breath skirted her cheeks and neck. "Shut up, bitch."

Michelle held her breath as her mind scrambled.

"Be a good girl. Don't scream. Don't say a word."

The man's words rattled through her thoughts.

"Who are you?" she tried to ask, but the movement of her lips intensified the sourness from his hand.

"I told you to shut the fuck up."

She wouldn't go down without a fight, kicking her feet and turning her head until she stopped due to a sensation. There was something sharp against her neck. Fear overtook panic and Michelle became stoically still.

He's going to kill me?

"Don't worry. You're only going to sleep."

Will I wake up?

What is he going to do to me?

These thoughts and more flooded her mind. She recalled something she'd learned about never allowing anyone to take you away. Being taken to a secondary location drastically decreased your chance of survival.

Michelle wanted to survive.

The needle prick didn't come.

The gun. The one from her dad.

She shoved with the full force of her hands at the unmoving attacker. He cursed and released pressure on her lips as he simultaneously reached for her hands. He had an iron grip on her wrists. The other hand returned to her mouth.

The pillow shifted but not enough to see her attacker. In the darkness of her bedroom, Michelle silently prayed for strength. She recalled the sharp sensation. If he was holding her wrists and mouth, the sharp object wasn't in his hands.

Although she tasted blood, she continued to fight —thrashing about.

The commotion continued as she struggled to get away from his hold. Grunts and curses competed with the racing circulation in her ears.

A second, then more. Five, six, seven, Michelle gasped for air.

The pressure on her wrists and against her mouth eased. Shadows moved as she scrambled for the gun. Knocking over her glass of water, she found the pistol.

Everything happened so fast.

The mattress of her bed sagged and moved. Blinking once and then twice, she hurried off the side of her bed, her body temperature plummeting. Straightening her arms, she held the gun with both hands.

"Stop," she yelled toward the giant dark shadow. It was at that moment that she saw a man lying on her bed.

There were two.

THIRTEEN

Michelle's voice was surprisingly strong. "Don't move. I'll shoot."

She blinked once and then twice. There was something familiar about the man standing before her. She tried to reason. Her heartbeat echoed in her ears. She struggled to breathe, fearing that she might faint. The shadow moved closer. "Fletch." His name came in a shocked whisper.

"Shelly, you're safe. Put down the gun."

His voice was a relief, until it wasn't. She kept the gun elevated. "What are you doing in my house?"

"Please put down the gun."

"Were you going to hurt me?" Michelle's eyes had adjusted to the dim bedroom.

His hands were raised in front of him. "Give me the gun." He took a step closer.

All at once her body gave out. Her arms became too heavy to lift as they fell to each side. Slowly, Fletch came closer and eased the gun from her hand. A smile spread across his face. "Next time, release the safety."

Michelle spun, facing the bed, or more exactly, staring at the unconscious man on the bed. "Who is he?"

Ignoring her question, Fletch seized her shoulders, turned her toward him, and steadied her. "Are you all right?" He moved his hand, ran his thumb over her swollen lips. "Fucker. I should kill him."

A tear slid down her cheek. Fletch pulled her closer.

Her tense muscles relaxed in his embrace. For a moment, Michelle listened to the steady beat of his heart before taking a step back. She wiped her cheek and looked down. Her bare feet were on the carpet. She was still standing, despite her trembling knees. With a sigh, she met Fletch's dark stare. "I think so. You saved me again."

A gleam sparkled in his black orbs. "I didn't expect you to go all Annie Oakley on him and me. I'm proud of you." His expression sobered. "You aren't safe here."

She turned again toward the stranger lying on her bed. "Who is he?"

Fletch turned on the lamp on the bedside stand before going toward the man and flipping him onto his back. First, Fletch removed a revolver from the man's waistband and placed it in the pocket of his hoodie. The man's closed eyes fluttered. Spittle and drool dangled from his open lips and tobacco-stained teeth.

Michelle took a step back, sickened by what she could see in the light. "He's not dead. Is he?" She'd read how sometimes involuntary muscle movements can happen with a corpse.

"No."

"What did you do to him?"

"Vulcan neck pinch." When Michelle didn't respond, Fletch added, "Dim Mak. I momentarily restricted his carotid arteries. There's no guarantee on how long he'll be out." Fletch's eyes widened at something on the floor. "This will help." He reached down, lifting a syringe that had fallen to the floor. His lips curled as he met Michelle's gaze. "I hope he wasn't trying to kill you. Either way, he's about to get a dose of his own medicine."

"Wait, what if that's deadly?"

"Better him than you."

Her hands were suddenly cold and trembling. Michelle hugged her midsection. Silently, she watched as Fletch moved with efficiency, lifting the man's leg up and removing the man's boot and sock.

Her stomach rolled as Fletch spread the man's toes. She winced when he injected the contents of the syringe between the intruder's second and third toe. After a moment, Fletch checked the man's carotid and hummed. "Still pumping. Not sure how long he'll be out."

"What the hell is happening?" Michelle asked, letting out a breath as Fletch slipped the man's sock and boot onto his foot.

Fletch patted the man down, retrieving a car fob, a pack of Marlboros, and a lighter. "No wallet or ID." He looked up at Michelle. "I don't know who he is or who he works for. Ten bucks says that he's connected to Perkins or someone associated with him." Fletch pulled out his phone and took a picture of the intruder. "When I have a chance, I'll see if he comes up on facial recognition."

Michelle shook her head and scrunched her nose. "This is insane. We should call the police." She remembered the card Officer McCoy gave her. "I only have the phone you gave me." She watched as Fletch stood. It wasn't that she hadn't realized his height and breadth or his strength while they were on the run. In her home, her bedroom, he seemed larger than before.

Fletch lifted the car fob. "No police."

The recent events had Michelle unnerved. "Why not call the police?" She furrowed her forehead. "Wait a minute, how did you get in?" She pointed. "How did *he* get in. The doors were locked."

"First, Perkins is the police. I'm saying you don't know who he's working with. Could be cops around here." He tipped his chin toward the man. "I'd bet he's either on the Iron Falls force or he's one of Perkins's bulldogs. Second, I didn't see him until he was inside. He left the front door unlocked."

Michelle inhaled, trying to fill her lungs. "It was locked." She looked at the unconscious man and back to Fletch. "If not the police, what am I supposed to do?"

"*We* will do it together. First, we aren't leaving him here in your house. I'll use his fob to find his car. It shouldn't be far away. He'll wake in his car, I'd imagine with a nice headache and a touch of frostbite." Fletch shrugged. "Not sure when, but he will."

Before Michelle could come up with a better idea, Fletch lifted the man over his shoulder. The man's arms dangled and the spittle fell to the floor. "Pack whatever is important to you. When I come back, I'm taking you with me." He headed out of her bedroom, the man's head banging into the doorjamb.

Michelle followed behind him. "Wait. Taking me? Where? For how long?"

"Too many questions," Fletch said as he carried the man toward Michelle's kitchen.

She was a step behind. "Fletch, I don't understand." Watching him carry the large man as if he weighed nothing reminded Michelle of how Fletch had carried her away from her father's home in the snow.

He turned, facing her. "Do you trust me?"

Michelle wasn't certain why, but she knew the answer. "I do."

A grin threatened his scowl as Fletch nodded toward her patio door. "Open that, would you?"

Michelle was too confused to argue.

Before Fletch disappeared into the line of trees behind her house, she heard his last demand. "Five minutes. Be ready to leave and not come back."

FOURTEEN

Not come back...the words sent a cold chill down her spine.

The cool night air wakened Michelle, bringing goose bumps to her arms and legs. She quickly closed and locked the sliding glass door before turning to her empty kitchen. This house was her home. She'd bought it after the settlement from the gas company. It wasn't palatial, just comfortable. Located in a quiet neighborhood, it was her safe haven—until it wasn't.

Pack whatever was important to her.

Those were Fletch's parting words.

Placing her hand on the granite countertop, Michelle closed her eyes as she doubled over. The happenings of the last hour hit like a sledgehammer. Her circulation stilled, and her stomach dropped.

Holy shit, she was almost kidnapped. Maybe

worse. The possibilities bloomed vividly in her wild imagination. Perspiration dotted her forehead as behind her eyes she saw the face of her attacker. In her mind, he wasn't unconscious but brutally determined as he threatened and restrained her.

Her fingers went to her swollen lips.

Opening her eyes, she looked down at her wrists, reddened and swollen from the attacker's intense grip. Tenderly, she probed the flesh and grimaced. In the illumination of the kitchen, she also saw bruises blooming on her legs where the attacker had held her down with his knees.

She recalled the rank stench of his touch.

Rushing to the nearby bathroom, Michelle fell to her knees with her head over the toilet. The contents of her stomach came up until her body racked with dry heaves. Flushing the evidence of her panic away, she stood. Turning on the faucet, Michelle cupped the fresh water and rinsed the sour concoction from her mouth.

Staring at her frazzled reflection in the mirror, the specifics of the attack were coming back to her. As if a scene in one of her stories, each moment bloomed in her memory with intimate detail.

The awakening.

The shock.

The pain.

The odor.

The sharp edge of a needle.

The anticipation of impending death.

Gaining strength, she began asking herself questions.

How did the man gain entry?

Had he gotten in as easily as Fletch picked the lock on the cabin door?

It was a mystery she didn't have time to solve. Fletch told her she had five minutes.

How many had already passed?

The last sighting of Michelle's suitcase was in the upstairs bedroom at her father's home. Scrambling, she found two carry-ons and a rolling duffel bag. The first thing she wanted to pack were her stories.

It wasn't family pictures—many of those were lost when her mother died. It wasn't family heirlooms. They'd met the same fiery fate. She hurried to her home office and shut down her computer. Without her laptop, she would need to take the desktop.

"What the hell are you doing?" Fletch asked as he appeared in the doorway. "I told you to pack what was important."

Michelle looked up. "Did you put him in the car?"

"I found his wallet in the glove compartment." He pressed his lips together. "The car's a rental. His name is Mathew Wilcox. Also saw his badge."

"His badge?"

"Iron Falls deputy."

Michelle slumped back in her chair.

Fletch lifted his wrist, pulled back his sleeve, and

looked at his watch. "We need to get out of here before whatever I shot him up with wears off. I told you to pack your things, not your computer."

Over the last few minutes, Michelle's life passed like a slide show in her head. Her parents were gone, but she had something else: her work. Her lips began to tremble. "Fletch, what's on my computer—it's my whole life. It's what I do, who I am. If I leave it all behind, it will be like cutting off a leg." She fought the burning in her eyes. "You said to pack what's important." She pointed at the screens. "This is what's important."

Closing his eyes, he exhaled. "Go throw some clothes and whatever else you need in a suitcase. I'll pack up your computer. Are there paper files?"

She nodded. "But everything is backed up either on the hard drive or the cloud. I can't think right now. I know not everything is on the cloud. I need the hard drive too—the whole computer."

"Fuck," he murmured. "Hurry."

Within minutes, Michelle brushed her teeth and changed into long yoga pants, a sweater, and warm socks. She slid her feet into wool lined boots. Grabbing clothes and cosmetics at random, she filled both of her carry-on bags. As she left the bedroom she met Fletch coming in from the door to the garage.

"My car is in there," he said. "I've got your computer, mouse, keyboard, and one screen."

"One?"

"One," he said matter-of-factly.

"Car?" Michelle asked. "You had a truck a few hours ago."

"Yeah. I traded it out."

"How?"

Fletch reached for her shoulders. "This goes against everything I do and everything I'm supposed to do, but I couldn't leave you. It felt wrong." His eyes opened wide. "Shelly, taking you away from here is what I need to do. It's what Denny would want."

Pressing her lips together, she nodded. "You haven't told me what you do."

His nostrils flared.

"Whatever you do, can you find out who killed my father? I don't mean just Sheriff Perkins. I mean *why* Dad was killed."

Fletch inhaled. "I'll do my best."

It was more hope than she had with the Iron Falls Sheriff's Department. She steeled her shoulders. "Then I'll go with you."

"We need to cover our tracks."

She felt a cold chill scatter over her flesh. "What does that mean?"

"Your house. It holds too many clues. I'm going to incinerate it."

"Burn my house." Tears prickled her eyes. "No more flames."

"Fire is the ultimate eraser."

Suddenly, Michelle remembered that she did have

something of importance—her mother's necklace. She'd borrowed it for a dance at Purdue. That was the only reason the keepsake had survived when her mother hadn't. "Just a second. I remembered something." She dashed off to her bedroom, pulled open the top drawer of her dresser, and began digging through boxes. A rush of relief filled her lungs when she opened the tattered hinged box. Inside sat the necklace—an outdated yellow gold locket. Prizing open the latch, she saw the two miniature pictures. One was of her parents. The other was of Michelle, taken the day she graduated high school.

Quickly, she clasped the necklace around her neck and stuffed it beneath her sweater. When she returned to the kitchen, her bags were gone. "Is everything in your car?"

Soberly, Fletch nodded. "Last chance. Is there anything else you want to take?"

Inhaling, she turned a complete circle. "I want it all." She shook her head. "I want to help you."

"Burn the house?"

"No," she replied quickly. "Find who killed not only Dad but my life."

He tilted his head toward the garage. "Go get in the car."

"Are you going..." She couldn't finish the sentence.

"I have a few things to retrieve, then I'll set the incendiary device. It will give us time to be far away when the fire starts."

FIFTEEN

Heading northwest and away from streetlights, a star-studded black velvet sky with a nearly full moon shone over the long stretch of highway. Indianapolis disappeared from their rearview mirror before the sound of sirens filled Michelle's neighborhood. Deep in thoughts she could barely navigate, she stared out the window. Under the silver illumination, harvested cornfields appeared dark and damp with patches of snow and ice.

Fletch had taken back roads out of the city, avoiding the interstate until outside Indianapolis limits. They traveled through a warehouse district on the west side of Indianapolis near the airport. The city was often referred to as the crossroads of America. Those roads brought large trucks delivering and transporting everything from pharmaceuticals to automobile parts. Their small white Toyota Camry intertwined itself with those of shift workers arriving to and leaving their jobs.

Driving through the inky darkness of an early January morning, a large semi-truck drove past them, causing their car to shudder. Michelle watched the dirty tailgate as it moved westward and out of reach of their headlights. "Fletch." she reached for his arm. "I trust you. I don't know who else to trust. Tell me where we're going."

From the light of the dashboard, she watched his Adam's apple bob.

When he didn't respond, Michelle retrieved her hand and turned toward the window. Staring into the dawn, she wondered if there was anyone she could call. No one. Her only phone was the burner Fletch gave her. The new phone wasn't supposed to arrive until later today.

She was now being driven across the country to a place unknown by a man she barely knew. "This is crazy."

Fletch turned to her. "Crazy beats dead."

Michelle mulled that over for a moment. He was right. But she wasn't a spy or whatever it was that Fletch was. When it came to survival skills, she hadn't thought far enough ahead to grab shoes when leaving her father's burning house in the middle of a snowstorm. Her days were spent creating stories. While those characters came to life within her head and on the pages of her books, they weren't real. Fletch had said the same thing about himself.

Reality struck.

No one was real.

She turned back to him, studying his profile in the green illumination of the dashboard. Silence prevailed as Fletch battled a war Michelle couldn't see or comprehend. She noticed how every now and then, Fletch would peer up into the rearview mirror and check the side mirrors. As they approached the Indiana-Illinois border, traffic was minimal.

Finally, he sighed and turned toward her. His voice was deeper and softer than usual. "You said this was crazy and you're right. But I know that you can do what you need to do. You have it in your genes."

"My genes?"

"You're smart, Shelly. And the gun. You were prepared."

She shook her head. "I forgot to release the safety." She exhaled. "I write stories. It's not exactly high-tech espionage."

He lowered his chin, his hooded dark eyes staring at her. "Your last book, *Broken Promises*..."

Michelle's mind filled with the crime thriller about the abduction of two teenage girls from the same small town. She'd loosely based the storyline off a cold case in Wisconsin. She'd read the news stories and listened to podcasts. Her editors helped to make sure the story was fictional, avoiding any legal questions. Nevertheless, most stories have some basis in fact. She blinked. "You read *Broken Promises*?"

Fletch nodded. "Where did you get the idea for the storyline?"

She told him what she'd done, the research and the work to fictionalize what started as real. The ending was fiction because the actual case in Wisconsin was still unsolved.

"You didn't get any of the ideas from your parents?"

Her forehead furrowed. "No. Why would I?" Her volume increased. "How could I?"

"Did your mom leave behind notes or journals?"

The sedan again vibrated with the force of another passing semitruck.

"No." Shelly shook her head. "Our house...like Dad's...fire. There was nothing left."

What had Fletch said?

The ultimate eraser.

The last sign she'd read said there was only one more exit before Illinois. "Isn't transporting someone over state lines a crime?"

Fletch scoffed. "Blowing up a house in a residential neighborhood is illegal. Placing surveillance equipment in your house without your knowledge was illegal. I have a long list of questionable actions that could be considered outside the scope of the law. As for transporting across state lines, it's only illegal if I'm taking you without your consent." He quirked a brow. "Do I have your consent?"

She shrugged. "It didn't seem like I had a choice." When he didn't respond, she answered, "Yes."

"Now, if you were underage and I was transporting you with the intention of sex, it could be illegal."

"Could? It would be."

"Really?" he asked. "It happens every day, and if there's enough money, it gets covered up."

"That doesn't make it right."

Fletch looked her way as his lips curled. "You're right. It doesn't."

Was he transporting me for sex?

The question was on the tip of Michelle's tongue when the red and blue lights of a state police car appeared behind them. The squeal of the siren caused Michelle to stiffen.

As Fletch slowed and pulled the car over to the shoulder, he said, "Let me do the talking. If they ask your name, it's Mindy. You're my sister. I'm Jason. Jason Martin."

Sister?

Jason Martin?

"Say you agree," he growled.

Michelle nodded as her pulse kicked into overdrive. She couldn't help wondering if she'd been wrong to trust this man.

Was anything real?

Fletch nonchalantly removed his gun from the

waistband of his jeans and placed it under the seat before lowering his window. They both squinted their eyes in the beam of the trooper's flashlight.

"Can I see your license and registration?" the policeman asked.

Fletch shielded his eyes, seeing the Indiana State Police uniform. "Yes, sir. Is there a problem?" Fletch nodded toward the glove compartment.

Michelle's hands trembled as she reached forward, wondering how Fletch was going to get out of this. "It's dark." She fumbled with the papers within.

Fletch hit the dome light.

To Michelle's amazement, the registration had the name Jason Martin. With wide eyes, she handed it to Fletch. He'd removed an ID from his wallet and handed them both to the officer.

"Looks like you're a ways from home."

Fletch nodded. "Visiting folks in Champaign. We got an early start."

What state was the license plate? Michelle couldn't recall if she'd even looked at it.

"Miss?" The flashlight's beam was on Michelle. "What's your name?"

Shit. She tried to remember.

"Miss, are you with this man of your own free will?"

She feigned a laugh. "He's my brother and some-times...but yeah, I'm here willingly. My name is Mindy, Mindy Martin."

The deputy studied Michelle for a moment. "You look familiar. Let me see your ID."

"You see, Officer, I don't have it with me. That's what Jason's upset about. I left my purse at home..." She was a fictional writer. She could do this. "If he wouldn't have insisted we leave so early...I've wanted to turn around, but Jason said it was a waste of time. You see, our grandfather is in the hospital."

"What hospital?"

"He's in Carle Foundation in Urbana," Fletch replied. "As for the purse, Mindy would forget her head if it wasn't attached."

The trooper shook his head and handed Fletch back the fake ID and registration. "Listen, I pulled you over because your left rear tire looks low. Stop at the next exit and check it out. Don't want you to have an accident out here." He shone the beam back on Michelle.

She lifted her hand over her eyes.

"You sure you're okay?" the trooper asked.

SIXTEEN

Michelle couldn't think too much about the trooper's question. If she did, she'd scream that she wasn't okay, but that wasn't what she needed to say. Taking a deep breath, she replied, "Just upset about our grandpa and my purse."

Again, the trooper nodded. "Can't shake that I've seen you or your picture. You're not a runaway?"

Michelle scoffed. "I guess I have one of those faces. Redheads all look alike." She feigned a smile. "I'm not a runaway. I'm almost thirty."

He waved his hand. "My shift's about over. Move along and we'll call it a day."

"Thank you, Officer," Fletch said. He waited a moment before rolling up the window. In the rearview mirror, he watched until the state trooper got into his car and turned off the overhead red and blue lights before he started the car. "Shit, Shelly," he said in a low growl as he pulled the car back onto the country road. "Less is fucking more. Our grandfather is in the hospital? I was half expecting you to go into his diagnosis. Will Grandpa make it?"

"Well, he's had heart issues for years. Grandma's cooking has about done him in. High fat and cholesterol. We've been telling them for years to eat oatmeal instead of fried eggs and bacon every morning. And now, they have to do a bypass procedure after that incident a few days ago." She laid her hand on her chest. "Thank goodness he listened to Grandma and went to the doctor." She smiled. "How did you come up with the name of a hospital?"

Despite his stress, Fletch laughed. It was a full-force belly laugh. "When you lie, you need to remember your lie. The hospital is real."

"I make up stories for a living. Although, I almost forgot my name."

He nodded. "I was about to say it."

"Do I have a fake ID too?"

"No. You were supposed to be home, tucked in bed right now."

She sighed, turning toward the window.

Fletch continued, "I have a reservation at a hotel outside Peoria under another name. It's best to travel at night and sleep during the day."

"How do you know this?"

"Common sense. There's another vehicle waiting

near the hotel. We'll take off in that after we get a few hours' sleep." He pulled the car back onto the highway. "We should lie low. If that trooper thought he recognized you, that could mean that IMPD or Iron Falls has an APB out on you."

Michelle turned toward him, her lips agape. "You have reservations in *another* name? This is insane. How many names do you have? Who are you? What do you do?"

"The same thing your parents did." He exhaled.

Michelle tried to see beyond the car windows, yet the conversation inside the car was too intense to leave even in thought. "You're telling me that my parents were some kind of spies." She laughed. "That's impossible."

"I can't tell you any more. Not yet." His lips curled. "All I can ask is that you trust me." He reached toward her, laying his palm upward.

She looked at him skeptically. "Did my parents trust you?"

"Denny did. I never knew Tracy."

Michelle took a deep breath before she laid her hand in his larger one and closed her fingers around his. "I trust you."

His smile shone in his black eyes as his inked fingers encased hers. "Then we're in this together."

It wasn't a question, and Michelle wasn't sure what *this* was, but at the moment, her decision felt right. "I guess we are."

A few miles later Fletch took the exit and pulled the car into a space near a large truck stop. "Stay in the car."

"I need to use the bathroom."

His nostrils flared as he reached into the back seat and grabbed his stocking cap. "Put this on. We need to alter your appearance. Your hair is memorable, and we don't know about the APB yet."

Michelle pulled the cap over her hair. Using the mirror on the back of the visor, she shoved rogue orange curls under the material and turned toward Fletch and lifted an eyebrow. "Is this sufficient?"

He cupped her cheeks, bringing their faces close. "Listen to me. This isn't a game. The goal is to go unnoticed."

"Not a problem. I'm mostly unnoticed."

Fletch shook his head. "That's not true." He nodded toward her bag. "Do you have sunglasses?"

"Seriously? The sun isn't up."

"Do you?" His voice was sterner than a second before.

She dug down into her bag, finding a pair of sunglasses. "Yes, sir."

"Keep your head down. Go straight to the bathroom and back out. Don't shop or talk to anyone."

She wanted to argue that she wasn't a child and didn't need all the warnings. Yet her age was irrelevant when it came to whatever they were doing. Fletch was right; this wasn't a game. "Just so you know, you're freaking me out."

"Good." He opened the driver's door, got out, and walked around the car.

As Michelle got out of the car, she heard him curse. "What's the matter?"

"The cop was right. I need to find out if they have a flat repair kit and get some air in this tire."

Keeping her face down and stuffing her hands into the pockets of her coat, Michelle entered the truck stop through the large glass doors and quickly scanned the interior. At this early hour, it was still relatively busy. There was a mother with three children near the donuts, an older woman near the coffee, and a man at the counter buying a pack of cigarettes. Michelle did a double take, making sure he wasn't her assailant from the night before.

He wasn't.

She spotted the sign for the restrooms off to the left. Doing her best to avoid other people, her pulse increased with each step. By the time she entered the ladies' restroom, her palms were damp with perspiration.

In the mirror under the bathroom's bright illumination, Michelle saw a greenish color around her lips. Bruises were also getting more colorful on her wrists. As she was washing her hands an older woman entered, pausing at the sight of Michelle's sunglasses and bruised lips.

"Are you okay?"

Michelle played it off, relying on her creativity. "Horrible headache. Probably should blame it on the cheap wine last night." She didn't wait for a response as she hurried out of the restroom with freshly washed hands still dripping. Unwilling to take the time to dry them, she wiped them on her yoga pants.

As she hurried through the store, a stand filled with burner phones caught Michelle's attention. The one Fletch gave her only had the capacity to call and text. She saw other prepaid smartphones, advertising full internet access via cellular data or Wi-Fi. If she purchased one, she might be able find out what happened at her house. What type of incendiary device had Fletch set? Was the house destroyed? Maybe she could learn if there was an APB out on her.

This brought more questions. How would she pay for it? Her credit cards were destroyed in her father's house. She had a little bit of cash that she'd had on hand, but it wouldn't last forever.

Michelle startled at the sound of Fletch clearing his throat as he walked past her.

Exhaling, she walked away without a new phone and made her way out to the car.

When Fletch returned, he handed her one of the smart phones and a cup of coffee. "Cream and sugar," he said. "I remember you saying the way you like your coffee."

"Thanks." She took the coffee and the phone.

"I'll set the phone up once we're in the hotel. Don't do anything with it yet. As soon as I patch this tire and add some air, we'll be on the road."

Michelle nodded and sighed as he closed the door. It was comforting that he remembered her coffee preference. But really, how could she be comfortable with a man she'd just met, one who claimed to burn her home and who was taking her to the unknown?

After repairing the tire and filling it with air, Fletch sat behind the steering wheel. "We should make it to our hotel before nine. It's about another two hours."

"Thanks for the coffee. I can repay you." She shrugged. "I brought the cash I had on hand."

The tips of his lips curled upward. "Don't worry about that."

Heading west, the sun was bright enough for Michelle to continue wearing the sunglasses. Traffic picked up as commuters rushed to their jobs and large trucks continued their drives. Lack of sleep, combined with the waning adrenaline, found Michelle having difficulty keeping her eyes open. She was nodding off as Fletch tuned into a true-crime podcast. It was *Crime Daily Podcast*, hosted by two women, Kenzi and Ali. It was one of many podcasts she'd listened to off and on for research.

Michelle was almost asleep when she heard something that sparked her interest—her name.

"*...Michelle Holdcraft, the author.*"

CHAPTER

SEVENTEEN

Sunday night before the fire

Dennis Holdcraft acknowledged his guest as he brushed the snow from his heavy coat.

Arrow nodded. "I got your message. Is this about the boy?"

It wasn't, but Dennis had information. "All the evidence is pointing to a professional. They nabbed him quicker than his mother could report him missing. I was so fucking close with the Jensen girl."

"Bratva?" Arrow asked.

Dennis shook his head. "I'm working on another theory. Remember Crossroads Network?"

Arrow nodded.

"This feels the same. It feels deep. I think the

network is transporting kids up to Nova Scotia via yacht. There's a lot of money involved. The question is who's controlling the local law enforcement, not just in Foxborough, but all over New England?"

Arrow was listening.

"We've known for a while that this operation caters to the oligarchs in Russia with deep pockets. It was my belief that the network facilitated the transportation of the children, either to Russia or Saudi Arabia. They take them north to where they can fly the victims over Russian airspace.

"I've been watching the marinas and shipyards. There was a yacht docked at Hingham Shipyard Marinas that caught my attention. It's called *Dayushchiy*—Russian for *The Giver*. I've been watching it for weeks. Yesterday, a two-man crew took off, reportedly for Nova Scotia."

"Any sign of the Wells boy?"

Dennis shrugged off his heavy coat and sat on the chair before multiple keyboards. "Here's the video of the crew preparing *The Giver*." He slowed the video footage. "See those large containers?"

Arrow inhaled. "Big enough for an eight-year-old boy."

"If he's in there, he's alive. Probably drugged. It's a two-and-a-half or three-day sail to Nova Scotia. With this nor'easter, I'd say three days is generous."

"Did they file a destination port?"

Dennis shook his head. "No, but there are a

number of privately held marinas capable of docking *The Giver*. And from there—"

"They're a plane ride away from Russia," Arrow said, interrupting. "Fuck, this is just like the Jensen girl."

"Hannah," Dennis said. "We were so fucking close to getting her before she was flown away. I think the storm might help us with Timothy. I've contacted headquarters. Peterson sent a team to Nova Scotia. They're in agreement that *The Giver* will head for a southern marina. There's one in Shelburne that's privately owned and less crowded than others. It would make sense for them to dock there. There's also a private airfield in the hamlet of Deerfield."

Arrow crossed his arms over his chest and leaned against another desk. "You've reported this to Peterson. Why did you want to meet with me?"

"A couple of reasons. Perkins has been acting stranger than normal lately. I heard a rumor in town that he's making cash on the side."

"Security?"

"Not the kind you put on the books. He's been out to my house a couple of times for bullshit reasons. Gloria at the diner said he was asking questions about me. I even got a call from a colleague back at IMPD saying that the sheriff called for information on my tenure. My old colleague thought I was getting back into law enforcement." Dennis stood. "I'm not. There's no reason for Ralph to be asking those questions unless..."

"He suspects you. Why would he do that? He can't know about the agency."

"He doesn't. I'm still afraid I fucked up."

Arrow's dark gaze narrowed. "What the hell did you do?"

Dennis stood and inhaled. "A few weeks ago..." He ran his hand over his gray hair. "I was following a lead. Our software is top of the line. I should have been able to pass through firewalls like a damn ghost."

"What happened?"

"I came across chatter about an evacuation. I had hoped to find the details so we could preemptively warn security. A contact going by the handle of @Recon729_Adam kept appearing. It hit me as a connection to "Code Adam.""

Arrow nodded.

"All of a sudden, Patrick Lehman's name appeared."

"Lehman?" Arrow groaned. "The Massachusetts senator? Did you take that information to Peterson?"

"Yes, I did. But first, alarms went off and the transmission disappeared. I shielded my end, but I'm afraid that I let someone know I was looking into their shit."

"What did the transmission say?" Arrow asked.

Denny shook his head. "It was there and then disappeared. I didn't get the chance to read or copy it."

He shrugged. "All I have is my word. And Perkins's sudden interest in me isn't reassuring."

"You're absolutely sure it was Senator Lehman."

"I am."

"And you think the Iron Falls sheriff is connected?"

"Feels like Crossroads. They have people in all levels. Fuck, if Lehman is in it, he's got some big money behind him." Denny shook his head. "Just seems damn coincidental. I told Peterson about the breach. He was pissed and said that our IT people would find out what happened. I've got a bad feeling."

Arrow's nostrils flared as he looked around. "Who knows about this place?"

"This back shed? The agency knows I've built something. No one from the complex has been here to inspect it. That leaves you, me, and Leo. If they were able to trace me, they won't find anything in the house."

"You think there's a network that includes law enforcement and elected officials?"

"Small-town cop goes dirty. It's not exactly an original story." Dennis sighed. "I'm not saying that Ralph's involved with the kids, but he could be part of a network that makes transporting them easier. All I know is that he smells dirty. I'm not sure Iron Falls is where I should stay."

Arrow looked around. "Shit, you've put a lot of work into this place to pull up stakes."

"I have. I've moved before. I can move again.

Bringing down monsters who deal in people as commodities is my repentance. I'm not ready to stop. Lehman could be our link. I don't think he's the top. He's not smart enough or rich enough. But he needs to be watched. He has contacts and we need to find them."

"I'd like to be part of that."

Denny sighed. "Hey, there's something else—someone." Arrow didn't respond. "When I reported the information on the Wells boy to Peterson, he told me you and Leo were close by. You've helped me with my daughter in the past."

Arrow set up some security in Michelle's home for Dennis to watch. It gave him peace of mind to see that she's safe without him seeming overprotective.

Arrow stood taller, pulling himself from the desk. "Shelly? What about her?"

"She's here."

"Here?"

"At my house. She surprised me." Dennis stood and turned in a circle. "I'm fucking surprised. The thing is, I wanted her to get back on the road but the damn snow. She stayed for dinner and now she can't leave until the roads are safe. She was up in the guest room working on her laptop when I snuck out. If anything would happen..."

"Shit, Denny, what do you think will happen?"

Dennis scrunched his face, making his wrinkles

turn into caverns. "It's a gut feeling. I don't want anything to happen to Shelly."

"You want me to drive her out of here in this blizzard?"

"No. If I thought the roads were safe, I would have already done that. I'm asking you to continue to keep an eye on her. If I'm right and Ralph comes after me, he was told to do it by someone else. That someone else could know my history and Tracy's. Shelly's books have some information in them that I wish she wouldn't have shared. Fuck, she doesn't realize it's factual, but if the wrong people..."

Arrow stood taller. "You have my word."

"If I'm reading the clues wrong and a week from now Ralph Perkins has a new obsession, then chalk this conversation up to a paranoid old man."

"You know what they say about paranoia?" Arrow answered his own question. "Just because you're paranoid, it doesn't mean someone isn't out to get you."

"Get her home and back to her own life. I've worked to atone for things I can't undo. I lost too much to the agency. I'm not losing Shelly."

CHAPTER

EIGHTEEN

Wednesday before sunrise

"Are they talking about me?" Michelle asked as she sat forward. She'd been right about the name of the show. *Crime Daily Podcast* was on the screen.

Fletch didn't answer, nodding toward the display.

They both continued to listen as Ali explained. *"D. Valentine—the same."*

"Oh, I didn't know that wasn't her real name. I love her books."

"The Wishing Well is still my favorite."

"Have you read Broken Promises?*" Kenzi asked.*

"It's on my TBR."

"It's terrifying and good. Wait, no, don't tell me something happened to D. Valentine."

Ali laughed. "Well, this isn't a BookTok podcast, so yeah, I brought her up for another reason."

"What happened?"

"Honestly, they don't know what or if anything happened to her."

"Is she missing?"

Ali replied. "This morning, I saw an all-points bulletin stating IMPD—the Indianapolis Metropolitan Police Department—issued a missing person's report for Michelle Holdcraft."

"An APB. Why?"

"Well, the police confirmed she'd been home last night and early this morning her house exploded."

Michelle gasped.

"Exploded?" Kenzi questioned. "How?"

"Methane gas, possibly. If you ask me, for something as severe as an explosion, the local police aren't being very forthcoming with answers."

"Oh, this is interesting," Kenzi said. "You said D. Valentine's real name is Michelle Holdcraft."

"Yes. I confirmed that off the record with a source at Broadway Publishing."

"Ali, there was a Dennis Holdcraft found dead in a house fire in Iron Falls, Massachusetts, only a few days ago."

"No way. They can't be related, can they?"

"The fires or the people?"

"Both," Ali answered. "Stay tuned. We will dive into this new unsolved mystery."

"Come back tomorrow, and we'll tell you what we learn."

Fletch turned down the volume as a legal statement was read. "I guess that answers our question about the APB."

"You blew up my house," Michelle said incredulously. "My pen name wasn't supposed to be revealed. They know that at the publishing house. They wouldn't give out that information." Her mind was running in circles. "I should sue."

"Can't sue if you're missing—or dead."

"I can't help but wonder if you're threatening me."

Fletch tapped his fingers on the steering wheel. "Not threatening you. Reminding you about what's at stake."

"Nothing. I have nothing left." Her volume rose. "You blew up my house. Not just a fire, but a full-out explosion. Oh, that's subtle."

"It wasn't meant to be subtle. It was meant to call attention to both you and Denny." Fletch grinned. "I can always count on *Crime Daily*. Those ladies scour the outlets for any little tidbit. They'll get people talking."

"I don't understand. One minute you're telling me to lie low and keep my head down. Now you're happy that my name is being broadcast all over the world in a true-crime podcast."

"They won't be able to hide the fact you're missing or that your father was killed. That's what they wanted. They wanted to sweep both of you under the rug like they've been able to do to others. They don't want justice. They want silence. This is the opposite of silence."

"Who are *they*?"

Fletch leaned back, extending his arms and intensifying his grip of the steering wheel. "There are lots of *theys*. We need to find out which they this is." She didn't reply. "We have about twenty minutes until we arrive at the motel. I'll check us in." He looked in her direction. "Put the stocking cap back on."

"Aren't most people checking out at this time of day?"

"The reservation called for a morning check-in. It was also for only one person. I'll be a gentleman and take the couch."

Michelle scoffed. "It's probably too late for the gentleman act."

"Shelly..." The muscles in his cheeks pulled taut. "I never thought I'd see you like that again. What happened the other night was selfish of me."

She pressed her lips together as she recalled their one night in a snowstorm, the adrenaline of running for their lives, and the safety of the cabin. It was easier to have a one-night stand when you didn't remain with that person. "You can have the bed. I'll sleep on the couch. Things are different now. That night will be..." —she thought for a moment— "special." When Fletch didn't disagree she asked, "Tonight?"

"Tonight, we'll be back on the road."

"If you're going to be putting in hours driving, I definitely want you to have the bed."

Michelle couldn't believe her eyes when they pulled up to the two-story motel outside of Peoria, Illinois. After leaving the interstate, Fletch drove a few back roads that seemed too narrow for oncoming traffic. If Michelle were asked, this would be the last place she would rent a room. "You can't be serious. This looks like it belongs in an episode of *Criminal Minds*."

"I guess it depends on who you think the criminal is, me or someone else."

Her eyes widened as she took in the rundown parking lot, the sign advertising television, and the front office with bars on the windows. "Do they rent rooms by the hour?"

"Probably. Think of it as shabby chic." He turned in her direction. "They also don't have an issue with people paying cash. Most likely, they won't check my ID. It's not the Ritz, but it will do for a place to sleep."

She shivered. "If you say so."

Fletch parked as far away from the front office as possible. He went around to the back of the car and opened the trunk. When he walked toward the barred window, Michelle noticed that he had his hair all tucked under a ball cap. In less than two minutes, Fletch was back with a key in his hand—an actual key.

It was attached to a plastic tag labeled with the number 108.

It was the room right in front of where he'd parked.

When Michelle opened the car door, she had to kick a fast-food bag out of the way. Wrinkling her nose, she hurried from the car and met Fletch at the door. Her red hair was covered with the stocking cap.

Michelle's expectations for the interior were nonexistent as Fletch opened the door. To her surprise, other than everything being outdated and worn, the room was clean and thankfully, didn't reek of smoke.

"No couch," they said in unison.

The furnishings were standard fare: one queen-sized bed, two bedside stands, a tiny table with two vinyl-covered chairs, and a TV stand. The closet was a metal rod attached to the far wall. The vanity was visible. Undoubtedly, the toilet and shower were off to the side.

Fletch closed the heavy curtains and walked back, checking the bathroom. When he returned, he said, "I'll take the floor."

"No. We're both tired. We can share the bed as…" She hesitated and motioned between them. "Whatever this is. What is this, savior and victim? Friends after a one-night stand? Kidnapper and kidnappee?"

"I'm not a fan of labels, but if you can sleep next to me" —he grinned and quirked a brow— "and only sleep, I'll do my best to follow suit."

"Deal."

"Which suitcase do you need?" he asked.

Michelle flung the covers back on the bed. "No bedbugs." She looked up. "I didn't put that much effort into packing. Could you bring all three in? I'll get them more organized after a shower, some food, and sleep."

Fletch returned with Michelle's bags, a backpack, and a duffel bag, Fletch opened the duffel bag and removed a small gun. "Since you're familiar with guns…"

Her eyes opened wide. "I didn't shoot the one last night. I had to do a YouTube video to remember how to load it."

"This one is a Glock 19." He handed it her direction. "It's heavier than your Sig Sauer due to the double-stack magazine."

Michelle took a step backward. "I brought mine."

Fletch's eyes opened wide. "You did?"

She shrugged. "Dad gave it to me. I decided it was important." She lifted one of her bags and unzipped the zipper. Clothes and items spilled onto the bed. "I'm not certain which bag it's in. Besides, as long as you're here, I won't need it."

"I'm going out for supplies."

Her heartbeat quickened. "Dad taught me to shoot a rifle in a field with clay pigeons. He took me to the shooting range to learn how to safely handle my Sig Sauer. I've never shot at a person."

"I'd like to get some sleep. Let me show you this gun and you can look for yours later. If you have to use this, it will be to save your life." Fletch came closer, placed the Glock in Michelle's hand. "You're experienced. I'll just show you the ins and outs of the Glock. It's not complicated."

For the next few minutes, Fletch explained the parts of the pistol, the way to load and unload the magazine, and how to depress the trigger safety. His instructions were thorough and patient. They also sparked memories of her dad's lessons years ago and more recently, the lady on the YouTube video.

At the end of their lesson, Michelle was only ninety percent as scared as she'd been at the beginning. The fear wasn't necessarily of the handgun but of being alone. Which was crazy. She hated sounding needy, but she still asked, "How long will you be gone?" Michelle carefully laid the gun on the TV stand.

"Not long. I told the front office I wasn't to be disturbed. Keep the door locked, and don't open it for anyone but me. I'll have the key, but I recommend you lock the deadbolt while I'm gone."

Michelle eyed the pistol and looked back at Fletch. "Please hurry."

He came closer and reached for her shoulders. "You've got this, Shelly. Most likely, you won't need to use that. I don't want to leave you without some protection." He glanced at the open carry-on cases.

"And it could be months before you straighten all of that out."

Pressing her lips together, she shook her head.

Fletch pulled the stocking cap from her head. Michelle's fiery hair fell from captivity, cascading over her shoulders. He ran a lock between his thumb and finger. "The first time I saw you in person, I couldn't look away from your hair. You were so vibrant, full of life." He inhaled. "I want to keep you that way."

"Alive is good."

"I'll be back with food and water." Surprisingly, he placed a kiss on the top of her head.

As Fletch headed toward the door, Michelle asked, "Is it really this dangerous? Do you think they're coming after me?"

"After what happened last night—yes, it's dangerous. Until you're where I know they can't find you, we aren't taking any chances."

Michelle followed behind him. Once the door closed, she turned the knob to engage the deadbolt and leaned her forehead against the cool metal door.

"How can this be my life?" she asked in a whisper.

Under the spray of the shower, she studied her wrists, now a deeper purple from the attacker's grip. There were tender bruises on her thighs, and her lips were still sore. Michelle couldn't help wondering what would have happened if Fletch hadn't been watching.

She would have had to pull the trigger.

As she shampooed and conditioned her hair, she

inventoried everything that had been taken from her over the last few days.

Her father.

Her home.

Her safety.

The life she knew.

At 9:40 in the morning, she was dressed in sleeping pants and a t-shirt with her wet hair combed out. Sitting cross-legged on the bed she opened her mother's locket and stared down at the small photos. The one of her parents curled slightly at the edge. Michelle pressed it down with the realization it was her only photo of her parents. Swallowing her emotions, Michelle latched the locket, slipping the necklace over her head and began going through her luggage.

She had her things in a semi-state of organization when her cocoon shattered at the distinct rattling of the doorknob.

Peering out from the edge of the curtain, she saw in the parking spot that had held the sedan was a dusty black truck. The knob rattled again.

Steeling her shoulders, she went to the TV stand and picked up the Glock.

NINETEEN

Michelle hadn't thought she could be more frightened than she was during the attack in her home. Her visceral reaction to the rattling doorknob proved she was wrong. Call it PTSD or shattered nerves, the results were the same. As she stared down at the pistol in her grasp, her hands trembled—her entire body shuddered. Her stomach rolled as she tried desperately to recall Fletch's lesson.

It was a gun, not too unlike her own.

All she needed to do was point and shoot.

With the Glock in her grasp, she set her sights on the door and extended both her arms. Michelle tried to steady herself as she released the safety. With the potential of harming someone, the pistol felt heavier in her grasp than it had during Fletch's lesson.

She saw the movement of the doorknob. The

sound was muted by the rush of circulation thumping in her ears.

A voice came through the chaos. "Shelly."

The breath she was holding rushed from her lungs at the familiar timbre. Laying the pistol back on the TV stand, she hurried to the door. Peering through the peephole., a bird's eye distortion of Fletch came into view. His baseball cap covered his messy mane, and his dark eyes stared back at her.

Quickly, she unlocked the deadbolt and opened the door. Her entire body sagged as he slipped inside the room and closed the door from the winter chill.

"You scared me."

After dropping the shopping bags on the small table, Fletch's gaze assessed the room milliseconds before turning his attention to Michelle. The darkness of his orbs intensified as he took in her expression and reached for her cheeks. "You're shaking and pale. Did something happen?"

As she closed her eyes and shook her head, a rogue tear slithered down her cheek. "I picked up the gun, like you said." She looked up at him. "I released the safety, but as I stood there waiting for someone to charge inside, I didn't know if I could shoot."

He wiped away the tear with his thumb. "That's okay. You did the right thing by picking up the gun. Didn't you hear me say your name?"

"Not at first. I just heard the doorknob rattle, and my mind went blank."

Fletch wrapped his arms around her, holding her against his cool hoodie. The steady beat of his heart beneath the soft material, combined with his signature scent, allowed Michelle's frayed nerves to mend a bit.

With a grasp of her shoulders, Fletch moved her to arm's length and feigned a smile. "Hey, you reached for the gun and removed the safety. Those were the right moves."

Inhaling, she nodded.

"I have food and supplies. The truck outside is our new ride. I made a stop at the junkyard for a different license plate."

"I don't know how you know what to do."

"Years of practice." He dipped his chin toward the small table. "Have a seat, and I'll bring in the food. Then we need sleep."

"How long until we reach wherever it is we're going?"

"This time of year, we have Mother Nature on our side. There're more hours of dark than light. We'll set off after the sun sets tonight and get a good twelve hours under our belt before we need to stop. That will give us one more day of driving. We should arrive to the complex Saturday."

"Complex? What is that?"

"We have time, Shelly. Let's concentrate on food and sleep."

Michelle wanted to argue, but the last seventy-two hours had drained her. They'd done more than that. Since falling asleep at her father's house, her life was completely upended. She wasn't certain she'd ever have a normal life again. Mentally and physically, Michelle was exhausted. During the few seconds of Fletch's embrace, she could have been lulled to sleep.

After consuming a breakfast sandwich and orange juice, Michelle lay on one edge of the queen-sized bed and pulled the blankets over herself. One deep breath in and out. She told herself that she was safe as she listened to the rush of water through old pipes and thin walls.

Fletch was showering.

She didn't know what the future would bring, or if Fletch would stay a part of her life. Currently, she wasn't reliving the magic they'd shared that first night that now seemed a long time ago. Instead, as her cheek settled into the soft pillow, Michelle only knew that Fletch's presence reassured her—which was bullshit. Since the loss of her mother and her father's move to Massachusetts, she'd been happily independent, not relying on anyone.

That didn't mean she didn't have friends. She did. She even dated sometimes. Michelle had a few friends with benefits but spending significant amounts of time together wasn't either of their goals. Going home to a quiet house after a night out with friends gave Michelle comfort. If she were into personality types, that would probably make her an introvert. She suspected that most authors were.

That life was gone.

The realization hit and combined with the memory of her father on the floor as flames climbed the walls of his living room. The emptiness within her felt cavernous—a deep dark hole that she wasn't sure how to navigate. More memories returned. Her nose scrunched at the one of the man's dirty hands on her mouth. Phantom cold prickled her feet. Tears burned her eyes, as if there wasn't enough room in her heart for more pain.

When the sound of the shower stopped, Michelle turned, burying her face in the soft pillow and trying to hide her breakdown.

"What the hell?" Fletch's deep tenor seeped into her consciousness as a warm hand came comfortingly to her shoulder. "Shelly."

She shook her head. "I'm all right." The clean scent of the motel bodywash filled her senses.

The side of the mattress dipped. "Turn around."

Slowly, she did as he asked and wiped the tears from her cheek. Opening her blood shot eyes, Michelle took in the half-naked man. A towel wrapped around his waist was his only attire. His dark hair was wet, releasing droplets of water on his broad shoulders. His lack of shaving over the last few days was accumulating into a nice dark beard over his cheeks and jaw.

"Really." She tried to sound convincing.

Fletch's lips pressed together. "It's okay not to be all right. It's probably the way a normal person would react to all that you've been through."

Michelle shook her head. "I don't know what to do. When I close my eyes, I see things I want to forget. I feel...alone."

Fletch stood and turned. The towel fell to the floor showing Michelle his fine ass. While the firm cheeks and dimple at his lower spine were gawk-worthy, her focus went to his shoulders, specifically to his tattoo, one like her father's. The view added to her distress. When he turned around, he was wearing black boxer briefs and a half smile. "You're not alone, Shelly. I promise to be a gentleman if you want to let me rest close to you, so you know you're not alone."

"Fletch," she began. "This isn't who I am. I'm not needy or weak."

"Okay, it's me. Let me fall asleep knowing that no one can get to you."

Swallowing, Michelle nodded. Although she barely knew this man, Michelle trusted him. And that was what mattered the most.

After turning off the lights, Fletch slid under the covers on the other side of the bed. He scooted in. "Are you going to meet me halfway?"

She contemplated his question. "I don't want your pity."

"How about just a shoulder to cry or sleep on?"

Exhaling, she scooted closer, feeling his heat and

inhaling his clean scent. His arm came around her, pulling her closer. This wasn't the mad passion of the other night. It was something different—not sexual. It was reassuring. Michelle laid her head on his hard shoulder.

No more words were said. In the warmth of his embrace, she closed her eyes. To her surprise, sleep came.

Time passed, but she didn't know how much when Michelle woke to the sound of Fletch moving about the motel room. After blinking her eyes, she remembered where she was and why she was there. Pushing herself to sit against the headboard, she noticed the unmade bed to her side. Fletch must have slept.

When he turned to see her awake and sitting, a smile curled his lips. "I wasn't certain what kind of magical spell I'd need to wake you."

"Magical spell?"

"You know, in the fairy tales, the beautiful woman is awakened only by..." He scoffed.

Michelle pressed her lips together, certain she didn't fall under that description. Shaking her head, she threw back the blankets. "I can't believe how soundly I slept." She stepped from the bed and stretched. "I owe it to you."

"My goal is for you to have many more restful nights."

"Did you get enough sleep?" she asked. "What time is it?"

"I got about six hours. That's more than I normally get. We keep gaining an hour as we head west. I mapped out our next stop near Rapid City. We should be able to check in before sunrise."

There were so many questions running through Michelle's thoughts, yet it was her realization before falling asleep that kept her content. She trusted Fletch.

Less than twenty minutes later, they were sipping gas station coffee in the dusty black truck. The clock on the dash read a little after five in the evening. With a cooler in the back seat filled with deli sandwiches, water bottles, and caffeine drinks, there would be no reason to stop except to fill up the gas tank and take bathroom breaks.

Beyond the lights of Peoria, the dark sky prevailed and the cab of the truck filled with country music.

Michelle turned to Fletch. "I just realized, I don't know your last name."

"You know my real name. That's more than most people know."

CHAPTER

TWENTY

Wednesday in Iron Falls

"Sheriff," Deputy Britney McBride said as she opened the office door. "Rick Lehman is on line two."

Ralph crushed out the remains of a cigarette and fanned the smoke. Smoking within the station was prohibited, but he was fucking sheriff and the one in charge. If anyone complained, it would fall on deaf ears. He'd given up the disgusting habit about ten years ago. The last few days his nerves were so tight he was ready to jump out of his own skin. The nicotine was welcome.

"Sheriff?"

"Yeah, yeah. I heard you."

"He said it was urgent."

"Rick Lehman, right." Ralph gritted his teeth and mumbled under his breath. He confessed to Rick about Shelly late last night. Ralph knew this call was coming. He just hoped Wilcox's call would come first. "Thanks, Britney. Close the door, will you?"

Ralph's tie was suddenly too tight around his neck. Tugging on his collar, he felt the too-familiar rage boiling in his stomach. It wasn't only focused on the congressman but on his own inability. The scene at Dennis Holdcraft's unraveled. He was fucking sure he'd seen Shelly Holdcraft that night.

The manhunt came up empty. The only possible incident that could possibly be connected was a report from Old Man Evans. He called the station midday on Monday, when most of the town's sheriff and fire personnel were still out at Holdcraft's place. Evans reported his snowmobile was stolen from beside his fishing hut while he was inside. According to the report Skiles took later that day, Evans admitted to leaving the key in the ignition. He also claimed to have shot at the thief. He couldn't give any details about the perpetrator due to the blizzard conditions.

There were multiple other fishing huts close to Old Man Evans's. The deputies conducted searches of the huts Monday. The snowmobile incident gnawed at Ralph. Despite his knee acting up, on Tuesday morning, he went out on Iron Reservoir himself and personally checked each of the nearby huts. Nothing was out of the ordinary other than a half pot of cold coffee and two unwashed mugs found in one belonging to a local resident. Ralph had a call out to the owner to find out if he'd been out there recently. The owner hadn't returned the call.

Strangely enough, Tuesday afternoon, Old Man Evans called again to say his snowmobile had been returned—no worse for wear. Definitely a head scratcher. Ralph didn't know if Shelly knew how to drive a snowmobile or if or how she made it to Iron Reservoir. Hell, he didn't know if she was the snowmobile thief. More likely, the thieves were some punk kids having fun on a day off school due to snow.

If he was right about seeing Shelly, she likely saw Denny. She saw him shot. Until Ralph had Shelly quieted, she was a loose end. With each passing minute, Ralph was losing his patience. He never thought she'd make it away from the fire. After all, it was a fucking blizzard. Yet, somehow, she made it from Iron Falls to Indianapolis.

He received confirmation via a call from IMPD officer Darla McCoy late last night. The officer verified that she and her partner contacted Ms. Holdcraft. Shelly claimed to have been working and hadn't checked her phone or heard the doorbell. Officer McCoy said Shelly's reaction to the news of her father was normal under the circumstances. Officer McCoy said she prompted Shelly to call Sheriff Perkins.

She hadn't.

Ralph's problem was with Shelly's alibi. He was certain she wasn't working in Indianapolis. She was here in Iron Falls, where she wasn't supposed to be. He knew in his gut that he caught a glimpse of a woman running from Denny's house and lost her in the trees. The damn fire burned bright, making everything around the perimeter too dark to see.

Taking a deep breath, he lifted the receiver and pushed the button. "Rick, Sheriff Perkins here."

"Tell me it's done."

Ralph's eyes scanned his cramped office. Thirty-five years in this department, twenty-two as sheriff, and this was all Iron Falls could do for him—a ten by twelve box with a window facing the courthouse. He lifted his third cup of coffee to his lips and had a drink. "This line. It's not—"

"I'm not saying specifics, Ralph. You know what I'm talking about. Give me a fucking yes or no."

"I'm waiting for word. I sent the best."

"Waiting? Jesus Christ, it's after nine in the morning. I've called you twenty times and you're not answering. You told me it would happen during the night. Why haven't you heard from your man?" Rick's voice lowered. "You know this isn't just about me. These are people we don't want pissed off. You fucked up, and you need to make it right."

Ralph's tone was more of a growl. "You told me to get rid of a problem. I got rid of it." Denny Holdcraft was a *him* not an *it*. At this moment, Ralph wished he'd never accepted the assignment.

"Sloppy. We can't afford to have a possible witness."

It was Ralph's career and reputation on the line. The possibility of Denny's death being tied to Rick was slim, unless Ralph told.

With each passing second, Ralph was aware that he was becoming more expendable.

Ralph knew damn well what was at stake. He stood, pacing as far as possible while tethered to the telephone cord. His jaw ached from the pressure of his clenched teeth. "We're working on leads. Just let me do my job and get off my ass."

"Like I said, I'm not taking the fall for your incompetence. Listen to me."

Ralph clenched his teeth. He felt his circulation heat as crimson filled his neck and cheeks. "Rick, I'll call you when I have news. Until then, shut the fuck up."

"Do you know what I could do to your department or more specifically, take away from it? Federal funding goes through the appropriations committee. And that's a light punishment. If you upset those above me, it could be worse."

Ralph's knuckles blanched as he gripped the receiver tighter. "I'm going to pretend you didn't just threaten me. You're going to pretend everything is going as planned." With that he slammed the receiver on the base.

Hanging up on someone was more satisfying with a good old-fashioned landline. Hitting a red button wasn't near as fulfilling.

Ralph pulled his private phone from his pocket and brought the screen to life. Three missed calls from Rick Lehman—not twenty. No calls or text messages from Deputy Wilcox. Matt Wilcox had been with the Iron Falls Sheriff's Department for nearly ten years. He understood the way things worked. Ralph trusted him with special duties—those off the books. He sent Wilcox to Indianapolis Monday morning on a plane out of Boston, even before the report of the stolen snowmobile. The assignment Wilcox was on wouldn't appear in any official documentation.

Lehman was a hot-headed asshole. Calling Ralph on his office phone was reckless. Of course, it would have been avoided if Ralph had simply answered his earlier calls.

Pouring himself another cup of Britney's coffee, Ralph went to the window in his office and stared down the three stories to the courthouse lawn. The bright sunshine combined with the snow was blinding. The snowstorm the night in question left over fourteen new inches of accumulation. The sidewalks and streets were clear and wet.

The last seventy-two hours ran through his brain. Rick was right that Ralph fucked up. If he'd known Shelly was with her father, executing the plan could have waited. It couldn't have waited long. Denny was up to something. According to Lehman's contact, the IP geolocator or whatever was never wrong.

This side gig was too lucrative to lose, after Ralph's financial woes. It was the answer to his problems. What concerned Ralph the most was that the people above Rick didn't give a fuck who they eliminated. If he didn't get Shelly, he could end up like Denny.

Denny was a retired cop with too much time on his hands. He shouldn't have stuck his nose where it didn't belong.

A knock on the door brought Ralph back to the present. "Who is it?"

Deputy Tom Skiles appeared as the door opened, his forehead wrinkled, and eyes opened wide. "Have you seen the news out of Indianapolis?"

"Come in, Deputy." Ralph narrowed his eyes. "What news?"

Tom lifted his phone, showing Ralph the screen. "House explosion."

"What?" Ralph grabbed the phone. "What the hell?" He quickly scrolled through the news article.

Massive explosion rocks Indianapolis, Indiana, suburb. At 5:18 a.m., residents in this neighborhood on Indianapolis's South Side were awakened by a loud blast. One home was destroyed. Witnesses say it sounded as if a bomb went off.

Two nearby homes were damaged by debris. No injuries in the neighboring homes. At this time, it isn't known if the resident was present at the time of the explosion. No names will be released until family members are contacted. This is an active investigation and ongoing story. WTHR will update the story when more facts become available.

"Tell me it's not Shelly's house."

Tom nodded soberly. "I confirmed the address with IMPD." He lowered his tone. "What the hell was Matt thinking? He was supposed to go in and get her. Nothing to bring attention to her disappearance." He grasped Ralph's arm. "This is getting out of hand."

Ralph looked down at Tom's hand and back up, sending a wordless threat from his dark orbs.

Slowly, Tom released the sheriff.

"Rick has already chewed my ass this morning. I haven't heard from Wilcox and now this shit." Ralph threw Tom's phone onto the worn leather couch piled high with case files.

"When did you last speak with Matt?" Tom asked.

Ralph found his phone where he'd left it on his desk and scrolled his recent calls and text messages. "I spoke to him at one this morning, after I got the call from IMPD. He said he'd staked out her house all day and didn't see anyone. He said he'd go over to see if things changed." Ralph inhaled and met Tom's gaze. "I told him to make an extraction. Not to set off any alarms."

"He fucking blew up her house," Tom said in an angry whisper. "That's a mighty loud alarm."

"At 3:47 a.m.," Ralph said, "he sent a text saying he was going in."

Tom shook his head. "Why blow up the house an hour and a half later? He should have been on his way back here."

Ralph's cell phone vibrated. "It's Matt." He hit the green button. "What the fuck happened?"

"I don't know..."

TWENTY-ONE

"Your real name," Michelle said. "What do other people call you?"

"Arrow."

She leaned against the crook between the window and door and stared. Based on Fletch's expression and body language, she'd guess he was telling her the truth. "Why Arrow? Are you like the male version of Katniss from *Hunger Games*?"

"I shoot straight." He turned toward her and winked. "I hit my target."

"Come on, there's more to the story."

"You're the one who makes up stories," Fletch said. "Why do you think people call me Arrow?"

"Because that's the name you've given them, or they've heard others use it, and you never corrected them because you do whatever it is you do. You don't want to get close to anyone enough to tell them your real name."

"And here I thought you had a pre-law degree not psychology."

"I took psychology classes. I think the workings of the human brain are fascinating."

Fletch turned down the radio as they followed the red ribbon of taillights. "Tell me about your childhood."

Looking down, she picked at the frayed material of her blue jeans. There was nothing wrong with Michelle's childhood memories. It was that she wasn't sure if she could talk about them without breaking down at the loss of her father. Instead, she decided to give a short answer. "It was normal and boring." She looked up. "What about yours?"

"Not normal nor boring. So, I can't relate." He turned briefly, his eyes meeting hers. "You can give a long-winded answer to a question about the color of the sky, but your childhood gets five words. Did you ever want siblings?"

"I had an older sister. Her name was Sarah."

Fletch's lips pressed together. "Denny never mentioned her."

"He wouldn't. Sarah passed away before I was born. I didn't know anything about her until I was in high school. She was only four years old."

"What happened?"

"Mom said it was a tragedy. Dad said it was an

accident." Michelle sighed. "Sarah was the only topic my parents wouldn't discuss." She lifted her cheeks. "It's funny. When I was little, my mom said I had an imaginary friend, and I called her Sarah. She asked me how I came up with that name, and I apparently shrugged. I honestly don't remember any of that."

"Maybe you overheard your parents talking."

"Maybe. It's hard to understand what a child thinks. I'd forgotten about my imaginary friend until I learned about the real Sarah. It's one of those memories that seems real and at the same time you can't quite reach. It's fuzzy." She turned toward Fletch. "How about you, siblings?"

"One brother. My story isn't as tragic. We lost touch in the foster system. He was a year younger than me. He got adopted. I didn't."

The winter night felt suddenly cooler.

"What happened to your parents?" Michelle asked.

"From the records I've found, no name was listed for the man who helped make me. The woman who birthed me wanted her heroin or other drugs more than she wanted to be our mother. It's like you said, I can't remember the specifics. I don't even have memories of what she looked like. I've seen her picture, but when I do, it's like looking at a stranger."

Michelle reached over to his arm. "You weren't kidding when you said your childhood wasn't normal or boring. I'm sorry."

Fletch pressed his lips together and shook his

head. "Don't be. I learned from a young age who I could trust. That lesson made me the man I am today."

"A man who would save someone he barely knew."

Fletch looked Michelle's direction and quirked his lips. "I knew who I was saving." He relaxed his shoulders. "You're not officially safe yet."

"I'm alive. That says a lot." She paused, staring out at the passing scenery before turning back. "Sheriff Perkins sent a deputy to kidnap me."

Fletch nodded.

"What if he doesn't give up?"

He turned and met her gaze. "He won't find you where we're going."

"Which is...?"

"For now, just think of it as my home base."

"Your house?"

"I have an apartment."

"How many women have you saved and taken away to your place?" Michelle meant for the question to be funny, but by Fletch's expression, he didn't hear her humor.

"I've never taken a woman to my place."

"Never?" She remembered what he'd said a few moments ago. "Is that because you don't trust anyone?"

"There are a few people who I trust. The list is comfortably short. I'm good with keeping it that way."

At the next gas stop, Fletch changed from

streaming country music to the *Crime Daily Podcast.* He began today's earlier broadcast from the beginning.

Michelle wasn't the lead story. Instead, it was about a child who disappeared last Sunday from an NFL game in Foxborough, Massachusetts. The little boy was eight years old, Caucasian, four feet, two inches tall, weighing about fifty-five pounds.

After the game was over, Timothy Wells told his mother he needed to use the restroom. According to Mrs. Wells, she would normally take him with her, but the line to the ladies' room was extra-long. He went inside the men's bathroom, and his mother waited outside. There were a lot of people coming and going, yet she never saw her son exit.

After seeing men come and go, Mrs. Wells sent another man in the bathroom to find her son. He returned with the news she didn't want to hear—Timothy wasn't in the restroom. Mrs. Wells immediately contacted the stadium's security. All exit doors were closed, and the remainder of the fans were required to pass through security checkpoints before leaving. Timothy wasn't found.

The nab happened too fast.

Security cameras later identified a person of interest, a man wearing a Patriots hoodie, carrying a sleeping child in his arms. The man kept his head down, not allowing a clear view from the cameras. While the child's face was also well hidden from the cameras, Mrs. Wells confirmed that the shoes the child wore matched her son's.

The man with the sleeping child left the stadium before the security was notified of the missing boy. The Foxborough Police Department and the Massachusetts State Police have reached out to the FBI for help in finding Timothy.

He's the fourth child to be reported missing in New England in the last six weeks.

As Kenzi and Ali spoke about the leads, Fletch's grip of the steering wheel tightened. His fingers blanched beneath the grip.

When the podcast went to commercial break, Fletch mumbled, "Professional."

"Professional what?"

"Kidnapper, probably child trafficker."

In the illumination of the dashboard, Michelle saw the strain in his clenched jaw. "What do you think has happened to the boy?"

Fletch hit the steering wheel with the butt of his hand. "If he's lucky, he's in some other country adopted by someone who could pay for the child they wanted."

"If he's not lucky?" Michelle asked, her stomach twisting.

"If he's not lucky, he wishes he was dead."

"Welcome back," Kenzi's voice came through the speakers as she and Ali continued the most recent broadcast

of Crime Daily Podcast. *"Remember the author we spoke about yesterday, D. Valentine."*

"Michelle Holdcraft," Ali corrected.

"I wish they'd stop saying that," Michelle said.

"Right. Well, Ali, I wanted to lead with the Timothy Wells story because things are getting even more interesting. Yesterday it came to our attention that a man with the same last name—"

"Holdcraft."

"Right. Dennis Holdcraft was identified as the victim of a house fire in Iron Falls, Massachusetts. Tell our listeners what we've learned about Mr. Holdcraft."

"He served in the Indianapolis Metropolitan Police Department for over thirty years with many commendations. After the death of his wife, he retired and moved to Iron Falls. Get this...his wife died in a house explosion eight years ago."

"Whoa, that seems like a coincidence."

"It gets more interesting with their only daughter's home exploding. On top of that, Iron Falls is two and a half hours from Foxborough."

Michelle gasped. "They can't possibly be insinuating my father had anything to do with that boy's kidnapping." Her comment made them miss a little of the podcast.

"...happening in Massachusetts?"

"And Indiana, Kenzi. That was where Ms. Holdcraft lived. The Iron Falls sheriff, Ralph Perkins, told sources that Ms. Holdcraft was seen in Iron Falls prior to her father's

demise. When the sheriff couldn't locate her, he contacted IMPD to notify Ms. Holdcraft of her father's passing and request she contact him."

"Contact him?"

"Yeah, IMPD made a statement that Sheriff Perkins wanted to talk to Ms. Holdcraft about possible involvement in her father's death."

"You don't think Michelle is involved in her father's death?" Kenzi asked.

"I don't know, but she's missing, and her mother and now her father perish in house fires- slash-explosions."

Kenzi inhaled. "Three fires."

"I think we need to take a trip to Iron Falls."

Kenzi laughed. "It's like you can read my mind. I hear it's cold, so pack some boots and a warm coat."

"We'll be back after a word from our sponsor."

Fletch turned down the volume. "Fuck, that took a turn I wasn't expecting."

"Are they saying...? Is Ralph Perkins insinuating I was involved in my father's death? Are the podcasters?" Her voice rose an octave. "There's no way my father was involved in a kidnapping or child trafficking. Is there any way the two events could be connected?"

Fletch inhaled.

CHAPTER

TWENTY-TWO

The motel in Rapid City was similar to the place they'd stayed a day before—threadbare carpet, an outdated television, cracked-vinyl-covered chairs near a worn laminate table, and thin towels. The difference was that this motel room had two standard beds instead of one queen. Fletch wouldn't say he was disappointed, but he was.

While he didn't know what the future would bring, having Shelly near let him know she was safe—safe from Perkins and whoever he worked for. Fletch had been thinking about his last conversation with Denny. The old man's gut was right. If Fletch hadn't stayed out in Denny's work shed, he didn't want to think about what would have happened to Shelly.

He knew. There would have been two bodies in the house instead of one.

He kept his word to Denny. After a few days of

being with her, it had morphed into more than keeping his word. Fletch knew about dangers others never noticed. People disappeared every day. Shelly could have been one of those statistics. Hell, she was. He was the one who knew she was alive. His plan was to make sure she stayed that way.

Last night, when he held her as she fell asleep, the closeness was as much for him as it was for her and completely out of character. He was possibly getting attached. In his line of work, that wasn't a good thing. Having someone you cared about was a liability. Once he got to the complex, they would sort it out.

Fletch knew he needed to come clean with Shelly, tell her more about where they were going and what her future may be. He heard the water in the shower running. They'd had a long night of driving and now was time for sleep, not the time to start a conversation that would most likely take hours. Assuming Denny was right, Michelle Holdcraft would need to stay missing. It wasn't fair to keep her in the dark.

"The water is hot," Shelly said as she came from the bathroom.

Despite their impending discussion, Fletch smiled as he scanned Shelly from her head to her bare toes. Water droplets came from her crimson hair, leaving spots on her sleeping clothes. The soft shorts and oversized t-shirt were the same as he'd seen her wear many nights on the secret cameras. Her lack of a bra was evident by the way her nipples tented the shirt.

Shelly surely didn't see herself the way Fletch saw her. Her smile was infectious, her laugh a melody. He'd always been attracted to women with curves. Stick-straight, boobless women weren't appealing in his opinion.

Fletch couldn't remember the last time he'd spent three consecutive days with anyone. A week ago, he would have said it was unimaginable. During this escape, he'd shared more with Shelly than any other person he knew. It was natural to talk with her. The more time they spent together, the more he wanted it to continue.

"Water, right. Glad it's hot. That's one star for this dump."

Shelly laughed. "Two stars, it's also clean."

"I have everything we need in the room and the door's locked." He took the Glock from his holster in his jeans and laid it on the TV stand.

Michelle's blue eyes opened wide at the sight of the gun. Her lower lip disappeared between her teeth. "Are you leaving?"

He shook his head. "Just showering. You know how to use that if you need to."

"Knowing and wanting to are two different things."

Fletch fought the urge to touch her and reassure her. Instead, his shoulder brushed hers as he went into the bathroom. They had enough happening without a repeat of the other night. While the shower's water was hot, he turned the temperature down—cool to colder. The shivering didn't help his hard cock. Closing his eyes he took matters into his own hands as he jacked off to the memories of their night together. His body trembled as he came. Fletch doubted it was the first time someone had masturbated in this sleazy motel shower.

When he came out after showering, the lights were all off. With the heavy drapes closed, the room was mostly dark. At first, he assumed Shelly was asleep.

As he crawled into the bed beside hers, Shelly's voice cut through the dim motel room. "You never answered me about the podcast. Are people suspecting me?"

There were many things he hadn't answered her about or told her about. Fletch needed to resolve a few issues. Peterson was one. He wasn't happy that Fletch went back for Shelly Holdcraft. He was even less pleased that Fletch planned to take her to the complex.

"Fletch?"

"We have all night to talk."

The morning sun created a brightening frame around the heavy curtains. Heat hummed from the large radiator beneath the window. Instead of going to sleep, Shelly turned toward his bed. Lifting her head to her fist, she asked, "The things you know how to do. You said it's from practice, but you had to learn them somewhere."

"Good night, Shelly." It was actually Thursday morning, but he wanted the conversation to end.

It didn't. Shelly continued, "My dad was always good at everything he tried. Once when I was little, I caught him in our basement with a hand radio. It was a relic, but he was talking on it."

"Can this story wait until we've slept?"

"That memory came back to me today after the crime podcast. Dad told me the radio was a hobby, but I heard him talking about a high-profile child abduction. He was talking in letters, like Alpha, Gamma..." She sighed at the memory. "I didn't know what his conversation was when I heard him. Later I saw a news bulletin about a kidnapping and..." Her voice trailed away. "I don't know why it stayed with me. I think it's why I wrote *The Wishing Well*."

"You said *The Wishing Well* was based off of a true crime in Wisconsin."

"That was *Broken Promises. The Wishing Well* came to me while I was interning at the Indianapolis courthouse."

He was glad it was dark because the memory of Shelly in that courtroom made him grin. Something he was doing more and more of these past few days.

"My dad didn't have anything to do with Timothy Wells's disappearance. If anything, I'd say he was somehow trying to solve it."

"Denny was retired."

"From IMPD," she replied. "I can't shake the

feeling that he was still involved in something." She sighed.

Fletch lay on his back, staring up at the popcorn ceiling. Shelly was close. Maybe he could explain it all to her. He didn't have a choice. She couldn't enter the complex without understanding what the agency was.

She continued talking. "He didn't want me to stay the night he was killed, but I couldn't leave with the snow. I think he was worried that something would happen."

Fletch didn't respond. If he did, they'd be talking for hours, and they both needed to get some sleep.

It didn't take long until he heard the even breathing coming from her bed. Shelly was asleep. Her questions sparked a memory of something she'd mentioned in the truck. It was about having a sibling. One that died before Shelly was born.

Fletch reached for his phone and searched for Sarah Holdcraft. He found the record of her birth to Dennis and Tracy Holdcraft at a hospital in Beech Grove, Indiana. The date would indicate that she would be four years older than Michelle. There was no other information, including no declaration of death.

He sent a text message to Leo.

"A favor – off the record?"

Leo responded immediately.

"Other than working to calm Peterson? What?"

Leo had access to the agency's computers. Fletch would also in another twenty-four hours. He hesitated. Maybe he should wait until he could run the search himself. A question mark appeared on his screen.

"Look into Sarah Holdcraft for me. Don't mention it to anyone else."

"Relation to Denny?"

"Yes."

"Okay."

Fletch turned off the ringer on his phone. He'd wake if it vibrated, even from a sound sleep. Years of working for the agency had him constantly alert. It was dangerous to be anything less.

TWENTY-THREE

Ralph Perkins was closed in his office trying to figure out a way out of this mess. Every damn domino was falling in the wrong direction. Take his plan to secure Shelly Holdcraft. Matt Wilcox was back in Iron Falls with a concocted story about securing Shelly and losing her. Matt said he entered the house without issue, picking the lock and carefully blocking the doorbell camera. Inside, he found Shelly asleep on her bed. Matt claimed he had her secured and was about to inject the sedative when she started fighting, kicking, and bucking. The next thing Matt remembered was waking up in his rental car to the sound of sirens. He circled around. The streets were blocked by emergency vehicles. Matt saw the debris from Shelly's house and fled the scene. Once he was a few miles away, he called Ralph.

Unlike Britney, who had a fancy degree in criminology, Matt's experience came from the job. While he was usually dependable, he wasn't exactly the brightest bulb in the box. Nevertheless, it seemed that even Matt could make up a better story about his failure to procure the target. Turned out he wasn't lying. The urine sample Matt delivered after his flight back to Massachusetts corroborated his story. It came up positive for Propofol, the drug in Matt's syringe.

The question was how a twenty-eight-year-old woman overpowered and drugged a man dumber than an ox and as strong as one. No one had an answer to that mystery.

The door to his office opened. Britney stepped inside. "Sheriff, you have a call from Indianapolis Metropolitan Police, an Officer Darla McCoy. She's on line one."

Well, shit, Ralph thought, wondering if Wilcox screwed up and left some trace evidence around Shelly's house. He'd deny sending Wilcox to Indianapolis. Then he had another thought. Maybe they found Shelly's body in her destroyed home. Can't get much more silent than dead. Ralph was almost giddy when he picked up the telephone receiver. "Officer McCoy. Do you have news for me?"

"Thank you for taking my call, Sheriff. What I'm about to tell you is currently classified. I know you were upset about what happened in your city to Dennis Holdcraft, and I believe our departments can be of assistance to one another."

She had Ralph's attention.

She continued, "My captain authorized me to speak with you. You, however, must agree, for the time being, to keep this information confidential."

He sat forward on his chair, believing this nightmare was almost over. "You have my word, Officer McCoy. I'm assuming this is about Shelly Holdcraft and what happened at her house. Did she go on to meet her papa in heaven?"

"Only if the road to heaven is west on I-74 in a 2017 white Toyota Camry."

"What?" His volume rose.

"We received a call late yesterday from an Indiana state trooper named Warren Stephenson. Before getting off duty Tuesday morning, he pulled over a 2017 white Toyota Camry with Ohio plates."

"Shelly was in the car?" he asked in disbelief. He was certain Shelly's car was in Denny's garage. Of course, it could have been a rental.

"*Possible* sighting." She emphasized the word. "Trooper Stephenson said the woman in the car looked familiar, but he admitted to being tired. His shift was about over. The woman didn't have an ID. She'd said she'd left her purse at home. Something about leaving early and being on their way to visit a grandfather in the hospital."

Ralph didn't care about an old man in the hospital. "Did this Stephenson run the license plate?"

"No, sir. He didn't pull them over due to any violation. Stephenson informed them of a low tire and sent them on their way."

Fuck, Ralph growled. "Wait." His volume rose. "Did you say *them*? The woman wasn't alone?"

Officer McCoy hummed. "A man was driving, carrying an Ohio ID with the name Jason Martin. The car registration matched. The woman who looked like Ms. Holdcraft said her name was Mindy Martin, Jason's sister."

Ralph shook his head. "This sounds farfetched."

"I'd agree. However, yesterday after Trooper Stevenson woke, he saw Ms. Holdcraft's picture on our APB and remembered the stop. Stephenson was so sure the woman was Ms. Holdcraft, he contacted two truck stops in Oakwood, Illinois. That's the first exit after he pulled them over.

"He figured the driver would've stopped at one of the two locations to fix the low air pressure. There's a Pilot and a Love's. Sheriff, we have video of Michelle Holdcraft in the Love's truck stop with a time stamp of 5:13 a.m., Wednesday morning. Trooper Stephenson's shift ended at six. Time changes over the Indiana-Illinois border."

"I'll be damned."

"She was wearing a stocking cap and sunglasses."

"Sounds like she's trying to be incognito," Ralph said.

"The location of the traffic stop also suggests she wasn't at home when the house exploded." Darla

McCoy lowered her voice. "Sheriff, what if Ms. Holdcraft caused the explosion at her own house? Why would she do that?"

Ralph couldn't pass up the opportunity. It was as if the good Lord Almighty was clearing away his troubles. "There's people talking they saw Shelly up here before Denny's fire." He hesitated. "No, Shelly wouldn't hurt her father."

"I pulled Ms. Holdcraft's file. I don't know if you're aware. Eight years ago, in Johnson County, just south of us, there was an incident."

"An incident." he repeated. "What incident?"

"Ms. Holdcraft was twenty years old at the time and a sophomore at Purdue University. She was home on holiday break, spending the night at a friend's home when her parents' home exploded. The police accused Ms. Holdcraft of tampering with the gas stove. That stove was believed to have ignited the explosion, the one that killed her mother. Now her father dies in a fire, and her house explodes. Sheriff, I'm starting to think we could have a serial arsonist on our hands."

He sat taller. "I think I should tell you, the fire marshal determined accelerant was used in Denny's house fire. Place went up quicker than a dead cat can fall out of a tree." Ralph debated about the wisdom of what he was saying, but this story was writing itself. "We haven't released COD. Confidentially, Dennis Holdcraft died from a gunshot to the head. We were leaning toward suicide, but..."

"Sheriff, would you be open to bringing ATF in on your case. Our chief has called them about the recent explosion at Ms. Holdcraft's house. Due to the burn pattern, our fire chief believes an incendiary device was used. If that's the case, Ms. Holdcraft could have been able to set the device to explode once she was out of the city."

Ralph was glad they weren't talking in person. He never would have been able to hide his grin. "I would never suspect Shelly..."

"It seems too coincidental. Three family members. Three fires. Occam's Razor."

"Let me consult with our fire chief, and I'll get back to you."

"Hard telling where Ms. Holdcraft is now. Chief said to broaden the search. We're still calling her a missing person. Once we get the ATF in on this, Ms. Holdcraft will officially be a suspect."

"Thank you for your call, Officer McCoy." A two-ton weight came off Ralph's shoulders as he hung up the call.

TWENTY-FOUR

Petroleum County was the least populated county in the state of Montana, the sixth least-populated county in all the United States. The last census had the county's population at just over 500. While that number shifted from time to time, most everyone knew everyone else. What wasn't included in the recent census were the people within a complex on three hundred and twenty acres of officially uninhabited ground.

In November of 1952, the National Security Agency was created with a seven-page top-secret memorandum. The plan was that the NSA would operate outside the guise of bureaucracy. Not everyone was content with the achievements.

In 1963, three hundred and twenty acres north of Winnett, Montana, was purchased for $40,000 by a wealthy rancher. That would be equivalent to almost half a million today. The land sat empty until the spring of 1967. According to county records, the land was sold for $100,000, over double its value. The new owner was hidden beneath multiple layers of business names, what today would be considered shell companies.

The idea of the agency was concocted in back rooms and think tanks with like-minded people who included military generals, elected officials, bureaucrats, successful business leaders, and motivated citizens. The country—no, the world—needed a department that answered to no person, party, or special-interest groups. This *agency* would work independently for the betterment of the people—all the people. They'd weed out corruption while fighting social injustices. It was a high-minded objective.

In November of 1968, a new federal agency to accomplish what NSA had not was born with the stroke of the president's pen. Even the date of the creation was planned. If any news of this new agency leaked out, it would surely be overshadowed by the results of the 1968 presidential election.

That top-secret status was still the case, despite its growth and development over the last fifty years.

It was important for the founding members of the agency to keep their activities off the public's and governmental agencies' radar. While the agency was funded through governmental diversions, its classified existence was known by relatively few. This status allowed the agency to do its work without the bureaucracy so often associated with other official departments.

No one from the agency was or would be called to testify before Congress nor had their picture and title on a website. While construction on the original structures began in 1967, the agency didn't fully bloom into what it was today until the summer of 1972.

America was in crisis with rising inflation, social unrest, and the hugely unpopular Vietnam War. A monumental scandal was brewing after a nightguard at a D.C. hotel and affiliated offices named Watergate Complex noticed a door taped open. There had been a break-in at the Democratic National Committee headquarters.

The great American experiment was failing.

In 1972, the agency stepped in, puppeteering a series of seemingly unconnected events.

In August of 1972, Americans watched as their president resigned.

Three years later, Saigon, Vietnam, fell.

The agency had grown since its humble beginnings. Today, there were thousands of agents throughout the world. The complex in Montana, where the agency began, was now one of many facilities throughout the country and world, while the agency had connections in all layers of government.

Dennis Holdcraft entered the agency over his

desire to fight human trafficking. He knew there had to be more than what he could do as a police officer.

It was Tracy who recommended Dennis. They shared the desire to make a difference. Her specialty was research. Even in the early 1980s, she was more skilled than most within cybersecurity—decryption and analysis—when it came to getting results. Not all the members of the agency carried guns. There were scientific researchers working on medical research that had unnecessarily been defunded. Agents filled vital roles in humanitarian efforts. The agents who possessed similar capabilities to Arrow were often shipped around the world, tasked with squelching problems before they got out of control.

An overaggressive dictator.

A terrorist cell.

A rogue warmonger.

There were rumors in Petroleum County about what went on behind the fences and guard shack. Some people thought it was a prison that housed the worst of the worst. Others said it was a research facility, specializing in infectious diseases. The local law enforcement personnel were told the facility was under federal jurisdiction. Most locals only knew that whatever it was had been there for as long as they could remember, and their workers contributed to the economy.

Pretty much, the people of Petroleum County coexisted with what they didn't know or understand without much thought. The people from the agency who made it into nearby towns such as Winnett, Grass Range, or Mosby were good-natured enough and didn't cause a fuss. Their money was accepted at the local taverns or grocery stores.

Those agency employees swore an oath to never divulge anything about the agency.

When Fletch woke, his first thought was of that oath. Sitting up, he saw Shelly's hair fanned over her pillow, appearing more auburn than copper in the dimness. Tonight, he would break that oath for her. The information he would share would change her world forever. Technically, her decision to visit Iron Falls and surprise her father did that.

Denny asked Arrow to take Shelly back to her life. He'd tried that.

Perkins sent a deputy to her house. If Arrow had left her alone, Perkins wouldn't give up.

The sun was fully set by five thirty as Fletch and Shelly made their way out of the motel room and into the black truck. Tonight, Shelly's hair was secured in a long braid. She'd said it would be easier to hide it under his stocking cap.

After the incident with the state trooper in Indiana, Arrow had considered getting her hair dye. He'd almost bought it the first night of their cross-country drive. But as he held the box, he imagined changing her hair from flaming copper to brown was like extinguishing Shelly's fire. He put the box back.

"How much longer?" she asked as he pulled out of the parking lot.

"A little over six hours."

"Are you going to tell me where we're going?"

Fletch clenched his jaw, feeling the muscles and tendons pull in his neck. "First, we're going to stop for coffee. The machine in the hotel looked questionable." He handed her his stocking cap.

Shelly didn't argue as she pulled it over her head. "It's too dark for sunglasses."

"Just don't look at the person in the window. Those blue eyes are too pretty to forget."

Shelly turned toward the window.

"You always turn away from compliments."

"Because I don't believe you."

"You said you trust me."

She turned back. "To keep me safe. You don't have to lie. I see myself in the mirror."

"I'm not lying. You're beautiful. We can agree that perceived beauty is subjective. However, I'd argue that my opinion is based on empirical evidence. I've watched you for years."

"That's kind of creepy."

Fletch couldn't help but laugh. "You're right."

"You say it like you've been stalking me."

"Watching, not stalking. Let me finish about my evidence."

Although she felt the warming of her cheeks, Michelle nodded.

"When I say you're beautiful, it's not only your outward appearance, which is, in fact, attractive. It's also the person you are, who I thought I knew but didn't." He reached over and laid his hand on her denim-clad thigh. "I'm not going to argue about this."

Shelly looked down at his hand. "I won't argue. It's that I don't see myself that way. I'm not like the women I write in my books. They're all in great shape. They run and exercise. I detest running. I sit for hours not realizing that time has passed." She turned to him and smiled. "And I like snacks. You probably figured that out by the things you bought."

"The women you write aren't real. You're real."

"But you're not?"

"We're getting to that," Fletch said before he drove up to the screen at the drive-thru and ordered two coffees and two cheeseburgers. As they waited for their food, Fletch searched for the *Crime Daily Podcast*. "Maybe we'll learn something."

To their disappointment, the podcast was a replay from a few days ago.

Once they were back on the road, she asked him again where they were going.

He exhaled. "I want you to listen. You'll have questions but try to hear me out first."

She took a sip of her coffee and then removed the lid and blew. "Is this some top-secret operation?"

"As a matter of fact, yes."

He watched as her blue eyes widened and waited

for her next comment. When it didn't come, he began. "Remember me telling you that I don't exist?"

"Is this where I listen or answer?"

Fletch furrowed his brow. "Work with me."

"I remember. Obviously, you exist."

"Fletcher Weir died seven years ago. It was declared a military training accident. The helicopter I was in went down."

"Were you really in an accident?"

"No. Three of my friends were. The flight wasn't training. It was a special mission. They died. My name was added to the manifest, allowing me to take another position with a different agency."

"Your family thought you died?" Her voice rippled with emotion.

He shook his head. "Remember, no family. That made me the perfect candidate. I'm also good at what I do."

"Which is?"

"Whatever I'm told. Until the other night."

"What is this agency?"

"It doesn't have a name. We refer to it as the agency."

"I don't understand. Is this like the CIA, FBI, or NSA?"

They were now headed northwest on Highway 212. "Those agencies have specific roles. The CIA focuses on foreign intelligence gathering and covert operations. The FBI focuses on domestic law enforcement and counterintelligence. The National Security Agency concentrates on signals intelligence and cybersecurity. There's also DIA, NGA, NRO, Coast Guard Intelligence, DHS, and more. The agency I work for does all of that and more. We do the jobs that don't go on the books—no official record. There are no checks and balances for what we do."

"Are you the bad guys or the good guys?"

"We know we're the good guys." He scoffed. "Or we've been brainwashed into believing what we do is for good."

"Have you killed people?"

He nodded.

Shelly shook her head.

"Those of us in the agency get things done. Most of us have military or law enforcement backgrounds, but not all. There are agents like me who work independently. We don't have liabilities, and that allows us to take greater risks, all for the good of humanity.

"There are also agents who function within societal norms, get married, have children, and work real jobs. Hell, they probably coach Little League. They also answer the call when it comes."

Shelly's forehead furrowed. "You asked me about my mom. How did you know about her?"

"Mostly from Denny, but Tracy Holdcraft is legend."

"You're crazy. My mom was a librarian, not military."

"The agency isn't all about brawn. It takes brains. Tracy had those."

Michelle looked at Fletch as if he had two heads. "You're saying it was my mother who was involved with the agency, not my dad?"

"They both were."

TWENTY-FIVE

Michelle couldn't believe what she was hearing. This wasn't like when she didn't believe Fletch's compliments. She enjoyed hearing them and while she didn't totally agree, hearing them was nice. She was more than pleased that he saw her the way he did. Because to be honest, she hasn't been at her best the last few days. What Fletch was saying about her parents was impossible or at least highly improbable.

"You're saying my parents were agents for this no-name agency while they pretended to be normal parents."

"I don't know what kind of parents they were. It's why I asked you about your childhood. I didn't know them then, but if you thought you had everyday parents, they were very good at hiding what they did. I never wanted what they did—to live a double life. It's risky in its own way. You were a liability for them. If they had been discovered…" He inhaled. "Denny called me to meet with him the night he was killed. He was worried about Ralph Perkins."

"Did he want your help?"

"Not with Perkins. He called me because of you. That's why I was nearby when the fire started. It's how I knew you were there. Hell, I was about to run into the blaze when I saw you."

"How did you see me and the sheriff didn't?"

"Sometimes there aren't answers. Maybe there's a higher being. Maybe your dad got one last wish. I told him I'd take care of you if anything went awry."

Michelle tried to make heads or tails out of what he was saying. "Can you tell me more about what they did? What you do?"

"I'm not supposed to, but I will. From what I've heard, Tracy was a master at navigating the web even before it was a thing. She had computer skills that the NSA would have wanted if they knew about her."

A smile tugged at Michelle's lips. She'd never thought of her mother as a crusader for justice. She had always just been her mom. Michelle recalled her mother's death and her smile faded. "My mom died in a house explosion on the night I came home for holiday break my sophomore year." She was recalling. "I was disappointed she wasn't home. Dad wasn't either." Her pulse kicked up. "Could I have been killed in that explosion? Was that related to this agency?"

His dark eyes flashed to her and back to the highway. A string of small reflectors lined the asphalt, highlighting the road. "If you had been there...then yes. As for it being related to the agency, Denny suspected."

Fletch's answer gave her a sinking sensation in her stomach. The cheeseburger she'd recently consumed churned. "You don't think it was the gas company's fault—or mine?" she added.

"It wasn't your fault. You wouldn't do that. Denny said the accusations were baseless. He couldn't tell them the truth. He couldn't tell them that he thought your home was targeted due to their work with the agency." Fletch swallowed. "It was one of the reasons he chose to move to Massachusetts."

She sighed. "I thought it was because I reminded him too much of Mom. I always got the feeling that while he loved me, it was difficult for him to look at me."

Fletch shook his head. "It was the agency, Shelly. Denny said he lost too much to the agency. He didn't want to lose you too."

Her voice carried a faraway tone. "I wish he would have told me."

"He couldn't. I can't."

Michelle turned toward Fletch. "Then why are you?"

"Because Denny was targeted. We believe... Denny did a lot of the research...he was searching for a possible network responsible for many of the abductions."

"A network?"

"They're happening faster and neater. Professionals. This network is large. Apprehending or stopping the kidnappers would only be a hiccup in their system. We want those at the top, those making millions or more by selling people. It takes individuals at all levels for a trafficking network to succeed."

"I've written a little about this."

Fletch nodded. "You have. Most of what you've written is damn close to reality. In fiction, it's easier to have fewer players. For one, it's easier for your readers to follow. Denny's learned over the years that there are the abductions, such as Timothy Wells. There are many other players. Social workers identify at-risk children and teens, especially ones without a support system. Law enforcement comes across a homeless mother with two babies. They all go missing and no one notices."

Michelle's nose scrunched. "I'd rather think it's one stoppable person who's responsible."

"The people who need to be brought down are the ones with the money. The ones paying for the yachts and private flights."

"That makes sense."

"Denny suspected that Sheriff Perkins is part of that network, a cog in the wheel, you could say. You were right about your dad wanting to help Timothy Wells."

That simple sentence revived Michelle's faith in her father.

"Denny's obsession was human trafficking, especially children," Fletch said. "He believed the Wells boy was taken and is currently being moved via yacht to Nova Scotia. He'd reported his findings to our boss at the agency. If your dad's hard work pays off, Timothy should be reunited with his family soon. Hell, today's Thursday. He could already be saved or on his way to a new country."

Michelle blinked, feeling the burn from salty tears she didn't want to shed. "Dad was a hero. Wait, this network doesn't kill children, as in *Broken Promises*?"

"It's an imperfect operation. Some end up in the wrong hands—they don't make it out alive. Some never adapt to the new life. Their whereabouts are unknown and unfathomable."

"Dad was the good guy." Thinking anything else was absurd. "Why would that get him killed?"

"If Perkins is part of a bigger network with powerful people at the top and he thought your dad was a risk to that endeavor, he'd kill him."

Michelle tried to come to terms with what she was being told. Her questions continued. "I've been all through Dad's house. He only has an iPad. That's not exactly high tech."

"There was an old shed about seven hundred yards

behind the house." Fletch shook his head. "Denny transformed it into a technological hub with a computer system your mom would have been proud to work."

"Do you think the sheriff will find it?"

He pressed his lips together. "No. My contact was supposed to clear it out. Ralph may have had his suspicions about Denny, but if his setup is found, it could lead a talented cybersecurity person to the agency. We can't risk that."

"Who is your contact?"

"He's one of the few that I trust."

"Will I meet him?"

"Eventually. Tonight, like I said before, I'm going to take us to my place. It's not much—an apartment in the complex. Think of it like a base. Sometimes it's easier to equate the agency with a branch of the military." Fletch shrugged. "I spend a lot of time traveling. This apartment is my home base, I guess you could say." He took a deep breath. "Shelly, taking you to the agency is a one-way trip."

The small hairs on the back of her neck rose to attention. "What does that mean?"

"If you're willing to stay and if the powers that be agree you can be an asset, Michelle Holdcraft will disappear. She already has."

"And do what? How could I possibly be an asset? I'm not a retired cop or a professional researcher."

"I would disagree with the second. You research

for your writing. Think of it as researching an idea for a book, but in this case, it's real life."

"What if I say no? What if I say, let me out at the nearest stop and I'll..."

"Do what?"

The emptiness in her chest opened to a chasmic void. "I can't go home." It wasn't a question. "You're saying that I would need to start over."

"Witness protection is an option, but you can't divulge the agency." He reached over to her thigh and squeezed. "I'm sorry, Chell. I made that decision for you. I should have talked to you about this sooner."

You think? She didn't say the words aloud, but they were there.

Leaving her life.

Michelle thought through everything she'd miss. It boiled down to her father, but he was already gone. There were her friends and her writing. Could she still write? Those thoughts and more swam through her brain. Michelle was quiet for a few minutes. "Dad's passion was saving children?"

"Oh." Fletch's voice became more animated. "He could rattle on about statistics for hours about missing children. Over 460,000 children go missing a year in the US. While the majority of those children are found safe, that still leaves hundreds who are never heard from again. When you broaden the statistics to adults, it's much higher. Technically, an eighteen-year-old is classified as an adult. It's not only in the US where children go missing. Consider war zones, migration, and weather devastation, people go missing and no one notices or has the means to report them."

Would she be missed?

Michelle pushed that thought away and concentrated on her father. A grin slowly formed. "You're right. He did talk about it. I think I used some of his stories in creating fiction. I loved to hear him tell stories about his time on the force. I was so proud of what he did." She shrugged. "I don't think I could do what Dad did, but if whoever is in power will allow me to stay, I'd like to try to help."

"The first step is convincing Peterson."

As they traveled, Michelle worked to settle her nerves. Her life was now in the hands of a person she didn't know. And there was nothing she could do to change it.

The clock on the dashboard read one o'clock Friday morning when they entered Petroleum County in the nondescript black Ford truck Fletch had secured. The license plate was from a junkyard, and the truck was streaked with the salt and sand they used to keep the ice off the roads.

TWENTY-SIX

It had been a long time since Michelle had depended upon another person. She couldn't recall the last time she felt so vulnerable. Her writing paid her bills. She shopped for her own food and clothes. She even managed to enjoy a few extravagances such as monthly salon visits. Her life was comfortable and secure. The reality of how drastically everything changed hit her with the force of a sledgehammer as Fletch drove down a narrow dirt road and came to a guard shack.

The things he'd told her about the no-name agency sounded more like fiction than reality. Yet here she was in a truck as Fletch got out and walked to speak with the guard on duty. While she couldn't hear their conversation, she was pretty sure it was about her. Finally, the guard acquiesced, and the gate opened.

"Problem?" she asked as Fletch got back inside the truck.

"Nothing that can't be handled."

She inhaled, unsure what to expect.

Beyond the guard shack, the truck's headlights cut through the dark night. For the next five minutes, there wasn't a light in sight, only the headlights cutting through the black night. The road wound between mountains leading into a cavern. Within was the first evidence of life. The settlement only had a few lights illuminating the complex. The structures loomed in the shadows of the higher elevations of land.

Michelle had never been on a military base. If she were to imagine one from books, movies, and TV shows, this complex would fit into that imagination. In the dark night, the buildings lacked color or differentiating features, giving the cluster an ominous uniform feel.

"It's not much," Fletch warned as they pulled up to what looked like a two-story apartment building. "I travel a lot." He shrugged. "And I wasn't expecting to bring anyone home with me when I left."

Michelle grinned. Fletch's usual self-assuredness was replaced by what she could only describe as self-deprecation. It was endearing. "Are you telling me your apartment might not be picked up?"

He pressed his lips together. "You won't hurt my feelings if the star rating is less than the last motel."

"It can't be that bad."

Outside the truck, Fletch opened the door to an apartment on the first floor and tentatively, Michelle entered. There was an odor of stuffiness that happens when a place has been closed for a long time. Fletch flipped the switches, bringing the interior into view. A small entry allowed them to go right into the kitchen, straight into the living room, or left to what she assumed were the bedrooms.

The counter between the kitchen and living room was covered with stuff. Michelle didn't have a better description. There were books, papers, and even an empty milk jug. There were dishes in the sink, even though there was a dishwasher.

"This is..." She spun around. "You said you've never brought a woman here."

Fletch was walking around, picking up blankets and pillows from the sofa. "You're the first."

Her laugh started as a nervous snicker and morphed into a full-belly laugh. It must have been contagious, because soon, Fletch was laughing too. "I know. It's a mess."

"Bedrooms?" Michelle asked as she tilted her head toward the left.

"Two, but one is...Let me show you." He led her toward the room with the open door and turned on the light.

It was a bedroom, all right. There was a bed—a king-sized bed with a fitted sheet, pillows, and a tangled knot of blankets. A television sat on top of a long dresser, where drawers were opened in disarray. Fletch went to the dresser and shoved the clothes inside the drawers as he closed each one. A bathroom was attached.

"There's a second bathroom in the hallway."

Michelle nodded, holding a nugget of hope that inside the closed door she'd find another bed, one not in disarray. While the space could be a bedroom, it was obviously Fletch's office. The room was overstuffed with computers and more computers.

Looking back into the main bedroom, she let out a breath and asked, "Do you have a laundry? Like a washing machine and dryer?"

"In the kitchen."

"How about extra sheets?"

He contorted his face in question. "You need more sheets?"

"No, different ones." She pointed at the coffee stain on the side of the bed. At least she hoped it was coffee.

Exhaling, he ran his fingers through his hair. "I'm fucking great at what I do. Cleaning isn't part of that."

"Not a problem. I think we found something I'm better at than you."

"It's the middle of the night," he reminded her. "Don't you want to sleep?"

She went to the bed and began pulling blankets from the pile. "You've totally messed with my sleeping schedule. How about some housework first?"

"Chell." There was a bemused apologetic tone to the one word.

Michelle stopped what she was doing and walked closer to Fletch. "Hey, I'm alive because of you. I don't care how you live." She shrugged. "But if you want me here—"

"Here is where you're safe."

"If you want me here, I have to clean." She pointed to the computer room. "I'm sure you have things in there that you want to do."

"Fuck," he said, "I can't let you clean my place."

Michelle's cheeks lifted with her smile. "For now, it's *our* place and yeah, I'm going to clean."

The first thing she did was to strip the bed and pillows and start the sheets in a wash. Thankfully, he had detergent. Next, she decided to tackle the kitchen. It appeared that instead of cooking, Fletch preferred microwaving. It took boiling water inside the microwave for her to begin to chip away at the layers of the last fifty food items he'd heated.

She rummaged through his cabinets, finding mostly nonperishable foods: soups, canned vegetables, rice, boxed macaroni and cheese. At least it was the kind with the gooey cheese, not the powdered cheese. To her surprise, Michelle found cleaning supplies.

Michelle didn't know where to begin with the countertops. Her goal was for organized clutter as she stacked papers. The books, much to her surprise, were thrillers, military and psychological, as well as multiple titles of non-fiction. The tomes she moved to an under-utilized bookcase in the living room.

Each room was an adventure.

Once the sheets were in the dryer, she started a load of towels, kitchen and bath.

She'd also collected an assortment of plates, silverware, and glasses and started the dishwasher.

While it wasn't exactly the glamorous life of a New York Times bestselling author, the menial tasks accomplished something Michelle desperately needed. They took her mind off the shit show her life had become and gave her achievable goals.

Each shiny or dust-free surface was an accomplishment.

The bed was made, the towels were in the dryer, and brewing coffee filled the apartment with a delicious aroma. Finally, she sat down on the sofa. The clock near the television read near four in the morning. Her days and nights were catching up to her.

Michelle laid her head on the soft cushioned arm of the sofa, pulled one of the recently folded blankets over her, and closed her eyes.

Her scream pierced the air. "Stop." She pushed with all her might against her attacker. The gun. She needed to get to the gun. "Stop." Her fists beat against his chest as he tried to carry her.

"Chell."

She opened her eyes, finding herself in Fletch's

arms, him staring at her with a bewildered expression. "Oh my God."

He'd placed her back on the couch.

Michelle sat up and buried her face in her hands. "I'm sorry. I think it was a nightmare."

He shook his head. "I shouldn't have snuck up on you. I wanted you to stay asleep." Fletch sat beside her and reached for her hands. "Fuck, you didn't show these to me."

He was talking about her wrists. It appeared as if she were wearing two large purple bracelets designed in the distinctive pattern of fingerprints.

Michelle tugged the cuffs of her shirt down. "They'll heal."

"Makes me wish I would have killed the motherfucker."

She knew she should be appalled by a death threat. She wasn't. In the short time she'd known Fletch, she'd decided that protecting was his way of showing he cared. "Hopefully, the deputy had a whopper of a headache."

"I didn't mean to wake you. I was going to put you in bed." He looked around the living room and kitchen area. "This place has never looked this good." He grinned. "Hell, I didn't know it could."

"After days of driving, it felt good to do something."

"How about that bed thing?" he asked.

She nodded. "I'm tired. Maybe a few hours' sleep, and we can get back on a normal cycle."

"I can carry you."

That made her smile. "I'm capable of walking." As they both stood, she turned to him. "What about you? Are you going to get some sleep?"

"A few hours. I have to meet with Peterson at 0900."

"What day is tomorrow?" Michelle asked, uncertain. The last week had been a blur that seemed much longer than one week.

"Today is Friday. Tomorrow is Saturday. There are no days off in the agency."

She nibbled her upper lip. "What if he says I can't stay here?"

Fletch didn't hesitate. "Then I go where you go. He's not going to want to lose me."

It was crazy how natural it felt when Michelle came out of the bathroom wearing her usual bedtime attire of soft shorts and an oversized t-shirt to find Fletch wearing only his boxer briefs.

He must have been waiting for her because he stood from the side of the bed and met her. Taking her hands, he squeezed them. "Thank you. I'm embarrassed you had to clean."

"Don't be."

He tilted his head, the tips of his hair curling near his wide shoulder. "I guess I'm normally a slob, but damn, even the bathroom's sparkling."

Michelle smiled. "It felt good to do something for you. You've done everything for me. I've been thinking about it. I grabbed the cash I had at home, but it's only a few hundred dollars. Will I be able to access the money from my accounts?"

"Not if you're officially missing."

"What about my father's estate? I don't know that he had a lot, but..."

Fletch shook his head.

Michelle closed her eyes and exhaled. "It was good to stop thinking for a while."

"Your legs are bruised."

Michelle looked down at the purple splotches on her thighs and back up to Fletch's concerned gaze. "They only hurt if I touch them."

His timbre changed, his tone deeper and words slower. "Maybe...I could take your mind off of them and everything else for a while."

The suggestion caused her core to twist and her nipples to bead. "I thought it was only one night."

"Chell, I'll let you sleep. I can even go out to the couch. When we were running, I was too concerned with keeping you alive to let my guard down. You're safe here."

She was also alive. That was evident by the way her circulation suddenly raced through her veins. "Don't sleep on the couch."

If cleaning had been cathartic, being in Fletch's arms was empowering. The bulk of his body surrounded her, creating a cocoon where she was not only safe, but satisfied. The unfamiliarity of their first night together vanished. They'd lived and breathed the same air in the same space for nearly a week. They were together in their quest for safety, bonded during hours of sharing, and forged by the dangers of their journey.

When Fletch offered to take her mind off things, Michelle wondered if the night they'd shared could be repeated. It wasn't. Tonight was more. Their days and nights were no longer threatened. Mutual pleasure was their only focus.

The secret agency, Sheriff Perkins, and even Michelle's father were momentarily forgotten. When Michelle surrendered to sleep, she was both satiated and exhausted.

TWENTY-SEVEN

Ralph didn't care for the visitors currently waiting for an interview in an interrogation room. Their names didn't ring any bells. He wasn't much into podcasts. Sports radio was more his speed. He stayed informed about the Patriots and Red Sox. Baseball and football were his favorites. Ralph cared if the Celtics won but didn't follow the team the way he did the others. True crime, hell, he dealt with that every day. He sure as hell didn't want to listen to it for entertainment, especially from some Nancy Drew wannabes.

Britney on the other hand was ecstatic that Ali and Kenzi from *Crime Daily Podcast* were in Iron Falls. She'd already set the pair up with water and cookies.

Joclyn Evans, Old Man Evans's wife, brought a big batch of snickerdoodles to the station to thank the sheriff for the return of her husband's snowmobile.

Ralph had no idea how the snowmobile returned, but he sure did like snickerdoodles.

Things were falling into place. Officer McCoy's call yesterday set a whole new string of dominos in play. ATF and the FBI were officially on the case. Shelly was still out there. She wasn't a scared woman running for her life. Later tonight, the two agencies will hold a press conference from the federal building in Indianapolis. They'll officially announce that Michelle Holdcraft was being sought as a person of interest—a possible serial arsonist.

While Ralph was relieved the blame was on Shelly and hoped it would take some of the heat off of him, he wished it wasn't getting the attention that it was. He detested publicity.

Now he had to deal with fucking podcasters.

The last thing the sheriff wanted was a spotlight on crime in Iron Falls. Taking one last puff of his cigarette, Ralph smashed the butt in an old plastic cup and threw the two into the trash can. He couldn't put off this interview any longer. Standing, he puffed out his chest, adjusted his belt, and made his way out of his office.

He worked out the kinks in his knee, walking with a slight limp. As he turned the corner, he saw Britney standing in the door frame to the interrogation room. With her hand on the doorknob, she was chatting and laughing with the podcasters. The sound of the three women cackling was enough to give Ralph a headache. The entire last week gave him a headache.

"Sheriff," Britney exclaimed excitedly. "Our little town is making the *Crime Daily Podcast*." She made it sound like it was an award or something.

If Iron Falls had to be made famous, Ralph would rather have it be recognized for Winston Hunting Lodge or the catfish Gloria served at the diner. Being on a true-crime podcast wasn't exactly a sheriff's dream.

Britney pushed the door farther open. "Sheriff Perkins, this is McKenzie Shaffer and Allison Buckley, better known as Kenzi and Ali." Her smile grew, splitting her face in half. "Kenzi and Ali, this is Sheriff Ralph Perkins."

Years on the force gave him the ability to read people. During the overly enthusiastic introduction, he made a few quick assumptions. These girls were young and pretty, looking like any one of the Insta-gramers or TikTokers that he avoided. Their smiles were plastic. Their hair was long and shiny, one blond and the other a brunette. If Ralph were to guess, the two weren't any older than Britney, probably younger. His most confident assumption—there was no way they were qualified to solve true crime.

"Thank you, Britney," the sheriff said as he stepped inside the room and pulled out a chair on the opposite side of the table. When Britney remained, he motioned with his chin. "Shut the door on the way out, will you?" He sat and turned his attention to the visitors. "Well, Britney sure seems pleased to meet you. Tell me, what can I do for you girls?"

They both shifted in their seats. The one with brown hair spoke first. "Deputy McBride was very nice."

"Now, which one are you?"

The same girl answered. "I'm Kenzi." She gestured to the blond. "She's Ali. As you know or Deputy McBride informed you, we host a true-crime podcast."

Sheriff Perkins grunted a response.

"Sheriff," Ali began, "we came to Iron Falls to learn more about Dennis Holdcraft's death."

"Sad." He pressed his lips together and shook his head for effect. While he would love to give these girls the scoop on Shelly, his lips were sealed by the feds. Instead, he went the original route. "Denny was a good ole boy. He moved up here about ten years ago, I think." He feigned a smile. "Don't quote me on that. Anyhoo, he was a quiet man. Kept to himself. Damn shame. He lost his wife before moving here and just never got over it. We're still investigating, but it's looking like he let loneliness and depression take over. You know, it gets mighty cold up here, and isolation can take a toll on some folks."

"You're saying it was suicide?" Kenzi asked. "But I read a statement from the Indianapolis police that you wanted to speak to Dennis's daughter—"

"Michelle," Ali injected.

"Right, Michelle." Kenzi referred to her notes. "You asked the IMPD to have Ms. Holdcraft contact you regarding" —she met the sheriff's gaze— "possible involvement in her father's death. Do you think Mr. Holdcraft was murdered?"

Sheriff Perkins crossed his arms over his chest and leaned back against his chair. It would be fun to play up that angle. However, it will be more dramatic to have it come out at tonight's press conference. "Listen, girls. It's real cute what you're doing, playing detective and all, but Iron Falls doesn't have murders. We have the occasional vagabond who breaks into hunting cabins. The other day, a patron tried to leave Gloria's Diner without paying." He uncrossed his arms. "Unfortunately, Denny's death was tragic. And then, on top of that, a tragedy struck in Indianapolis involving Shelly's house. We don't know her status." He shrugged. "I sure would like to be more helpful to you."

"Did you know," Ali asked, "that Michelle Holdcraft is an author of bestselling fiction?"

Ralph paused to think. "Britney told me. I do recall Denny saying something about it."

"Was Ms. Holdcraft in Iron Falls recently?" Kenzi asked.

"There's some debate about that. Some folks around here said they saw her. Britney found on Shelly's website that she'd been in Boston last weekend for some author thing. Truth is, we're investigating all possibilities. The fire at the scene made gathering evidence difficult. Again, this is an ongoing investigation, and I'm unable to share anything else."

"Deputy McBride," Ali began, "mentioned a shed found on Mr. Holdcraft's property."

Heat rose beneath Ralph's skin. "I know you're not from around here. Nothing unusual about a shed."

Ali and Kenzi looked at one another; Kenzi spoke. "She said you said it was filled with computers and such, 'a real big setup,' but when she and a few other deputies went back with you, it was empty."

Sheriff Perkins stood. That information wouldn't fit with the narrative. "I believe Britney was mistaken. Thank you for your visit. I'll be happy to see you out."

"Did Mr. Holdcraft have any other family besides his daughter?" Ali asked.

"I'd figure you girls would know the answer to that."

Kenzi stood. "The answer is no. IMPD confirmed Michelle's presence in Indianapolis late Monday or early Tuesday. If his only family member was a thousand miles away, who would have cleaned out his shed and why?"

When the sheriff didn't respond, Ali asked, "Why did Mr. Holdcraft have all the computers? Was he working for someone?"

Ralph opened the door. "Denny was retired."

The ladies gathered their things. It was Kenzi who smiled at the sheriff as they passed him holding the door. "Sheriff, Mr. Holdcraft had a net value of over two million dollars. I hope your pension is as good as IMPD."

The fuck?

Ralph didn't know that Denny had that kind of money. What was he up to with that shed?

"Tune in on Monday," Ali said. "You might learn something."

After the podcasters exited the station, Ralph pounded his fist on Britney's desk. "Come to my office."

TWENTY-EIGHT

S unlight streamed through the mostly closed blinds as Michelle's eyelids fluttered awake. For a millisecond upon waking, Michelle thought she was in her home—in her bed. The reality sped through her consciousness. She wasn't home, not in her home. This also wasn't a cheap motel. This was Fletch's apartment. Sighing, she lifted her head and saw the bed beside her where Fletch slept was now empty.

Before the worries of the day and Fletch's meeting could bombard her thoughts, Michelle rolled to Fletch's pillow. The soft sheets caressed her skin—all her skin. She'd fallen asleep without her night clothes. Though the pillowcase was cool, his familiar scent filled her senses. Memories from a few hours ago returned.

When she'd first encountered Fletch outside her

father's home, he seemed gruff, giant, and dangerous. His brute strength was evident in the way he was able to carry her. The man with her last night was still tall and strong, but that wasn't all there was to Fletch. There was a gentleness in his touch and passion in his kisses. Simply the memory tightened her core. Despite or perhaps because of Fletch's knowledge of Michelle's insecurities, his compliments continued as his deep baritone timbre whispered praises.

She'd thought of their one night in the cabin as the eye of the hurricane. Maybe the storm had passed, leaving danger and death in its wake. Could it be that sunnier days were ahead? Despite the looming realities, those wishes brought a smile to her face.

The stillness of the apartment was refreshing, no hum of a motel heater or sound of water through thin walls. Suddenly, Michelle wondered what time it was.

How long had she slept?

Slipping her nightclothes back on, she made her way into the bathroom. Water droplets inside the glass enclosure let her know Fletch had showered. She'd slept through it all. Out of the bedroom, she peeked into Fletch's office, hoping he was still home. That hope was dashed at the sight of the vacant room, dark screens, quiet computers, and empty chairs. In the living room, she checked the clock beneath the television. The time read 10:32.

After Fletch helped her forget the world, she'd slept for five or six hours.

Michelle spun a slow circle, taking in Fletch's apartment. With the sunshine streaming through the windows and the cleaning she'd done the night before, the apartment was less bachelor pad and unquestionably homier.

The star rating had gone up.

Michelle snickered at the thought.

It wasn't that Michelle was a neat freak. Cleaning was a matter of health and safety. She was relatively certain there were more than a few CDC violations before her intervention.

The thought of Fletch's meeting weighed heavily on her mind. She couldn't sit and do nothing. No matter how long she'd be staying with Fletch, she knew the one element she needed to truly feel at home.

Her computer was still in the entry where Fletch had unloaded it the night before. There was no room in his office for another computer. That didn't deter Michelle. Looking in his office reminded her that she longed to feel the keys beneath her fingers and to create stories, maybe as unbelievable as the one she was living.

She warmed a cup of coffee in the microwave and found the sugar. The refrigerator was a monster she hadn't tackled the night before. There wasn't much inside apart from condiments, a jar of pickles, and left-over pizza. Michelle thought it was pizza. Whatever it was, it was harder than the box that contained it. A shopping list was forming in her mind. The number one item was cream. Two would be milk. Today she'd settle for coffee without cream and dry cereal.

As she drank and nibbled, Michelle set up her new workstation on the table near the breakfast counter. Without Fletch's Wi-Fi password, she couldn't be fully operational. Nevertheless, simply seeing her keyboard, mouse, computer, and screen filled her with a sense of purpose.

After a second cup of coffee, Michelle unloaded the dryer and folded the towels. She made the bed and began to search through her luggage. She'd wait for the mysterious Peterson's decision before she unpacked her clothes. Her toiletries were something else. In no time, the vanity in the bedroom suite was filled with creams, cosmetics, and other items she'd grabbed from home. It wasn't much neater than when she arrived, but at least she was sure the surface was clean.

Nearly an hour later, while wrapped in a towel with her hair still wet, Michelle heard the door to the apartment open. Tentatively, she stepped into the bedroom awaiting the verdict. Fletch entered from the other doorway, his lips twitching as he scanned the towel. The scan went both ways. With an important meeting, Michelle expected Fletch to be dressed differently than to what she'd become accustomed.

Other than instead of hanging down, Fletch's hair was cinched at the nape of his neck in a small ponytail, he looked the same. Still handsome, tall, and muscular. A growing beard covered his cheeks and neck. His long legs were covered with blue jeans, and he was wearing his customary hoodie. This one was gray. The different color meant he'd gotten a clean one from the closet.

Placing his hands at her waist, he exhaled, tipping his forehead to hers.

His lack of speaking caused the small hairs on Michelle's arms to stand to attention and her pulse to race. This was the end of the line, as Fletch said, because entering the agency complex was a one-way ticket. If Peterson said no, Michelle didn't know any other options. Witness protection. The thought added to her trepidation. She didn't want to be completely alone.

Taking a step back, she met his dark gaze. "You're scaring me. What did Peterson say?"

"Do you want the whole story or just the conclusion?"

She needed the answer. The story could wait. Michelle blurted out her question. "Will they let me stay here with you?"

He exhaled. "Yes."

She exhaled as tears filled her eyes.

Fletch framed her cheeks between his large palms. "If you're willing to help the cause, Peterson would like to meet with you."

A lump formed in her throat. Help? She didn't

know if she could. Then again, Fletch said the agency wasn't all brawn; it was brains too. "This is what my parents did?"

"Yeah, Chell, it's what they did."

Michelle nodded. "When does he want to meet?"

"We have some time. He wants to meet on Monday. Before then, I'm supposed to take you to a lab we have here. Peterson wants data before anything is officially decided."

Her eyebrows arched. "What kind of data?"

"Before I was part of the agency, I was in Force Recon. It's a Special Ops unit of the Marines. To get to that level, I had to pass physical and mental assessments. Tests."

Michelle looked down at herself and back to Fletch. "If they want to see how many push-ups I can do, I'll save them the trouble. The answer is zero."

Fletch chuckled. "No push-ups. I told Peterson about your strengths and skills. The tests will be to determine your proficiency in the area of your mother's expertise."

"Research." She inhaled. "I can do that." She narrowed her eyes. "You promise there's no physical test."

"I promise, but..."

"But what?"

He arched his eyebrows and a gleam returned to his eyes. "From my experience, I'd say you're very fit."

She felt the heat rise beneath her skin.

"And endurance," he went on, "you have that."

Michelle smiled, walked to the bed, and sat on the edge with a sigh. "I was afraid he'd say no."

Fletch crouched near her knees. "I was prepared for his answer to go either way."

"This is what you do. You believe in it. I could never ask you to leave it behind."

He cupped her cheek. "You didn't ask me, Chell. I know I have marketable skills."

She leaned into his touch and smiled. No one had ever called her Chell before, just Michelle or Shelly. Staring into Fletch's dark eyes, she liked the way it sounded coming from his lips.

"Beyond the gate isn't safe for you. Until it is, I want to know that you're not in danger."

"What's behind the gate? Are there stores or restaurants?"

Fletch shook his head. "We need to go into one of the nearby towns for those things. There's a cafeteria, but the food we picked up from convenience stores tastes better."

"Did you get pizza from there?" When he didn't answer, she added, "I found some in the refrigerator. It was rock hard."

"Don't eat it. You might break a tooth. But if you do, we do have medical and dental services in the complex."

Michelle shook her head. "I don't mind cooking."

"If you make me a list, I'll go shopping this afternoon."

"I can go with you."

"There's an APB out on you. The complex is safest."

"I'll wear your hat," she said with a hopeful grin.

"Leo sent me some information I asked for. Now that I'm home, I can search the internet to find out what your status is."

"Fine. I need the Wi-Fi password."

TWENTY-NINE

Ali cautiously drove away from Iron Falls. "What a dick."

Kenzi laughed. "It started when he called us girls."

"Patronizing."

Kenzi agreed. "That was the highlight. It went downhill from there." She turned to Ali. "Do you think Dennis Holdcraft committed suicide?"

"First, the Sheriff told IMPD he wanted to speak to Michelle about possible involvement. Now he's saying suicide. What is he covering up?"

Ali shrugged. "Perkins shut up quick when we mentioned the shed."

"Why would Deputy McBride make something like that up?"

Ali's smile grew. "I don't think she did. That's what

we're going to find out. I put the Holdcraft address in the GPS. We're headed there now."

Kenzi checked her watch. "Our flight to Indianapolis leaves..."

"In four and a half hours from Boston. We have time."

"It's a crime scene."

"We're right here. We owe it to this crime to check everything out. The Sheriff wasn't any help. Besides, do you really think they have enough deputies in Iron Falls to have someone watching the scene twenty-four seven? And see how clear these roads are? There's been a lot of traffic back and forth. I think there's more to this than a sad man ending it all."

Kenzi took out her phone and began to film. "Hi everyone. It's Friday and I'm Kenzi."

"And I'm Ali."

"We're in Iron Falls, Massachusetts, to learn more about the Holdcraft mystery. Mother, father, and daughter all consumed by flames." She turned off the camera.

Ali laughed. "That was good."

"Thanks. It just came to me."

If it weren't for the parade of sheriff cars, trucks, ambulances, and fire trucks that drove these roads recently, the turnoff to the lane leading to Dennis Holdcraft's home would be easy to miss. As it was, the well-traveled lane was obvious.

"If anyone's here, we'll act casual and try to get some more information."

"And if no one is," Kenzi said, "we'll get as much footage of the property as possible. Then tonight in the hotel we'll go through it."

Ali brought the rental car to a stop about fifty feet from what remained of the home. Both ladies stared at the charred aftermath. While no one was patrolling the area, there was yellow police tape tied to posts surrounding what was left.

After shutting off the car, both ladies zipped their coats and opened the doors to the cold air. The stench of burned wood assaulted their senses. The ground beneath their boots was slippery with frozen water, and their breath crystallized in the air. "How big was the house before?" Kenzi asked.

"I read in the county assessment that it was two stories and two thousand square feet."

They stared in amazement.

"It doesn't even look like it was one story."

Ali pointed to what remained of the chimney. "That's basically all that's left."

"I can't imagine the condition Mr. Holdcraft was in when they found him."

"Probably not a lot left." Ali took out her phone and videoed what was left of the house. She didn't speak. The silence was appropriately eerie. When she turned the camera off, she looked from left to right. "Let's find the shed."

Kenzi asked, "Do you want to split up?"

"No," Ali answered immediately. "This is the middle of nowhere. I'm not prepared to meet a bear or an elk."

"I'm not prepared either."

"Yeah, but I can run faster than you."

Kenzi pushed playfully against Ali's shoulder. "Let's follow some of these boot prints."

"Wait." Ali turned the camera on her phone back on. This time, she spoke. "We're here at the sight of the fire in Iron Falls." She switched the camera and began to pan the scene. "This is where Dennis Holdcraft, the father of author D. Valentine, lost his life. There's very little left of his home." She turned the camera again. "Come with us as we search for more clues." After taping a few seconds of their walk, Ali turned off the camera.

Kenzi pulled a pair of gloves from her coat pocket and slipped them on. "It's cold."

Ali laughed.

The boot prints seemed to be taking them in a circle, until they veered away from the house. Kenzi brought out her phone. They'd walked what seemed like a mile. Although the charred bones of the house were no longer visible, the stench was imprinted in their noses. "I see something," she said, lifting her phone. "In Iron Falls, we heard that there was a shed on the Holdcraft property, spared by the fire. What was he keeping out there? We're getting close."

There was yellow tape over a broken window above the door and a yellow taped X over the door.

"Looks like we found the shed, Kenzi."

Both of their faces were on camera. "We came a long way," Kenzi said. "Do you think we should take a peek inside?"

"Let's do it."

They rotated the camera and pushed on the heavy door. "It looks like someone broke in. See the splintered doorjamb?" Kenzi made sure to record the damage.

The door creaked further open.

Nothing.

"It's empty." The ladies stepped inside. The soles of their boots echoed within. The space was vastly larger inside than it appeared from the outside. The concrete floor was spotless as if someone scrubbed it. "Someone took a lot of time to clean this place out," Ali said and began walking along the walls. "How could someone have technology out here? How do they get electricity?"

Kenzi recorded as Ali went to a plug and removed a charger from her purse. "Let's see if it works." She plugged the charger into the wall and then her phone into the charger—nothing. "No electricity."

"Or," Kenzi said, "whoever cleaned this place out disconnected the electricity. Why have plugs if there's no electricity." Her eyes opened wide. "I've heard the commercials for generators. Do they make them powerful enough to run whatever Mr. Holdcraft had here?"

Again, both of their faces were on the screen. "We'll find out."

Kenzi's eyes opened wide. "Do we both agree that the sheriff is hiding something?"

Ali nodded. "First, he insinuated Michelle killed her father, and then he insinuated suicide. What if whatever was in this shed got him killed?"

ALI AND KENZI boarded their nearly three-hour flight in Boston bound for Indianapolis at 5:16 p.m. Seated in the third row, they exchanged phones and watched each other's videos.

"I'm really curious what was in that shed and who cleaned it out."

Kenzi agreed. "Especially after Sheriff Perkins went ice cold when we mentioned it."

"Do you think we could call Deputy McBride for follow-up?"

"When we land, we'll check into our hotel. Tomorrow's Saturday. Hopefully, the Indianapolis police will be more forthcoming with answers to our questions."

CHAPTER

THIRTY

Friday afternoon, after a shopping trip where Fletch bought more food than he ever had, he settled into his home office and took a seat behind one of the desks. His setup was similar to what Denny had. With VPNs and browser extensions, Fletch had the ability to move about the web without leaving cookies or a digital footprint.

Peterson asked him a few questions earlier that had his mind racing. Denny's loss was felt by all, a fallen soldier in one of their many wars. Members of the agency were currently in Nova Scotia. Things were looking positive in the Wells boy's case. Denny's service was one of the reasons Arrow hadn't been reprimanded for bringing Chell to the complex and the agency.

He entered Chell's name, Michelle Ellen Holdcraft, into a special search engine. *Crime Daily Podcast* was the first site to come up. An article in *News Bulletin* confirmed she was the person behind the pseudonym D. Valentine.

Fletch debated sharing that with Chell. He knew she wouldn't be happy.

The *Indianapolis Star* was next with a story about the house explosion. Those were mostly expected. What wasn't expected was the *NewsBreak* announcement of an upcoming press conference broadcasting from the Birch Bayh Federal Building in Indianapolis, Indiana, tonight at five thirty.

Fletch checked the time. It was nearly three thirty, which meant it was five thirty in Indiana.

"Chell," he called.

Michelle appeared in the doorway, her sapphire eyes wide. "Is something wrong?"

A smile tugged at his lips as he scanned from her auburn hair to her sock-covered toes and everywhere in between. The blue sweater made her eyes pop, and he approved of the way she filled out her jeans. And then he remembered what was on his screen. "I don't know. There's a press conference broadcasting from Indianapolis. Come watch it with me."

She pressed her lips into a straight line, furrowed her forehead, and came closer. The citrusy scent of her perfume preceded her arrival by milliseconds. "What's it about?"

"I'm not sure. It came up in a search about you." Since learning Peterson's decision that Michelle could stay in the complex, Fletch sensed it seemed as if she appeared lighter, freer, or maybe just a little less burdened. When he arrived with the groceries, her glee while removing them one by one in the kitchen was as if he'd presented her with a rare collection of crown jewels. As he found the broadcast, he worried that whatever they were about to watch was going to take Michelle back to the trauma of the last week.

He reached over and rolled another chair beside him. "This is live." He tilted his chin toward the large screen. "Let's listen."

"Is it about my house?"

The ticker on the bottom of the screen read: **FBI and ATF joint press conference. Breaking news.**

Michelle took a seat in the chair beside Fletch.

He turned up the volume.

The woman speaking from the podium stood in front of the Department of Justice symbol. "Thank you for your attention. As most of you know, I'm Sandra Oaks, Attorney General of Indiana." She motioned to the people behind her. "And this is Special Agent Miles Beuford with the FBI and from the Bureau of Alcohol, Tobacco, Firearms, and Explosives, Special Agent in Charge Bradley Goodwell. My office is currently working in conjunction with the Office of the Attorney General of Massachusetts.

"We're here to announce the formation of a grand jury in what my office believes involves multiple cases of homicide with the use of arson, specifically incendiary fires—fires purposely set to hide homicide."

Michelle gasped. "They caught Sheriff Perkins."

"The connection came to our attention after the house explosion that occurred early Wednesday morning south of the city. Thanks in part to the exemplary work of the Indianapolis Metropolitan Police Department and that of the Iron Falls Sheriff's Department in Massachusetts, the convened grand jury will consider evidence and decide if Michelle Holdcraft should be formally indicted for the murders of Tracy Holdcraft and Dennis Holdcraft as well as for the incendiary fires that resulted in the recent house explosion, a house explosion eight years ago, and the recent fire in Iron Falls, Massachusetts, set to cover up Dennis Holdcraft's homicide. His cause of death has been ruled a gunshot wound. I'm willing to answer a few questions."

Fletch clenched his jaw and turned toward Chell.

Her eyes twitched as she tried to make sense of what was being said. "Wait. What? How?" Michelle stuttered, as if her thoughts were spinning out of control.

A man's voice. "Are you suggesting Michelle Holdcraft is a serial killer as well as a serial arsonist?"

Michelle held her fingertips over her lips as she stared in utter disbelief.

Attorney General Oaks replied, "I am not. I'm saying we believe we have enough evidence connecting three separate events to one person: Ms. Holdcraft. If the grand jury agrees, her guilt or innocence will be determined by a jury of her peers."

A woman's voice. "IMPD put out an APB on Ms. Holdcraft. Is she no longer missing? Have you located her?"

Chell's voice was low. "No. No. No. Please..."

Fletch reached over, placing his large hand over Michelle's blue-jean-clad thigh.

"No body was discovered in the aftermath of the explosion. Ms. Holdcraft is still missing. I'll let the FBI discuss her whereabouts." Attorney General Oaks stepped away from the microphone.

"Fletch?" His name came from her lips like a cry for help.

He scooted closer, cursing under his breath as he wrapped his arm around her shoulders.

Special Agent Miles Beuford stepped up. "We have evidence that Ms. Holdcraft willingly left the state and is evading law enforcement. She's been wearing disguises such as sunglasses and hats to cover her hair. We've contacted state police in multiple states and expanded our search. Once she is found, she will be detained as a probable flight risk."

"Fuck," Fletch growled.

"I don't believe this is happening."

Miles Beuford continued. "At this time, we consider Ms. Holdcraft to be possibly dangerous. If anyone believes they have any information about her whereabouts, please contact law enforcement. Do not approach her on your own.”

Michelle's hands went to her stomach. “I think I'm going to be ill.”

Fletch tugged her closer, her back against his chest.

A man's voice. “Wasn't Ms. Holdcraft previously tried for the explosion that took her mother? And if so, wouldn't trying her again be double jeopardy?”

“The original charges,” Miles Beuford replied, “were brought on by the State of Indiana as Attorney General Oaks can confirm. There was not a trial. The state prosecutor determined that he didn't have enough evidence to convict. As for double jeopardy, today we're talking about state charges; however, depending on the evidence presented to the grand jury, and the decision of the Massachusetts' attorney general, we could be looking at federal charges. The Supreme Court ruled that a state conviction or acquittal doesn't prohibit subsequent federal prosecution.”

“This isn't real. This can't be real.” Michelle's glassy eyes turned to Fletch. “What do I do?”

He lowered the volume on the streaming press conference and reached for her trembling hands. They were ice to his touch. “You stay here, with me.”

“And let everyone think I killed my parents—that I'm a serial arsonist.” She dropped her chin as her shoulders bowed forward. “I can't.”

"Listen to me," Fletch said, squeezing her hands in his. "You didn't do any of what they're saying. Hell, I'm guiltier than you." The struggle in Michelle's gaze filled Fletch with fury. He let go of her hands, released her shoulders, and stood, his chair sailing backward at his sudden movement. "I'm going to clear your name, Chell." His volume rose. "If it's the last thing I do, I'll clear your name. If I go to hell, I'm fucking taking Sheriff Perkins with me."

She stood, her lip trembling. "They think...I killed..." Michelle shook her head. "I couldn't. I wouldn't."

Fletch cupped her cheek. "I know that without a shred of doubt."

"But..." She backed away, her eyes unfocused. "Eight years ago..." Tears fell down her cheeks. "...the accusations and questioning... it was horrible. I can't go through that again."

"You won't."

"Then it was Mom and now it's Dad." She inhaled. "You were in Iron Falls. You know I didn't kill my father. I didn't set the fire. Hell, if I had, I would have taken shoes."

Fletch nodded. "I'll go to Peterson right away. With the agency's help, we'll clear your name."

"I should have admitted I was there when the sheriff called for me."

"No," Fletch said adamantly. "Chell, he would have killed you. I'm one hundred percent certain of that."

"But I ran. That looks guilty."

"Only because of the way they're painting it. We will find the real evidence."

Michelle clutched her chest. "The paper trail your associate made for me...what would they find if they check with Greyhound or American Airlines? Would they confirm my tickets and travel or is it another example to make me out to be more of a liar?"

"They'd find your tickets. If they scanned cameras and security, they wouldn't be able to find your image boarding or deboarding." Before she could speak, he added, "And that's not unusual. There are a lot of people at those gates. The paper trail would be backed up by the manifests."

She wrapped her arms around her midsection. "I hate that I lied. I'm afraid it will make me appear guilty when I'm not."

Her wide eyes had the haunting shadows Fletch wanted to chase away.

Michelle let out a long sigh. "Can I...? I want to help clear my name. Tell me what to do."

"First, we need to prove that someone else shot Denny." He wiped a tear from her cheek before wrapping his arms around Chell and pulling her to his chest.

THIRTY-ONE

"You may use your cell phones now."

Ali and Kenzi hadn't waited for the announcement. The second the wheels hit the tarmac, they both took their phones out of airplane mode. Even in silent mode, their phones vibrated with incoming notifications.

It was as they walked up the jet bridge that Ali's phone vibrated with an incoming call. She lifted it and looked at the screen. "Oh shit," she said. "It's Greta."

Greta Erikson was the producer of *Crime Daily Podcast.*

Ali hit the green icon. "Hey, Greta, what's happening. You knew Kenzi and I were traveling today."

"Is Kenzi with you?"

"Yeah, she's right here."

They'd now stepped into a boarding area within Indianapolis International Airport.

"Put me on speaker. Oh my God, you're not going to believe what happened. I've been trying to call" — Ali waved Kenzi to an area of empty chairs and put Greta on speaker— "right after your plane took off from Boston."

Kenzi and Ali wrinkled their foreheads in confusion.

"What happened, Greta." Ali asked. "You're on speaker now. We lost some of what you just said."

"You know that case you're working, the one with the author and her father. The fires?"

"Yes," Kenzi said. "It's why we're here in Indianapolis."

"Right after your plane left Boston, there was a press conference in Indianapolis. The Indiana state attorney general announced that her office is convening a grand jury with the intent to present evidence that Michelle Holdcraft killed both her parents. They're saying she's a serial killer and a serial arsonist."

"The fuck?" Ali questioned.

"They also said she didn't die in the house explosion. She's been on the run, using disguises."

Kenzi replied, "No way."

"And get this, the police accused Michelle of blowing up her house years ago when her mother died. But then, the prosecutor dropped the charges."

"Oh," Kenzi said, "can you get us the police records and court documents?"

"I'll work on that."

"I don't believe she killed her father," Ali said. "The sheriff in Iron Falls is hiding something. A day or two ago, the IMPD stated Michelle had an alibi for the time Dennis died." She nodded at Kenzi.

"Yeah," Kenzi agreed. "I know I have that report on my computer."

"And," Ali said, "there was a shed on Dennis's property that the deputy said was full of high-tech equipment. Then it was mysteriously cleaned out, and when we saw it, the place was spic-and-span clean."

Greta replied, "I'm just telling you what I heard. I sent both of you the link. You can watch the press conference. I think we should let this story fizzle and start something else. I'll keep looking for new topics."

"Let it fizzle?" Ali asked, astounded. "Are you kidding me? This case is getting more interesting by the minute."

Kenzi spoke. "I'm with Ali on this. Greta, once we're at the hotel, we'll send you what we recorded in Iron Falls. There's more to this story."

"You ladies are the stars. I'm still going to scour the police reports, public records, and media."

"Get us the deets on that case from..." Ali paused to think. "...years ago. The one where they dropped the charges."

"On it."

Ali hit the red icon. "Holy shit. I don't think this case is fizzling. I think it's catching fire."

"Let's make our game plan for tomorrow." They began walking through the airport. "I still want to talk to the two officers who interviewed Michelle before the explosion," Kenzi said.

IT WAS after nine at night when they stepped into their hotel room. High in the Indianapolis skyline, the small city sparkled through Ali and Kenzi's windows. The large sports arenas, tall limestone buildings, and variety of restaurants made for a visitor-friendly and walkable city. *The Crime Daily* podcasters weren't taking advantage of any of that.

After ordering room service, the two ladies went to work.

Ali started digging into the first Michelle Holdcraft accusation. Turned out that it was eight years ago. In Indiana, the statute of limitations for arson was expired. However, if that fire caused a death, there wasn't a statute of limitation.

Kenzi's voice pulled her attention away from her research. "You said you read *The Wishing Well*, right?"

"I did." Ali pursed her lips. "You said you read another one."

"I've read two, *The Wishing Well* and *Broken Promises*."

"How many books has she written?" Ali asked.

Kenzi opened another window and entered *D.*

Valentine. "Her website says four. *The Wishing Well* was her first. *Broken Promises* is the most recent. *Don't Say Goodbye* and *Until Tomorrow* are the others." She turned to Ali. "Why do you ask?"

"I have her Amazon page up." Ali sat back and sighed. "What do you enjoy?"

Kenzi laughed. "You can probably guess."

"Right. True crime. Me too."

"Well, I'm glad to know that. It works for our podcast."

"I've only read the one—*The Wishing Well*. It reminded me a lot of the Emily Madison case." Ali said.

Kenzi nodded. "Frank Loews." She shook her head. "I can see some similarities. He got away with it."

"Yeah, the accused abductor got off—hung jury."

Kenzi scrunched her nose. "But the trial resulted in uncovering a bigger trafficking network. I think it was somewhere around here."

"The trial was in Indianapolis. The media called the network Crossroads. A few months after the trial Frank Loews committed suicide."

"What does this have to do with Michelle Holdcraft?" Kenzi asked.

"I read *Broken Promises*, and that story had similarities to a Wisconsin abduction of two girls. Remember, we covered that on the podcast."

"I still don't—"

Ali went on. "Hear me out. I've got the synopsis of

the other two books here. They sound like they're stories about human trafficking. If Michelle Holdcraft a.k.a. *D. Valentine* is a serial arsonist, wouldn't she write about fires? I mean, you do what you enjoy."

Kenzi's eyes grew wide. "You think she's involved in the abduction of Timothy Wells."

"Shit, no. I just don't think she is what the attorney general is saying. She couldn't have been in Iron Falls and in Indianapolis, and that shed is bugging me."

"Me too. We need to prove she didn't do what she's accused of doing."

THIRTY-TWO

Safe in Fletch's embrace, in the middle of a secret compound, Michelle closed her burning eyes. She knew she wasn't guilty; nevertheless, the thoughts returned from eight years ago, the ones that sought to spread the seeds of doubt.

If Michelle questioned her own innocence, wouldn't a grand jury do the same?

The evidence was stacking up.

Three fires.

Two people dead.

Two explosions.

Michelle was the connection between all of it. She was the center of a Venn diagram.

Her temples throbbed. However, before she could break away from Fletch's strong arms, his doorbell rang. At the tones, Fletch stiffened. Michelle looked up to his dark stare.

"Go in the bedroom and shut the door."

Fletch's tone sent her frayed nerves into overdrive. "Could someone be coming after me?"

"That person would have to go through me first." He kissed the top of her head and led her across the hallway to the bedroom. "Let me see who it is."

The doorbell rang again.

"Do you get many visitors?" Michelle asked.

"Never."

She took a ragged breath. That wasn't the answer she was looking for.

Michelle reached for her own hands. They felt numb as if the circulation had stopped. Her body trembled as Fletch closed the bedroom door. Before it was fully shut, she saw him reach for his pistol from his holster. She backed away from the door, one step and then two. Her focus was on the doorknob. There was a small switch in the middle of the knob to lock the door. It wasn't enough. Michelle knew without a doubt that the flimsy lock was insufficient to keep Fletch or possibly anyone from getting in.

Tentatively, she stepped forward and laid her ear against the door, straining to hear what was happening in the other part of the apartment. She even longed for the thin walls in the cheap motels.

Michelle heard voices, Fletch's and someone else's —a man's—but she couldn't make out the words. There was no yelling or gunshots. After a minute, she sat on the edge of the mattress. Her thoughts went to the press conference.

Lying back, she laid her arm over her eyes.

She was certain the night in Iron Falls had occurred exactly as she recalled. How could anyone suspect her of killing her father?

Her father probably had guns. As a retired police-man, she recalled he was always fanatical about gun safety. The only gun she owned at the time her father was shot was in a gun safe on the top shelf in her closet in Indianapolis.

Not only couldn't Michelle have shot him, but she also wouldn't.

Her thoughts went to her mother's death.

After the explosion and her mother's death, Michelle agreed to be questioned by the police. In her mind, she had nothing to hide. Yet, the more she was questioned, the less sure she was of her own memories.

Yes, she was upset that her parents weren't home to greet her.

Yes, she canceled her last planned visit. It was because she was called in to work.

Yes, she chose to spend the night with her friends instead of going back to her home.

No, she wasn't rebelling. Her friends called. She missed them.

Yes, she missed her family too.

Yes, she had access to the gas stove.

No, she wasn't worried about her semester grades.

Yes, she was the last person to leave her parents' home.

A kernel of uncertainty was all it took to make Michelle begin to question her own memories. Then came the psychological evaluations. She answered honestly about her childhood.

How did she feel about being an only child?

Fine.

Did she consider herself selfish?

Was that self-centeredness why she was upset when no one was home?

Michelle didn't consider herself self-centered, jealous, dependent, or quarrelsome, or any of the qualities associated with an only child in antiquated psychological research. She didn't like or dislike her lack of siblings. It simply was what it was.

The evaluating psychologist asked Michelle for her memories of her older sister. If she hadn't learned of Sarah's existence a few years earlier, the question would have thrown her for a loop. Michelle answered truthfully; she had no memory of a sister. Sarah died before she was born.

On Michelle's currently overstressed brain, this train of thought was the beginning to a bottomless rabbit hole.

Moving her arm and staring up at the ceiling in Fletch's bedroom, other memories returned. As part of her attempt to avoid formal charges, Michelle agreed to court-mandated counseling. She recalled she liked the counselor at Purdue. Her name was Naomi. The last name was lost to her. A scene came back, during the second semester of her sophomore year.

The office in the Purdue Counseling and Guidance Center was simple with light gray walls and darker gray carpeting. There was a large round bright-white rug in front of the sofa. The bookshelf behind the counselor's desk was filled with books with colorful spines. The windowsill was lined with multiple thriving plants despite the gray winter skies beyond. Her standing appointment was every week after her economics lecture.

Naomi sat in a chair, and Michelle lay back on the sofa.

"What are some of your first memories?" Naomi asked.

Michelle was used to the routine. Sometimes it was cathartic as if she was regaining her ground. Other times it was sobering, making her feel melancholy when they were done talking.

She sighed at Naomi's question, trying to take her mind back in time. "I'm not sure what I recall from pictures and stories and what was real." She'd looked through scrapbooks her mother made. Though now after the explosion, those too were only memories.

"It's all right. Let's set the stage. What did your bedroom look like?"

"I probably had a nursery, but what I remember is a room with pink wallpaper. There was a border with princesses."

"Tell me more," Naomi said.

"There was a small chandelier over my bed. My bed was white wicker. There were two beds." She shook her head. "No, that's not right. Just one. My bedspread was frilly—girlie. I had one of those big dollhouses in the corner."

"Is anyone with you in your room?"

"Sarah." Michelle's answer surprised even herself. Catching herself, she sat up and smiled. "My mom told me I had an imaginary friend named Sarah."

Naomi peered back in her notes. "Wasn't that your sister's name?"

"Yeah, but I never knew her."

"You don't remember her?"

"My parents never said anything about her until a few years ago."

"All right. What are you doing in the bedroom?" Naomi asked.

"Playing with the dollhouse."

The opening of the bedroom door brought Michelle to the present. Startled, she sat up, watching as Fletch entered.

"Peterson is here."

The announcement didn't fill Michelle with optimism. "He saw the press conference?"

Fletch nodded.

"He wants me gone."

Fletch offered her his hand, his large palm facing upward.

She laid her hand in his, sensing his warmth as his long fingers enclosed hers.

"No. You're staying. Come, let me introduce you."

Michelle looked down at her blue jeans and sweater. Fletch may not feel the need to dress appropriately for important meetings, but Michelle did.

It was as if Fletch read her mind. "You're perfect the way you are."

"What do I say?"

The glint in his brown eyes offered support. "Be honest. Say whatever you want to say."

"Have you already told him things?"

"Some. He wants to hear from you."

She took a deep breath. "Okay."

Holding tightly to Fletch's hand, Michelle followed him out into the living room and toward the kitchen. A man with dark hair stood near the breakfast bar. His casual attire suggested that there wasn't much in the way of dressing up in this secret agency. The mysterious Peterson was a Black man in his forties—as suggested by the beginning of gray in his hair—probably three to four inches shorter than Fletch and equally as muscular.

"Ms. Holdcraft," he said in a deep, demanding tenor as he offered her his hand.

Michelle went forward and shook. Peterson's handshake was as firm as his tone. "Mr. Peterson, please call me Michelle."

The tips of his lips curled, if only slightly. There

was a twinkle in his astounding light-green eyes. "I've heard you referred to as Shelly, but if you want Michelle—"

No doubt, it was her dad who called her Shelly. "Shelly is fine," she interjected. "I believe I have you to thank for allowing me to stay here. Thank you, sir."

"Peterson is fine. No sirs around here. We don't have ranks in the agency. My condolences regarding Denny."

"Thank you." I didn't kill him, she wanted to add.

Peterson's gaze went to Fletch who was protectively at Michelle's side. "Arrow's the man to thank. He was quite convincing with his appeal and proposal."

She turned, giving Fletch a smile, and then turned back to Peterson. "You heard the press conference out of Indianapolis?" She knew the answer.

"I did. I'd like to talk to you for a few minutes, if that's all right with you?"

He had the voice of a man in control, as if his question wasn't really a question, simply a polite demand. Michelle had to remind herself that Peterson wasn't the police, she wasn't twenty years old. "Yes, we can speak." She met Fletch's eyes, silently questioning if he agreed.

Fletch motioned toward the living room furniture. "Why don't we have a seat? The table is a bit full of Chell's computers."

Peterson nodded as they walked the few steps to

the living room. "Arrow tells me you're a bestselling author." He sat in the lone soft chair.

Michelle took the sofa, and Fletch sat at her side.

She grasped her hands in her lap. "I am. I write fiction, not whatever is happening now." She shrugged. "It's supposed to be a secret that I write under the pseudonym *D. Valentine*, but with the events of the last week, that secret is out."

Peterson leaned forward, placing his forearms on his legs. "Shelly, is there any truth to the press conference we heard today?"

THIRTY-THREE

Michelle appreciated Peterson's straightforwardness. "Some," she answered truthfully. "My house recently exploded."

Peterson's gaze momentarily went to Fletch, making her believe this wasn't news.

"My father was killed by a gunshot. I was at his house, and the sound of the gun woke me. When I went downstairs, he was dead. His house was on fire. I ran out and hid. That's where Fletch...I mean, Arrow found me. My mother also perished in a house explosion. The gas company finally paid to settle the case. I think that would mean they took responsibility because I wasn't guilty."

Peterson sat taller. "The outcome of the events mentioned are true, just not the connection to you."

It wasn't a question, yet Michelle felt compelled to

reply. "I'm connected, but only by association. There were three fires, two explosions, and two people—people I loved—deceased." She inhaled while subconsciously wringing her hands. "I didn't shoot my dad, arrange the explosion that killed my mom, or blow up my own house. I'm connected, but not the way they made it sound."

"Before meeting Arrow, what did you know about the agency?"

"Nothing." She shook her head. "I'd never heard of it."

"Neither of your parents ever mentioned a word."

"I was completely oblivious."

"How did you get the storyline for *The Wishing Well*?"

His question took her by surprise, and then she recalled Fletch asking a similar question. "Um," she cleared her throat. "I had an internship at the Indiana State Courthouse the summer of the Frank Loews trial. It was a high-profile case, especially for Indiana. I followed it closely and tried to dig into the evidence or lack thereof." Peterson seemed interested, so she continued. "I thought he—Mr. Loews—killed Emily Madison. She was only eleven." Michelle didn't want to think about what she endured. She sat taller. "The jury was hung. Juror number seven was a holdout. No conviction. The more I thought about it, the more I wanted to convict him. I decided to do it in fiction. I changed names, location, and I added evidence that wasn't present in the trial. In *The Wishing Well*, my character Ernest Philps rots in prison. It was what I wanted for Frank Loews."

"What evidence?"

Michelle wouldn't have committed these details to memory if they hadn't struck her as important at the time. "During pre-trial discovery, the prosecution claimed to have trace evidence from Emily's bedroom connecting Loews. Emily was believed to have been kidnapped by someone who went through her window. The defense painted a picture of a pre-teen going out the window of her own volition. When it came time for the trial, that evidence was deemed contaminated and the judge threw it out. I kept that trace evidence in my book. It was the nail in the defendant's coffin."

Peterson's nostrils flared as he inhaled. "And the title?"

Michelle had to swallow the lump in her throat from the memory of the crime-scene photos. "Emily Madison's body was found at the bottom of a wishing well in Shakamak State Park, a state park in southern Indiana." She took a deep breath. "Why do you ask?"

Peterson nodded. "Arrow tells me that you agreed to work with some of our people to show them what you know about research."

"I will. If you still want me after the press conference, I'd like to help." She lifted her eyebrows. "Why ask about *The Wishing Well*?"

Peterson stood and spoke directly to Fletch. "I still want to see the data from the evaluations, but they won't change my mind. You were right." He turned to Michelle who was also standing. "Welcome to the agency, Shelly. Your parents wanted you to have a normal life. I'm afraid that's no longer possible. I also believe they'd be proud." The gleam was back in his hauntingly light-green gaze. "There's only one stanch, unbreakable rule. You can't tell anyone outside the agency about the agency or anything you do."

"I won't." She looked to Fletch and back to Peterson. "Is Fletch in trouble? He told me about the agency."

"You don't need to be concerned. As with most rules, there are exceptions. Talk to Arrow about why I asked about *The Wishing Well*. He worked the Loews case." His focus was back on Fletch. "Get Shelly to the testing center tomorrow. Then come to my office. Leo's back. We need to break down everything that's happened and what exactly got Denny killed."

"I'll be there," Fletch said.

Peterson turned toward the door and Fletch followed. Once Peterson was gone and the door was closed, Michelle asked, "What the hell? You worked the Frank Loews case? What does that mean? What did you do?"

He straightened his shoulders. "I contaminated the evidence and worked behind the scenes to get juror number seven seated."

Michelle stared in disbelief. "You got Frank Loews off? The agency let that monster go free?" She slapped her thighs. "You said the agency are the good guys."

"We are."

Her thoughts were spiraling. "Did I just agree to be part of something that lets child molesters and murderers go free?" She didn't wait for his response. "Because if I did, I've changed my mind. I want witness protection."

Fletch took a deep breath. "Real life isn't as simple as fiction, Chell."

"Real life is what Emily Madison endured at the hands of Frank Loews." Tears prickled her eyes. "I saw the postmortem photos and read the coroner's report." She straightened her neck. "Fiction is much simpler. My character Tiffany Moore didn't have to suffer because she was a name I made up."

He came closer and reached for her shoulders. "Frank Loews was later taken care of."

"He committed suicide."

"No, he didn't. And the bastard suffered if that makes you feel better."

Michelle pressed her lips together. "I don't understand. You—the agency—made sure he wasn't convicted to kill him?"

"Loews was a symptom of the disease. He wasn't a lone pedophile working the network. Most of the players don't make the sick decisions he did. What the press later dubbed the Crossroads Network was the cancer. If Loews had been convicted, the public would have been content with the one monster off the street. The agency had identified a network of monsters— abducting, transporting, raping, and selling. That network ran from as far north as Chicago and Detroit to as far south as Atlanta. The players ran the gamut from the woman behind the counter at the gas station to powerful names."

Michelle bit her lip as her eyes opened wider. "I read about that."

"Loews was a weak link. He led us to others. That network was shut down. Nearly one hundred people were identified, arrested, and prosecuted or are awaiting prosecution."

"It was one of the largest FBI stings in recent years," Michelle said.

"And it wouldn't have happened if Loews had been convicted."

She let out a long breath. "I was wrong."

"No, you weren't. You were right. That evidence would have most likely convinced even juror number seven. You couldn't see the full picture. That's what we do. We try to find all the angles. Once we have them, we dig deeper. Research is the backbone of the agency. Some of that is on the ground, listening, watching—"

"Spying?" Michelle asked.

"Yeah. The world today makes it a lot easier than it was when the agency was founded over fifty years ago. Today our geeks" —he smiled— "it's what those of us who do the legwork call the techies. They can literally watch a person of interest twenty-four hours a day. Hacking into home surveillance, doorbell cams, street cams, traffic cams, business security...the list goes on and on. People today don't realize how much of their life is being watched and heard."

"I want to watch Sheriff Perkins."

THIRTY-FOUR

Senator Patrick Lehman turned up the volume on the television in his hotel room. The press conference from Nova Scotia was live, interrupting the usual Sunday morning news shows. The assistant commissioner and commanding officer of the Royal Canadian Mounted Police—Canada's national law enforcement equivalent to the United States FBI—was speaking from a podium.

"Fuck," Rick mumbled under his breath. The scrolling words on the bottom of the screen read— **Breaking News, Timothy Wells found alive. Yacht seized. People of interest in custody. Ongoing investigation.**

He mumbled the expletive again. If the Royal Canadian Mounted Police were involved, then so were the FBI.

How had this gotten out of control?

It was the alarm in Iron Falls. Rick knew at the time that the alarm was bad. He'd taken care of the problem. Perkins admitted they got the right guy. Upon further investigation there was a shed on the property. The door was locked and sturdier than it appeared. The sheriff broke one of the blackened windows and found the interior transformed, equipped with top-notch technology. Of course, when the incompetent sheriff went back to collect the equipment with his deputies, the shed was cleaned out.

That meant Holdcraft wasn't working alone.

Thanks to some damn true-crime podcast, the two separate fires at two homes a thousand miles apart were getting national attention. He couldn't figure out why Perkins's man caused such a scene. That wasn't what Rick wanted. It sure as hell wasn't what the investors wanted.

To top it all off, yesterday, Indiana's attorney general announced she was calling for a grand jury to assess evidence that Holdcraft's daughter was responsible for her father's death and the explosion in Indianapolis.

Perkins let this situation get out of control.

One problem solved wasn't supposed to create ten more.

The investors had a lucrative operation trafficking

children around the world. The primary customers were in Russia, where people paid exceptionally well. Russia's birth rate had reached an unsustainable replacement level. While the world wasn't privy to the actual statistic, a recent report from National Bureau of Asian Research stated that the fertility rate was down to 1.4 from the 2.1 needed for population stability.

In other words, wealthy oligarchs wanted children of all ages. Anglo-Saxon children were in high demand, the younger the better. There were on average two children shipped overseas per day. It was the high-profile kidnappings that were to blame for part of this disaster.

Rick sat on the edge of the king-sized mattress and listened to the broadcast. The assistant commissioner was speaking.

"...believe that Timothy Wells wasn't an isolated case. Our investigation is underway."

A reporter shouted a question. "Do you think other disappearances can be connected to the Wells case?"

The commanding officer gripped the sides of the podium. "We do."

"What proof do you have?" another reporter asked.

"Due to the status of the investigation—"

"Fuck," Rick mumbled. He'd be hearing from the people higher up, the people who supplied the money, planes, yachts, and more. Rick didn't have that kind of money, but this operation was increasing his wealth a hell of a lot faster than his congressional paycheck. Rick was only a cog in the operation. His job was to provide cover in the New England area. He had counterparts throughout the country.

Rick scoured New England for the right people.

Utilizing the state's resources, Rick acquired demographic statistics. Income-to-debt ratio was particularly helpful. Take Ralph Perkins, for instance. He lost his wife about five years back after her bout with cancer. The wife's treatment drained their savings and put them underwater in debt. A man in that position was usually willing to make money on the side. Rick had both law enforcement and laypeople throughout New England on his payroll.

If the Timothy Wells case or whoever Holdcraft was working with brought more attention to the operation, Rick knew the damn liberal governor would call it terrorism. Then he'd get the feds involved. Rick needed to stop the bleeding before it became terminal.

He sent a text message to his man in charge of quotas.

"Quotas still present. Let this news cycle die. Concentrate on plan B. No plan A until further notice."

. . .

PLAN B WAS the most sustainable. No taking children from families with resources for the time being. Instead, his people would concentrate on homeless camps, socially and economically challenged neighborhoods, and Title One schools. Those children could go missing without the fanfare surrounding the Wells boy and the other girl...Jensen or Janson. Rick couldn't remember the name.

He preferred not to know names. Give him numbers.

Numbers paid.

Rick sent a text to Ralph Perkins.

"WHAT AM I seeing on TV? Call me."

HE LOOKED at his phone as if wanting and willing it to ring. Rick's patience with the good sheriff of Iron Falls was running thin. It might be time to do something about him.

Yes, if Rick took care of the Iron Falls problem completely, it would ensure the investors that the problem was solved. There were five more people out there for every one person on his payroll.

He looked up at the headline again. A particular part caught his attention. **Yacht seized.**

Shit, that was a problem.

Rick turned down the volume at the ring of his personal phone. The name *Perkins* was on the screen.

Rick hit the green icon and began speaking without a greeting. "The news out of your town continues to hit the national cycle."

"Listen, we're in good shape. They're framing Shelly for what happened up here. We're downplaying the damn shed. In a few days, the country will be talking about the serial arsonist who killed her parents. They'll probably make up a song. You know, like Lizzy Borden." He half sang, half spoke the Lizzy Borden tune. "Shelly Holdcraft struck a match."

"Fuck, Perkins, are you drunk?" Rick looked at the clock. It wasn't even ten in the morning.

"I'm not drunk. I'm relieved. The attention will be on Shelly and not on Iron Falls."

"What about the fucking press conference from Nova Scotia? All the evidence goes to your boy Dennis. I don't give a fuck what the country is talking about. Someone cleaned out that shed. Someone who was working with him. That means that someone else could know about your connection." He hated to say the next part. "And my connection." Rick lowered his voice. "The thing is, without you, no one can prove we're connected."

Ralph's tone lowered. "I'm doing my damn best here. I'm getting tired of your threats."

Rick's phone beeped in his ear. He pulled the screen away and looked at the name. Rick's stomach dropped and perspiration formed on his brow and palms. "I'll let you know when the next transport is coming through. Until then, try to stay off the fucking national news." He disconnected Ralph's call.

He answered the incoming one. "Sir?"

"We need to talk."

THIRTY-FIVE

While Fletch had taken Michelle on a walking tour of the complex on Sunday, Monday was her first official appointment. There were more people out and about the complex. Their breath crystalized in the frigid air as they walked to where Michelle would be tested. "What if I fail?"

Fletch reached for her glove-covered hand and squeezed. "There's no failing or passing. These evaluations help the agency understand your baseline understanding and skills. From there, you improve."

She sighed and laid her head against his shoulder. "I appreciate your belief in me."

"I could say it's from years of listening to Denny." He stopped walking and took both her hands. "That's part of it. I believe in you."

"I do better when I hide behind a made-up

persona. D. Valentine is more self-assured than Michelle Holdcraft."

"You're the same person. D. Valentine wouldn't exist without you. But when you're in there with Olivia, be whoever feels right."

They stepped through two sets of doors. Warm air swirled around them as Michelle unbuttoned her coat and stuffed her gloves into the pockets.

"This way," Fletch said as he led her down a hallway and to what appeared to be an office. He knocked.

A young woman with brown hair wearing a lab coat opened the door. "Welcome, you must be Shelly."

Michelle feigned a smile. "I am."

"I'm Olivia." Her smile bloomed as she peered up at Fletch. "Arrow's told me a little about you. Please, come in."

Olivia didn't look like Michelle expected. She'd imagined spies like Angelina Jolie from *Salt*, Jennifer Lawrence from *Red Sparrow*, or maybe Charlize Theron from *Atomic Blonde*. Olivia looked more like a middle-school science teacher. The science teacher was probably because of the white lab coat. She was petite. Her olive skin, shiny brown hair, and hazel eyes gave her a Mediterranean appearance.

Despite the warmer interior, Michelle's hands trembled. "You're in the agency?" Michelle asked.

Olivia's smile put Michelle at ease.

"I am," Olivia said. She tilted her head toward

Fletch. "Did he make it sound like the agency is filled with men like him, the kind that can break down a door as easily as pick the lock."

"No, he said the agency needs brawn and brains."

"Arrow has both. My strength is brains."

Fletch reached for Michelle's arm. "Are you all right? Olivia's cool. She'll help you figure things out."

"I'll be good," Michelle answered, feeling slightly less nervous.

When Fletch walked away, Michelle watched, realizing that this was the first time in over a week that she'd been with someone else without his presence. For a woman who relished her independence, multiple traumatic events seemed to have a way of zapping her autonomy. Forcing a grin, she turned back to Olivia who was also watching Fletch leave.

There was a split second of something new in Michelle's emotions. Jealousy. Proprietorship. The feeling hit her out of the blue. It was completely understandable that Olivia would find Fletch attractive. He was. More than attractive, he was handsome. And as Olivia said, he had both brains and brawn—a sexy combination.

Had the two of them dated?

Had they had sex?

Michelle didn't have any right to wonder those questions, much less ask them. And as for what her and Fletch's relationship was, she wasn't certain. Maybe they were roommates with benefits. With

Michelle's world falling apart, she'd come to depend on him. She had feelings for him. There was like and lust. She didn't trust herself to take it further. There were too many other matters at hand.

"Welcome to one of my caves," Olivia said. "As I said, Arrow filled me in a little about you. I'm sorry about Denny. I never met him personally, but we collaborated on cases over the years."

"Thank you." The response was robotic. "How long have you been with the agency?"

"Going on ten years."

Michelle's eyebrows shot upward. "Did they recruit you when you were in high school?"

Olivia laughed. "I was in college. I'd started my master's degree in computer engineering." She shrugged. "I never knew a department like the agency existed. Needless to say, I never finished graduate school, but after ten years, I'm confident I could teach my professors a thing or two."

"How does it work? Recruiting?"

"You're here."

Michelle sighed. "I'm relatively certain I didn't take the most traveled path. My circumstances were unusual. I didn't know the agency existed until Fletch told me. My parents did a great job of keeping it from me." She wondered what else they'd kept from her.

"Fletch?" Olivia turned her head. "Do you mean Arrow?"

Olivia didn't know Fletch's real name. That gave

Michelle a needed boost of self-confidence. "I do. He told me the name Fletch when we first met. Then he told me his name was Jason." She laughed, trying not to give away his secret. "He probably has multiple aliases."

"My work for the agency is all behind the scenes. If you're as good at research as he said, yours will mainly be too. It's not all cloak-and-dagger here. I'm sure Arrow and others have more exciting experiences. However, I think what we do is exciting, especially when we make a significant discovery.

"As for recruitment, I think each agent is recruited differently. There are more agents than you could imagine, considering the highly classified nature of what we do. I was recruited by one of my professors. She said she recognized my talent and well, the rest is history." Olivia took Michelle to a computer setup in the middle of the room. "Arrow said your specialty is research."

"Technically, my specialty is writing fiction—crime thrillers. I do research to create the most believable stories."

Olivia lifted her eyebrows. "Oh, this will be similar. First, I'd like you to sit here."

After Michelle removed her coat and laid it over another chair, she sat.

"I have a list of prompts," Olivia said, pointing to a piece of paper. "Let your mind and your fingers wander. One answer usually leads to ten questions.

That's a good thing. My team and I have fallen down rabbit holes and found answers to questions that hadn't yet been asked."

"How do you grade me? Do you want me to save the information?"

"You're not being graded. I can see on the back side everything you do. I'm curious where your thoughts and actions go." Olivia smiled. "I'll be back in an hour and see how you're doing." She took a step back. "Oh, there's a poor excuse for a lounge down the hall to the left. We have coffee. It's actually decent. I finally convinced Peterson to upgrade the coffee maker." She grinned. "It makes espresso. And there's a restroom the other way by where you came in." Olivia opened her hazel eyes wider. "Do you need anything?"

Michelle read over the prompts and shook her head. "I'll just wander."

"Perfect."

Michelle followed the prompts, searching for information. The computers at the agency were equipped in ways her personal computer hadn't been. Not only was this faster but with it, she had access to systems she'd never before been able to reach. She infiltrated traffic cams, searching for a silver Chevy Tahoe in the Minneapolis city limits.

One prompt reminded her of her alibi.

Olivia said to wander, Michelle justified.

She tried to infiltrate the airline's reservation

system. Each time she made it past a firewall, she shook her head in amazement and wonder.

While she couldn't recall the flight number that had been on the ticket, she recalled the date of her supposed flight. Next, she searched for flights from Boston to Indianapolis, finding there were three that day. She pulled up the manifest of the early morning flight. She wasn't listed. The midday flight was next. Again, there was no sign of her name.

Michelle was getting nervous about the alibi when she pulled up the evening flight. To her amazement, her name was listed. According to their records, she was seated in seat 3D. "Unbelievable," she murmured.

THIRTY-SIX

After escorting Michelle for testing, Arrow made his way to headquarters. It was only a little after eight on Monday morning, yet the building was electric with activity. As he walked the hallways, he saw and acknowledged fellow agents he hadn't seen in a while. He was almost to Peterson's office when Leo caught up with him.

"Arrow," Leo called. "Good to see you. I heard you were back."

Fletch turned around and met Leo's stare. His associate was six feet, three inches of solid muscle as shown by the bulging biceps beneath his short-sleeved black t-shirt. Fletch didn't know Leo's birth name. His friend adopted the name Leo because of his lethal fighting skills—like those of a lion.

Leo looked as if he'd already been to the gym and showered. His blond hair was cut in a short military style. After all that had happened over the last week, the friendly face was a sight for sore eyes.

"Thanks for your help back in Iron Falls," Fletch said, offering him his hand.

Leo took it in a firm handshake. "About that. I didn't want to say anything to you until you made it back, but the shed…"

Leo's pause set off alarms in Fletch's nervous system. "What about it?"

"When I got there, one of Denny's high blacked-out windows was broken."

Fletch wrinkled his forehead. "Blast from the house?"

"I don't think so. Prints in the snow indicated boots, a man's boots."

"Fuck, the sheriff?"

"My guess. Whoever it was, looked inside but didn't get in. I got it cleaned out before they could make it back."

"We all appreciate that, man. Perkins is too stupid to have figured out what Denny had going on, but that doesn't mean the people he answers to couldn't have done it."

Leo reached for Fletch's shoulder. "Before we go in there with Peterson, I looked into Sarah Holdcraft."

"Shit with all the crap, I forgot about her. What did you find?"

"Birth records indicating she would be four years older than Shelly. No death certificate. According to what I found, she went missing but not before Shelly was born. It was over two years later."

"What?" Fletch asked. "Missing? Police reports?"

"Yeah. Denny had them sealed."

"You need a judge for that."

"He already had years on the force. It wouldn't have been too hard."

"Was she ever found?"

"That took a little more digging, and honestly, the jury's out," Leo replied. "The remains of a young juvenile fitting Sarah's profile were discovered fourteen years after Sarah disappeared. The forensics team determined based on environmental factors that the remains had been buried for fifteen to seventeen years."

"COD?"

"C1 through C2 vertebrae fracture."

Fletch pressed his lips into a straight line. "Trauma." He shook his head. "Where did they find her?"

"A man driving a front loader for an excavation company was preparing the site for another distribution warehouse southeast of Indianapolis. The land had been farmland for generations. The remains stopped the project for a couple weeks. That made the news—local at least."

Fourteen years, Fletch thought. Chell told him she learned about Sarah while she was in high school. It was probably because that was when her remains were found. He shook his head. "Makes sense why

Denny had such a passion for missing and exploited kids."

"Yeah, but that's where it gets weird. Neither Denny nor Tracy officially claimed their daughter was deceased. They refused to acknowledge the remains were Sarah's. They paid for cremation out of respect for the deceased child."

"You said she was identified?"

"Possibly identified—inconclusive dental records. The remains were cremated prior to DNA testing. IMPD claims it was a mix-up in evidence. The Holdcrafts chose not to pursue legal action."

"Sounds like a cover-up," Fletch said. "If she was abducted, why wouldn't they want to know? Where was the investigation?"

"I couldn't find it. The case was closed not long after the cremation." Leo pressed his lips together and shook his head. "If I were to make an assumption, it would be with Tracy and Denny working for the agency, they didn't want the publicity."

"Damn, that would've been hard on them both. No wonder they didn't talk about her to Chell."

The door to Peterson's office opened, and Peterson eyed Fletch and Leo up and down. "Get your asses in here."

After a nod to each other, the two men followed Peterson into his office.

"We have a development in Iron Falls," Peterson announced. Before either man could reply, he said,

"After Perkins failed to show to the office this morning as usual, Deputy McBride went to Sheriff Perkins's home."

"No fucking way," Fletch said.

Peterson nodded. "Dead. Coroner puts the time of death somewhere between ten p.m. and two a.m. COD is unknown. They're doing an autopsy, but foul play has been ruled out. The old man probably had a heart attack brought on by stress. According to Deputy McBride, he'd been having problems with an old football injury."

Fletch shook his head. "I don't believe it."

"I checked. From 1973 to 1975, Ralph Perkins played quarterback for Iron Falls High School, Class C."

"Not the football injury. I don't believe he died peacefully in his sleep," Fletch corrected as he and Leo took the chairs in front of Peterson's desk.

Peterson stood before them and leaned against the desk, crossing his arms over his chest. "As we know, there're a lot of ways to facilitate a cardiac incident, ways that can be hidden from the standard toxicology screen. Then again, if he was having knee pain, the old bastard might have overdosed on painkiller." He shrugged. "No matter how it occurred, Perkins is no longer."

"He shot Denny," Fletch said. "Now getting a confession is out of the question; we have to prove it."

"I'm going to be upfront with you gentlemen,"

Peterson said, relaxing his arms. "There are those higher up who would rather the publicity around this case die down."

"No." Fletch stood. "If we let it go, Chell takes the blame."

"Arrow," Peterson said, "Michelle Holdcraft is dead too. For her to join us, she no longer exists."

"That doesn't mean she has to die suspected of crimes."

"You figure out how you can clear her name, and we'll talk." Peterson turned his focus on Leo. "Where's the equipment from Denny's shed?"

"A temperature-controlled storage container in Manchester."

Peterson nodded. "Get the address to the coordinators, and we'll get it moved."

"It's a lot," Leo said. "Impressive, really."

As the two discussed Denny's technological skills, Fletch paced, his mind on Perkins. The fucker wasn't going to get out of this by dying. There was no way Fletch would allow that to happen. It was when he heard one term that his attention went back to the discussion.

"...backed up the *hard drive*..."

Fletch turned to Leo. "I need Denny's hard drive, everything you backed up." Before either one of them could question, he went on, "Denny was onto something. His information saved Timothy Wells." He nodded as he spoke. "The night he died, he made a comment about Crossroads. I let it go in one ear and out the other until the other night." He turned to Peterson. "You told me to explain the Loews case to Chell. I did. Frank Loews was a small cog in the Crossroads Network. Denny said he thought he was onto something akin to Crossroads." Fletch ran his hand through his hair. "Fuck, I don't recall his exact words. I know he said Crossroads, and he talked about Patrick Lehman—"

Peterson lifted his hand. "Denny told me about the senator also." Peterson pressed his lips together and shook his head. "He didn't have proof."

"Denny was killed. That's enough fucking proof for me. He was on to something. He said he believed a new network had been created, linking professional kidnappers, laypeople, law enforcement, elected officials, and wealthy connections." Fletch's words were coming faster. "I read all about Crossroads. I began in the agency at the beginning of Crossroads' fall. After Frank Loews's trial, many layers were successfully peeled away, exposing money and power." He stared at Leo and Peterson. "The tip of the spear was never even questioned."

"Nelson, Arron Nelson?" Peterson asked. "He's one of the wealthiest men in the world."

"That doesn't mean he's innocent."

"Hell no," Leo said. "It means he can afford to get away with whatever he wants."

Peterson shook his head. "We couldn't connect

him six years ago. Nelson's wealthier and more powerful today than he was then. He just received some big governmental contract for defense spyware."

"And who's on the Defense subcommittee?" Fletch asked.

"Patrick Lehman," Peterson answered. "Guilt by association isn't evidence."

"Then let me find evidence," Fletch said. "Chell can help."

"Shelly isn't ready—"

"She can do it if we're part of a team. Baptism by fire. Put her to work on a case that matters to her."

"Emotional connections have a way of distorting objectivity. Hell, I'm not even sure you should work on this."

Ignoring that comment, Fletch turned to Leo. "You'll be my eyes on the ground."

"Wait," Peterson said. "Is this a witch hunt to bring Nelson down?"

"No," Fletch replied. "Denny told us that he was afraid he accidentally created a cyber breach, alerting either Lehman or Perkins. Personally, I don't think Sheriff Perkins would recognize a cyber breach if it loaded him up with ketamine or oxy."

Both potential painkillers that in excess amount caused cardiac arrest.

"But Lehman," Fletch went on. "If he's in this, he has the connections and manpower. Let me start with Denny's hard drive."

THIRTY-SEVEN

"Welcome back to *Crime Daily Podcast*. It's Monday. I'm Kenzi."

"And I'm Ali. We can't wait to tell our listeners what we learned over the weekend."

"First," Kenzi said, "we need to pay the bills. We'll be back in sixty seconds." She looked through the glass at Greta who motioned they were off the air.

Ali removed her earphones. "Shit, I know we planned to throw Sheriff chauvinistic asshole under the bus." She scrunched her nose. "But now he's dead."

"That doesn't refute anything we planned to say."

"It just seems like..."

Greta's voice came through Kenzi's earphones. "In ten seconds." Kenzi tapped the earphones.

Ali put hers back over her ears as Greta's count-down continued.

"Live."

"We're back," Ali said. "And if you've been following along with the Michelle Holdcraft—"

"D. Valentine," Kenzi interjected.

"That case has blown up. Literally."

Kenzi scoffed. "If you listened to our podcast last Thursday, you know about the explosion. We also have news about Timothy Wells. Let me recap. Last Wednesday morning the home of Ms. Holdcraft exploded."

"And a few days before, her father's house caught fire. His remains were found in the rubble."

"Yes, Ali, and eight years before, her family's home exploded. Her mother perished in that fire."

"That's what we knew last Thursday. Oh boy, have things progressed rapidly," Kenzi said. "Let's start with information about eight-year-old Timothy Wells that may or may not be connected to the Holdcraft case."

"Timothy is home with his family. The details of his ordeal haven't been released. What we know is that he was transported from Boston to Nova Scotia via yacht."

"Yacht? I'm assuming he wasn't a guest."

"I agree, not a willing one, Ali. Timothy was checked by medical personnel in Nova Scotia and flown back to the US. When we know more, we'll share."

"It isn't often we have good news."

"You're right. We're happy for Timothy and his family. Let's tell our listeners about our visit to Iron Falls."

"Friday morning, we arrived in Iron Falls, Massachusetts, to a warm reception—"

Kenzi interrupted, "From Deputy McBride of the Iron Falls Sheriff's Department."

"Deputy McBride may be listening. If she is, we want you to know your kindness was appreciated. Because..."

"Because the reception was less warm from the sheriff himself. As a matter of fact, Sheriff Perkins was less than informative. He did say one interesting thing, though, didn't he, Ali?"

"He did. On Saturday morning, the sheriff insinuated that Dennis Holdcraft had been depressed, never fully recovering from his wife's passing."

"Please," Kenzi said, "if anyone listening has similar thoughts, seek help. We have a suicide prevention hotline on our website."

"The sheriff insinuated that perhaps Dennis Holdcraft committed suicide."

"So, we know that was his original hunch."

"The thing is," Ali went on, "there's a lot that the sheriff didn't tell us. Dennis Holdcraft had an outbuilding on his property. The sheriff acted as though that wasn't unusual. I could agree if the shed contained gardening tools."

"Or even tools for home repair or fishing and hunting gear," Kenzi added. "That's what most people we spoke to in the Iron Falls area said they keep in their sheds or outbuildings."

"But according to a source we spoke with directly, Mr. Holdcraft's outbuilding was an elaborate techno-logical setup. Tell the listeners what we found when we investigated."

"The most moving sight was the ruins of Mr. Hold-craft's home. While prior to the fire it was a two-story home, it was basically reduced to ashes and a chim-ney." Kenzi paused. "We walked farther out on his property. It seemed like a mile, but it was probably closer to one thousand yards. That's where we found the outbuilding. It was as we were told: *empty*." She emphasized the word.

"As if someone had scoured every surface. And what looked rustic on the outside had recently been up-to-date on the inside. Electricity, heat, and air conditioning. I've done a little research based on what we found: conductors and wires. There were also voids in the snow, suggesting larger machinery had been removed."

"What did you learn?"

"I read up on ways to generate energy off the grid."

"Why do people do things off the grid?" Kenzi asked.

"It could be to hide their activity. It could also be that with how rural Mr. Holdcraft's property was, it was his best option. The thing is from what I've read, the kind of power he possibly had at that shed was enough to light a small town."

"Like Iron Falls?"

"Exactly," Ali replied. "What was Mr. Holdcraft doing in that shed that required so much power? What happened to the setup that was seen? How did it all disappear? Who cleaned out the shed?"

"We know it wasn't Ms. Holdcraft. And after this word from our sponsors, we'll tell you more." Kenzi sat back and sighed. "I know it's not up to us to decide guilt or innocence, but I still don't believe that Michelle killed her father. Why would Sheriff Perkins tell us that he possibly committed suicide?"

"I agree," Ali replied. "For now, let's stay with the facts."

"Three, two..." Greta cut in.

"We're back," Kenzi said. "After Iron Falls, Ali and I flew to Indiana to check out the crime scene in Indianapolis."

"You can go to our website to see our pictures and videos from both Iron Falls and Indianapolis."

"In Indianapolis, we met with Officer Darla McCoy from the IMPD. And if you're listening, Officer, thank you for seeing us."

"After the press conference the night before, she didn't have much more to add."

"Greta, can you play the audio from the press conference for our listeners?" Kenzi sat back and stared at her notes.

Both ladies knew what the audio said. They'd listened to it repeatedly, choosing the precise clips they wanted to share. Once the audio ended, the podcast went to commercial break. When they returned to broadcasting, their listeners would know that the Indiana attorney general, Sandra Oaks, was convening a grand jury to determine if there was enough evidence to indict Michelle Holdcraft of serial arson and the murders of both her parents.

"Welcome back," Ali said. "As our regular listeners know, Kenzi and I share the facts and our instincts. We try to see what others may have missed. We learned in that press conference that Mr. Holdcraft died from a bullet to the head, not by the flames that consumed his home."

"Right. Let's look at facts. Mr. Holdcraft was either shot by someone else or his own hand. In order for that someone else to be Michelle Holdcraft, she would have had to be present in Iron Falls on Sunday night. There was a severe snowstorm that evening. The IMPD confirmed they spoke to Michelle in her home near midnight Tuesday night, or early Wednesday morning. It is possible to drive between the two locations in that amount of time, but how could she have done it?"

"Officer McCoy stated that on that late Tuesday night, once they reached Ms. Holdcraft in person, Ms.

Holdcraft claimed she saw her father on Thursday, stopping on her way to Boston," Ali said. "And if you check D. Valentine's website, she was at an event Saturday in Boston. There are pictures of her on the event's website and social media. D. Valentine was seen by hundreds if not thousands of readers as well as other authors at the event."

"Officer McCoy also said Ms. Holdcraft claimed to have left her car at her father's and ended up flying home because of weather conditions."

"Do we know the airline?" Ali asked. "And if her car was at her father's, she couldn't have driven to Indianapolis."

"We found multiple flights between Boston and Indianapolis on Sunday. I'm not saying that a best-selling author wouldn't fly an inexpensive airline, but if she didn't that still gave her numerous options."

"I think we need to investigate if Michelle was on one of those flights."

"I couldn't agree more, Ali. Speaking of flights…or fleeing…where is Michelle Holdcraft now?"

"According to the Indiana attorney general, they're pursuing her as a person of interest. No human remains were found in Michelle's home. As we all heard in the clips from the press conference, law enforcement believes the explosion was ignited with an incendiary device that could have exploded after Michelle fled. A diversion."

"Wait," Kenzi said. "If she took a flight home, it

doesn't seem as if she was in Iron Falls, not at the time of her father's demise. Then why would she flee and ignite her own home?"

"How would she even know how to do that?"

"It's not exactly common knowledge," Kenzi said.

"And does this have anything to do with Timothy Wells?"

"We have more work to do. Come on, all of our cyber sleuths, please give us your theories on our website or social media. Use HashtagWheresD-Valentine."

"That will do it for today. Come back tomorrow."

THIRTY-EIGHT

Michelle spent about five hours wandering through cyberspace before making her way back to Fletch's apartment. She wasn't sure when he'd be back, but that didn't stop her from starting dinner. She was currently in the kitchen chopping vegetables from the groceries Fletch had gotten a few days ago. After surviving on truck-stop and fast food for a week, she was enjoying cooking real meals.

When she arrived back to the apartment, she placed two chicken breasts in a teriyaki marinade. Those were now in the oven. As it turned out, Fletch had never in all his years in the complex used his oven. Brown rice and chives were simmering on the stove-top, and the salad she was creating was almost complete.

Michelle reached for the glass of merlot she'd

poured earlier and took a sip. Her thoughts went to today's earlier episode of *Crime Daily Podcast*. Out of habit, she fidgeted with the locket hanging from around her neck.

Could her name really be cleared by two podcasters?

She popped the clasp open. Her parents' picture fluttered to the ground. There was another picture beneath it. Michelle strained, looking down at the faded child. A smile curled her lips. The little girl would be her. Her mother had it hidden beneath the other picture.

Michelle bent down, recovering her parents' photo as the front door opened and Fletch came home.

As he stopped inside the entry and inhaled, his shoulders straightened. With an exhausted grin, he walked to Michelle, took the glass from her hand, and placed it on the counter. Before she could say a word, his lips were on hers.

The concerns she had about Fletch and Olivia evaporated as his tongue tangoed with hers. She lifted her arms over his wide shoulders and pressed her breasts against his solid chest.

When he pulled away, his gaze was fixated on hers.

"I like how you say hi," she said with a grin.

Fletch stared, still silent.

She tried to read his thoughts, but there were too many to decipher.

Finally, his baritone timbre broke the spell his eyes had cast. "I want to tell you something."

"After that greeting, you can tell me anything."

"I've never in my recollection, ever, in my thirty-six years, come home to a home."

Michelle tilted her head.

"I've come home to a place I can rest, but damn" —he lifted his chin and inhaled— "when I was a kid getting moved from place to place, I imagined what it would be like to be like one of the kids on television, the ones with a family that sat around a table to eat." Fletch pressed his lips together. "I think I gave up on that dream when I was around ten." He cupped her cheek. "I forgot about it. And then, walking in here, the delicious aroma, the clean apartment, that dream came back to me."

She swallowed the lump in her throat. "I'm sorry you never had that growing up."

"Don't be. It makes me appreciate you all the more."

Michelle pushed up on her tiptoes and brushed a kiss over his lips. "I appreciate that I'm here. I wouldn't be without you."

Fletch reached for her wine glass and took a hearty sip before handing it back to Michelle. "I want to talk to you about what I learned today."

"Is it about the grand jury?"

"It's all connected." He went to the cabinet and found a second wine glass. As he topped off Michelle's glass and poured his own, he asked, "How did it go with Olivia?"

"She said today went well. I guess I'm supposed to meet with Peterson tomorrow and discuss the results."

"He's a blowhard, but he's a good man. Don't be concerned."

"I wasn't." She narrowed her gaze. "But now I am."

Since the dining table was now Michelle's office of sorts, she had two place settings on the breakfast bar. She set her wine glass at one of them. "Once the salad is done, we can eat."

"You don't have to cook for me. I can get us food."

She laughed. "You did that for a week. I've had my fill of burgers and breakfast sandwiches." Michelle opened the oven door, and the scent of teriyaki came out with a puff of hot air.

Soon they were seated at the breakfast bar. "I should move my computer someplace else," Michelle said.

"Where and why?" he asked between bites. "Damn, this is good. I usually buy frozen shit that tastes about as good as it sounds."

Her cheeks lifted at the compliment. "Thank you."

"You can take a compliment about your cooking but not your appearance."

She wasn't sure if it was a question or a comment, but she responded, "I enjoy cooking. It's even more fun to cook for two instead of one." She offered him a shy smile. "I'm getting more accustomed to the other compliments."

"Seriously, I can barely boil an egg. Who taught you to cook like this?"

"My mom." She turned to Fletch with a grin. "My mom who was also a secret badass agency spy, apparently. If she did both, maybe I can too."

"Is that what you want?"

"I think you were the one who said my choices were limited."

"If they weren't...?"

Michelle put down her fork and reached for the stem of the wine glass. "I can't think about it too much. Dad used to quote Aristotle—'Choice, not chance, determines your destiny.'" She shrugged. "I think it's both. I made the choice to visit him. You made the choice to stick around and help me. You chose to come back for me after the deputy tried to kidnap me. If those choices led me here, who am I to say it's not my destiny?"

"Ralph Perkins is dead."

Michelle reached for the globe of the glass to steady it from its sudden wobble and set it back on the countertop. "How? What happened?"

"No foul play is suspected. They'll know more after the autopsy." Fletch took another bite and swallowed. "I don't buy it. I think he fucked up. Denny's case and your disappearance shed too much light on Iron Falls and whatever operation they have going there. I'd wager they got rid of him."

"Who is they?" She'd asked him that question before.

Fletch inhaled. "That's what we need to find out."

"You don't think Sheriff Perkins was acting on his own when he killed Dad."

"I don't. I think Perkins was a soldier carrying out orders. He fucked up with you there. Think about it. If you hadn't been there, I wouldn't have been there. Leo wouldn't have known to clean out Denny's shed."

"I would have gotten a call," Michelle said, "from Sheriff Perkins, and I would have believed that it was an accidental fire." She shook her head. "He couldn't have convinced me that Dad took his own life, but an accident...I would've believed that."

"You also wouldn't be a suspect."

Michelle sighed. "How will the agency do it?"

"Do what?"

"Kill me. Make the world think I'm dead. I don't want to spend forever in this complex. I need to die and be given a new identity, like you, right?"

"They have their ways."

Michelle stood. "There's more chicken and rice. Would you like more?"

A smile spread across Fletch's face. "I'll lick the dish clean, and then do the same to you."

Warmth filled her cheeks as her core did its familiar twist. "We'll start with the chicken." Walking around the counter to the stove, she jutted her chin toward the dining table. "I started writing today when I got back from Olivia's lab." She dished more chicken and rice onto Fletch's dish and handed it across the counter. "In Olivia's lab, it felt good to be typing and researching. The access the agency has to infiltrate other sites is phenomenal. I even checked on my airplane ticket."

Fletch stopped eating and stared at her. "Why?"

"I wanted to see if the agency had the ability to make it look like someone was where they weren't. And I found my name." She shook her head and took her seat. "It's truly astounding. I thought this stuff was fiction."

"What did you start writing?"

"I know it will never be published, but I started writing what we've gone through. I'll change it some. No mention of the agency. I know that."

Fletch leaned back and stretched. "After your conversation with Peterson, I'd like you to help."

"Help with what?"

"Leo backed up your dad's data on a hard drive. I spent most of today weeding through it. I believe Denny was on to something. That something got him killed."

"The Timothy Wells case?" she asked.

"He's one of hundreds if not thousands of children. I remembered something. Denny mentioned Crossroads the night before he died."

"That network that was exposed due to Frank Loews's trial?"

Fletch nodded. "Denny believed there is a new one. I hope he had the proof and didn't realize it. Will you help?"

"If you answer a silly question for me."

He lifted his brow. "Oh, we're making conditions now."

"I was just curious. You and Olivia seem to know one another."

"You'll know everyone here soon. Many agents come and go, like I do. The ones who stay here everyone knows. Olivia stays here."

She lifted her glass to her lips, suddenly feeling foolish for her concern. "Oh."

Fletch studied her face. "Are you asking if I've fucked her?"

"No." She batted her eyelashes. "I mean, like you said, there aren't a lot of people here, and she's pretty and petite."

"She's built like a teenage boy." He turned his stool and twisted Michelle's until her knees were between his. After taking her wine glass and setting it on the counter, Fletch leaned closer. "I've never fucked Olivia. I prefer women who are shaped like women." He leaned closer until their noses touched. "I like breasts, curves, and a sexy ass." His lips curled. "There is one asset that makes me do a double take every time."

Michelle wasn't sure if she wanted to know. "What is that?"

Fletch reached for a stray curl of Michelle's hair. "Gingers make me hard."

Her smile grew. "I don't know how in all this trauma I ended up here with you, but I'm glad I did."

"I'm not letting you go, Chell. We're going to be a team like Denny and Tracy."

THIRTY-NINE

"Happy Thursday. I'm Ali."

"And I'm Kenzi."

"We haven't discussed the Holdcraft case since we announced the sad news about Sheriff Perkins in Iron Falls. Is that because there's no new evidence?"

"As we've discussed before, in the case of a grand jury, there's no disclosure of evidence. However, thanks to a tip out of Indianapolis, a network analysis found hours before the explosion, someone on Michelle Holdcraft's internet searched in incognito mode."

"Who would be using her internet besides her?" Ali asked.

"Remember how we questioned how a fiction author would be able to create a device to time-delay an explosion?"

"Can you get that information online?"

"From what I've been able to tell," Kenzi said, "if you know the right places to look, yes."

"Oh." Ali sounded genuinely disappointed. "That doesn't look good for Ms. Holdcraft. Speaking of whom, what is her status?"

"Still missing. The authorities have broadened the search nationwide. They're watching airports and borders."

"If she's innocent she should come forward."

"Let's go to our sponsor and when we return, I have another conflicting bit of evidence. I swear, the pendulum swings one way and then the other."

"I can't wait, Kenzi."

"Thirty seconds," Greta said.

"We're back," Ali said. "What additional evidence did you have to share with our listeners?"

"It turns out that we have a cyber sleuth who works for a nationally recognized airline. Anonymously, this sleuth confirmed that Michelle Holdcraft flew from Boston to Indianapolis at 5:37 p.m. on Sunday, before Dennis Holdcraft's death. She arrived in Indianapolis at 8:09 p.m."

"Are you sure? That isn't normal for an airline to disclose such a thing."

"It isn't. However, once the information was leaked, the airline made an announcement on Twitter. Ms. Holdcraft was seated in 3D." Kenzi's smile was audible.

"You're right. Now I'm back to believing it wasn't her. But then, why would she blow up her own home?"

"Are we sure she did?" Kenzi sighed. "I wish we could ask her."

"Do you think with the proof of an airline ticket, the Indiana attorney general will change her mind about the grand jury?" Ali asked.

"I'm sure the ticket will be evidence. Even though it doesn't help the prosecution, now that it's public, they have to disclose it. It might be enough for the grand jury to decide not to take this case to trial."

"Shout out to our cyber sleuths. Let's go back to Dennis Holdcraft," Ali said. "You and I saw his house. The analysis determined accelerant was used."

"Definitely arson."

"There's no way Michelle was there. And don't forget the shed."

"I haven't forgotten the shed. Do we believe that Mr. Holdcraft was suicidal or that whoever cleaned out that shed could be the person who killed him?" Kenzi asked.

"And, I keep wondering, what was in that shed. Everyone we spoke to said Mr. Holdcraft was a loner and quiet. Back to one of our original discussions on this case. Could there be any link between retired police officer Holdcraft and the child abductions in the New England area?"

"I don't know," Kenzi said, "The good old sheriff would tell us we're playing detective and Iron Falls doesn't have murders. It couldn't possibly be a stop along a trafficking highway."

"Before it was cleaned out, the shed was sustainable."

"As in keeping someone there? Maybe a child?"

"What has Timothy Wells revealed about his ordeal?" Ali asked.

"His parents are keeping him away from the press."

"I can't blame them."

"We'll be back after a break with new information about the Delphi case from Indiana."

"Thirty seconds," said Greta.

CHAPTER

FORTY

Days passed as Michelle and Fletch searched the excessive quantity of files from the hard drive. They spent hours in the complex computer lab only to come home, eat dinner, and resume work in Fletch's office.

Late one evening, Michelle asked Fletch for his help. "Multiple paths take me to this zip file. It's encrypted and I've been trying for over a day to open it."

"You think it's important?" he asked, scooting his desk chair next to Michelle and peering at her screens.

"I hope so. I don't want to leave any stone unturned."

"Have you tried the decrypt program?"

She nodded. "I used the decryption program one you showed me. It's run a million different number combinations."

"What if the encryption phrase isn't numbers?"

Michelle sighed, twisting her long hair and restraining it on top of her head in a messy bun. "The rest have been only numbers. Is there a program for combinations of letters, numbers, and symbols?"

"Let me show you."

Michelle scooted her chair to the side as Fletch took over her keyboard. With her elbow on the long desk supporting her head, she closed her eyes. Olivia said this was exciting when a discovery was found. Michelle would describe the last few days as tedious. She opened her eyes and watched as Fletch's long fingers flew over the keyboard. With his hair untethered, it hung near his chin. He'd shaved recently, and his chiseled jaw was set with determination. His focus was on the ever-changing screen.

"There," he said. "There're billions of combinations. I'd say let the program run and we'll check it in the morning."

"All right," she said with a yawn. "I'm glad Dad was a good guy. All this information he had could make him look like he was part of the network."

Fletch stared at Michelle. "I've known your dad since I started with the agency. He was a good guy, Chell. Don't doubt that."

"I'm not." She shook her head. "I'm just tired. You know when they accused me of setting the fire that killed Mom, there were times I questioned my own innocence. I wasn't guilty. I knew that. But when you look at something from another point of view…" She shrugged. "Dad was obviously obsessed with these abductions. I compared one of his lists with the data from NCRB. Dad had information on children they didn't have."

"Those databases usually lag twelve to eighteen months behind."

"He had a small notice about a family reported missing from a homeless camp in Detroit. Mother and three children reported missing. No follow-up. Nothing."

Fletch covered her hand with his. "This isn't easy work. It can be emotional. I think my empathy was never strong. I see cases. I try not to see people."

Michelle thought about that. "I don't want to do that. I think seeing the people will ingrain the importance of what we're doing. Do you think Dad felt empathy?"

"He was a police officer and an agent in the agency. Denny saw unimaginable things." Fletch sighed. "Fuck, I keep forgetting to tell you something."

She sat up in her chair. "What?"

"You mentioned you had a sister."

Michelle nodded. "Before I was born."

"Chell, that's not true. She went missing when you were two years old."

Michelle's eyebrows knitted together. "No. I never knew her." Her mind scrambled. "Mom said Sarah was my imaginary friend."

"Leo ran a search using the agency's resources. Sarah Holdcraft was born four years before you were born. She disappeared when she was six years old."

"Disappeared. I thought she died."

Fletch pressed his strong lips together. "Did your parents say she died?"

"Yes." She stretched her neck and twisted her sore shoulders, trying to recall. "They said gone." Her head shook. "Mostly, neither of them would talk about her. You said disappeared, as in abducted?"

He nodded.

"Was she ever found?"

"Have you ever tried to search for information about her?"

"No. I think that was out of respect for my parents. The subject was too difficult for them. Mom said it was a tragedy. Dad said it was an accident." She met his dark stare. "Was she found?"

"I truly don't know. There were remains found not far from where you lived. They weren't found until fourteen years after her disappearance. It was suspected to be Sarah, but the body was cremated before DNA testing could be conducted."

"Why?" she asked puzzled.

"IMPD said there was a mix-up in evidence."

"But Dad worked for IMPD."

Fletch nodded. "Maybe as agents within the agency, your parents didn't want the publicity that would come from such a discovery."

Michelle stood. "I can't believe my parents lied about her."

Fletch stood too, reaching for her hands. "Maybe they misled you."

"But if those dates are right, I knew her."

"I'm not sure what we can recall from our early childhood. I don't know. Maybe acting as if she didn't exist was easier for them than living with the idea that she was taken from them."

Sighing, Michelle tipped her forehead to Fletch's chest. The steady thump of his heart was reassuring. She looked up, meeting his gaze. "The remains. Did they determine the cause of death?"

"Spine fracture."

"An accident. A tragedy." Michelle's lips gaped open. "What if she wasn't kidnapped?"

"What do you mean?"

"Mom told me it was a tragedy. Dad said it was an accident." Her hands began to tremble. "I can't fathom my parents would hide the death of a child, much less their own child."

"Chell," he said softly, "with your writing and what we do here—it's easy to let our imaginations run wild. Your parents experienced a horrible tragedy and made the choice not to share that with their young daughter. They were protecting you."

She pressed her palms over her temples. "It's like I was saying about when the police questioned me. Learning that my parents hid the agency from me and now, Sarah. What else did they hide?" The computer screen caught Michelle's attention. "Look."

"It looks like a match was found."

Michelle eased back into her chair and began typing. "It's a huge file." She read off the numbers. "Can this computer handle a file that large?"

"We're better off taking it into the lab tomorrow."

Michelle sighed. "I know you're right. I have a weird feeling, like I could learn things I don't want to know about my dad."

Fletch offered her his hand. "Let's go to bed."

FORTY-ONE

Michelle tossed and turned throughout the night. Despite her exhaustion, her mind swirled with the new revelations about her parents. What kind of people could live a double life the way they had done? The kind of people who could lie.

There was no getting around the fact that Tracy and Dennis Holdcraft were liars.

If she asked Fletch, he'd tell her that they lied to protect her. And in his mind, they were heroes. Michelle reminded herself that her father was the reason Timothy Wells was home with his family.

Sleep came on and off. The slumber was fractured and filled with unwanted dreams. During times of wakefulness, Fletch's information would come back. Sarah was six when she went missing.

Six.

Suddenly, Michelle had the need to learn more.

Quietly getting out of bed and not disturbing Fletch, Michelle made her way to his office. Her computer on the table didn't have the ability to search undetected the way his did. Sitting back in the chair she'd left hours ago, Michelle brought the computer to life and entered the name of her sister.

There was more than one Sarah Holdcraft.

She narrowed the search to Indiana.

The birth announcement appeared. Sarah Louise Holdcraft.

Michelle's heart seized. She hadn't even known her sister's middle name.

Born at Saint Francis Hospital in Beech Grove, Indiana. She'd been born at the same hospital. However, by the time Sarah was born, the hospital was in Indianapolis. They'd built a new modern facility.

Fletch was right about the date, four years before Michelle was born.

Next, Michelle accessed the community school system's database. Michelle attended Eastwood Elementary. If Sarah was six, wouldn't she have attended the same school?

The only Holdcraft was Michelle.

There were a couple of private schools in the area, one Christian and the other Catholic. Michelle discovered Sarah Holdcraft attended Holy Mary's. She was enrolled in kindergarten and first grade. There was no further record of her attendance.

She stared at the screen.

Michelle had always considered her parents loving. What kind of parent loses a child after loving them for six years and forgets them—erases them as if they never existed. She racked her brain for any memories of Sarah. For the life of her, Michelle couldn't recall as much as a picture.

Sarah's name didn't come up in relation to a missing person.

She went to IMPD. If the agency was as good as they claimed, they should be able to access police records. Surely, her parents reported Sarah missing. There was a file. It was sealed.

Was that her father's doing?

Michelle knew police officers didn't have that power. In her father's position, he would know people who could.

Olivia was right. One answer led to ten questions. Michelle had another idea. She went to the *Indianapolis Star*, Indianapolis's newspaper, and entered Sarah's name. Her birth announcement came up first. The next hit was a prayer service at Holy Mary's for missing Sarah Holdcraft. Tears filled Michelle's eyes at the black and white photo of a little girl. It was as if she were seeing herself at six years old. They could have been twins, born four years apart.

The girl in the locket.

The counseling session from years ago at Purdue came back to her. She'd told the counselor her bedroom contained two beds. Had they shared a room? Michelle was two years old when Sarah disappeared. Wouldn't Michelle be in a crib? There wouldn't have been two twin beds.

Was Sarah her imaginary friend, or did young Michelle remember having an older sister?

"What are you doing?"

His voice made her jump. Michelle looked up, seeing Fletch. He filled the doorframe, wearing only his boxer briefs. "I'm doing what everyone wants me to do for the agency. I'm researching."

"Denny's files?"

She shook her head, her focus back on the screen. "I'm looking at a picture of Sarah." She looked back up. "Sarah Louise. I never knew her middle name."

Fletch padded toward her on bare feet. His large hands came to her shoulders, gently massaging as he looked at the photo. "She looks like a young you."

"I thought the same thing." She craned her neck and looked up at Fletch. "I know they were also heroes, but all I can think is that my parents lied to me my entire life. I don't know what to believe or what's real."

Fletch crouched down beside Michelle's chair. His dark stare looked up at her. "Denny loved you. You were his last concern." When she didn't reply, he said, "Let's go back to bed. Maybe you can get a few hours of sleep before we head to the computer lab tomorrow."

The emotion building within Michelle was different than simply the loss of her parents. It was the realization that she never knew them in the first place.

Standing with her hand in Fletch's, she said, "Will you help me take my mind off of what I'm learning?"

His lips quirked and he tugged her close. "I can do my best."

FORTY-TWO

Fletch, Leo, and Michelle stood around a large screen scrolling though picture after picture. The bounded, gagged, and unconscious children ranged in age from roughly two years old to seventeen years old. Some of the children were identified with names, others weren't. Each picture had a date and time stamp. The pictures weren't of the children prior to them going missing, such as would be on a missing poster. These pictures were of children during the abductions.

"How the hell did Denny get these?" Leo asked.

Fletch stared in disbelief. "There are hundreds."

Michelle walked away and spun, her eyes glued to the screen. "Did you know that some arsonists are firemen?"

Fletch and Leo turned toward her.

"Really. There's something called a hero complex.

The fireman rushes in and saves the kid or the puppy. He's a hero. Murderers are known to participate in the search for their victims. They want to know if they've gotten away with the crime. They get a psychological thrill in being part of the excitement. In a case study for one of my criminology classes, the unsub was identified because he attended his victims' funerals. Multiple people in different states—he showed up to all of them."

"Chell, no."

Her heart was beating in her chest, but she had to say what she was thinking. "My father was obsessed with child abductions. You said it yourself. He'd rattle off statistics. He told stories of horrors that he witnessed."

Leo looked at Fletch and back to Michelle. "Denny wouldn't."

Michelle lifted her hands, as if in surrender, and backed away. "I don't want to be right, but what if I am? What if Sheriff Perkins found out?"

"He would have arrested him, not killed him," Fletch replied.

"Maybe the sheriff went there for that, and things took a turn. The sheriff panicked and started the fire." She was talking fast. "Now Sheriff Perkins is dead. He can't tell us what happened—neither one of them can."

"First thing," Fletch said, "before we accuse anyone, we need to understand what Denny was doing with these pictures. And once we confirm the identities of the children, we find out if they were recovered or are still missing. There are families out there that deserve answers."

"I'll work on that," Leo said, "...keep going through Denny's information. We can't rule out Chell's concern. However, there might be an explanation if we keep digging."

"I need a minute," Michelle said as she stepped out of the lab. Going down the hallway to the lounge, she poured herself a cup of coffee. Olivia was right that it was pretty good. She needed a break from life-altering revelations. Somehow, she'd have to come to terms with the fact she didn't know her parents or her sister.

"Shelly."

She turned, finding Peterson standing in the doorway. "Hi."

He nodded, stepped into the small room, and motioned toward the table. "Can we talk?"

It was like the last time he asked. Michelle felt the need to comply. She nodded in return and pulled out a chair.

Peterson sat across from her and placed his hands on the table. "You've had some large discoveries."

"How did you know? Fletch—?"

"Arrow didn't tell me. We monitor the work that's done here at the agency. When something is flagged, it's brought to my attention."

"My dad..." A ragged sob lodged in her throat. "He wasn't what I thought he was."

"Dennis was a good man. He and Tracy told my predecessor about Sarah. It was tragic, but due to the agency, they handled it the best they could considering the circumstances."

Sarah.

That wasn't the subject Michelle expected. "They never mentioned her. It was as if she never existed."

"It was easier for them that way. You were so young. You weren't responsible for what happened."

She sat straight. "What? I was two. Of course, I wasn't responsible."

"Your parents didn't want you to know, but I'm afraid that your skills are as good as Arrow said. Now that you have the power of the agency behind you, you could learn the truth. I thought it would be better if you heard it from me."

"My sister was abducted."

"No, your sister fell down the basement stairs after she tripped over you. It was an accident."

An accident.

A tragedy.

"Tripped? Over me? I don't understand."

"Your mother was home with the two of you. She went down in the basement to do laundry. The two of you were running around and playing. The next thing she heard was a scream and then the falling. She tried to get to Sarah in time, but her little body was contorted. Her neck was broken."

Spine fracture.

"You'd fallen too. According to what was recorded, you didn't make it to the bottom of the stairs. You stopped on the landing; however, Sarah continued the fall."

Michelle was frozen, unable to move or speak, paralyzed by this information.

"Because of the agency, Tracy and Dennis chose not to alert the authorities of the accident. Instead, they constructed a tale about her playing in the yard and disappearing."

Words began to form. "The body that was found, was it Sarah?"

"They believed so. Dennis was able to facilitate the mix-up in evidence. DNA testing was never done."

"They cremated her." Michelle's voice was a mere whisper.

A chill scattered over her.

Flames.

Peterson nodded. "It was a horrible situation. If the police would've gotten involved with the accident...your parents didn't want you to grow up with the knowledge you facilitated your sister's death. Imagine how that would look now, with the current grand jury."

"I was two. I wasn't responsible." Michelle felt the

way she had when she tried to defend herself regarding her mother's death. "I've been lied to."

"Not anymore. Now you know the truth." Peterson's chair scooched across the vinyl floor as he stood. "We do good things here. I didn't want you to spend any more time on a case that will remain closed. We need you to concentrate on the cases that we can affect."

Michelle sat in silence as Peterson walked away.

Her coffee was lukewarm.

Her parents covered up the death of her sister. They were secret spies. And her father was not only involved in the prevention of child trafficking, but quite possibly in the assistance of child trafficking.

"Chell," Fletch said, a bit out of breath. "I've been looking for you. Come see what we found."

Michelle wanted to share what Peterson told her, but it was too new. Instead, she picked up her coffee and followed Fletch back to the computer lab.

FORTY-THREE

"Do you remember," Fletch began, "how the picture file was encrypted differently than Denny's other files?"

Michelle was having difficulty focusing. "Encrypted? Yes. The other files were coded with only number sequences. The picture file had numbers, symbols, and letters."

Fletch's smile bloomed and his dark eyes shone. "Further analysis determined the reason. The picture file wasn't Denny's."

She stopped walking. "Wasn't Dad's...how do you know?"

"Come on." He hitched his jaw and quickened his step.

Michelle was a step behind Fletch as they entered the lab. Leo was sitting at the computer where they'd opened the horrible pictures. The pictures were gone and in their place were rows and rows of codes, multi-plying exponentially. "What's happening?"

Leo turned with a smile as large as Fletch's. "Chell, those photos weren't taken by Denny. He may not have even realized he had them."

"I don't understand. They were on the hard drive you made from Dad's computers."

"They were on the hard drive. I copied that folder from his computers, but when Arrow started talking about the different encryption, it made me wonder why it would be different. If you know this, stop me."

Michelle took the chair next to Leo. "I'm so out of my league right now. Please explain."

"That's how you found the file," Leo said. "You didn't know what you were looking for."

"I thought we were looking at everything."

"Yes," Fletch said. "Honestly, with the different coding, I would've probably overlooked that file unless I noticed the size. The point is that you didn't overlook it."

"All files have invisible extensions," Leo said. "It's a defining sequence that carries additional information. Denny's file extensions were similar to each other because they came from the same computers, the same VPNs, the same geolocation."

Michelle nodded. "I'm following. You're saying the picture file had different extensions."

"Yes." Leo looked up at the screen. "We're about to find out where the file came from."

"How would it be on Dad's computer?"

Fletch answered. "I have a theory. A couple of weeks or so before Denny was killed, he intercepted a transmission. He believed it was between Sheriff Perkins and Patrick Lehman."

"Am I supposed to know who that is?" Michelle asked.

"A Massachusetts senator."

Her eyes widened. "The network, like Crossroads."

"I fucking hope so," Fletch said.

Leo spoke, looking up at the screen. "The file has been rerouted through multiple VPNs. I hope the code hasn't been severed."

Michelle wasn't sure what that meant, but it sounded bad.

The three continued to wait. The tension rippled through the air in invisible waves.

Finally, the program stopped.

The code was cracked.

Leo began to type. The click of the keys echoed through the lab. "Fuck."

"What?" Michelle and Fletch asked in unison.

The screen filled with a satellite image. They zoomed in on the house. It was more like a compound with a massive house in the middle flanked by a large swimming pool, tennis courts, and manicured lawns.

"Where is that?" Fletch asked.

"East Texas. Old-money country."

"No fucking way."

"Who?" Michelle asked.

"Arron Nelson," Leo said with a grin.

"Oh my God," she said. "He has the money to fund a network, right?"

Leo pushed back from the desk. "We need to go to Texas. We can't be sure until we physically check his network. If we can prove this is correct, we get Nelson and all the people under him, including Patrick Lehman."

"Wait," Michelle said. "Isn't this enough? You can't go to his house. He's not going to just let you in."

Fletch's lips curled into a grin. "We don't knock on the door."

"You're going to break into the home of one of the wealthiest men in the world. That doesn't sound safe or smart."

"We only need to confirm his network's extensions," Leo said. "His system is well protected. We need to be in close proximity."

Michelle reached for Fletch's hands, the fears of the past few weeks surfacing. "Please don't go."

"Leo and I have pulled off more dangerous jobs. This will be a quick trip."

"Are you going now?"

"We'll coordinate with Peterson," Fletch said. "I've been wanting evidence on Nelson since Crossroads. We're so damn close." He smiled at Michelle. "Because of you and Denny."

Satisfaction bloomed in her chest. It felt better

than the doubt she'd had earlier. "My father didn't take those pictures."

"I doubt Nelson took them. He must have them sent to him after each abduction," Leo said. "Let's take this to Peterson."

FORTY-FOUR

Michelle sat at the dining room table, the story in her head coming out as she typed. Every now and then, she looked at the clock. It was nearly midnight. She didn't know where Fletch and Leo were. They'd left after six p.m., before she'd been able to tell him Peterson's news about Sarah. There was too much happening with the possible connection to Arron Nelson.

Unlike their cross-country drive, the agents flew to East Texas via an agency plane. What Michelle imagined was happening fifteen hundred miles away was the thing of spy thrillers. While part of her wanted to accompany them, Michelle knew her strengths didn't lie in on-the-ground reconnaissance. That was Fletch's strength or one of them.

She let her mind go back to her story. It was about an author who found herself living an unbelievable chain of events. As in all Michelle's stories, there was a love interest. Handsome and dangerous, he was a man the heroine would never imagine having in her life, but Michelle knew by the end of the story, they'd be together. She was writing their first meeting. It was easy to describe her character's reaction because she was describing her own feelings the first time she encountered Fletch.

Michelle shivered, recalling the frigid air, the ache in her feet, and the blazing flames.

After she finished writing the scene, she saved and closed her manuscript. Telling the story felt cleansing and cathartic. Remembering the sheer terror of that night was too much, especially with Fletch out on a mission.

She settled in the large cool bed and was almost asleep when she heard the door to the apartment open. Her mind told her it was Fletch. She was safe in the complex. No one would hurt her. At the same time, her body trembled, reliving the horrors of the night her father died.

Her focus went to the bedroom door, mostly closed but not completely. There was someone out there. Staring, she waited for Fletch to enter the bedroom.

As more time passed, Michelle's alarm intensified. She quietly slipped out of bed and tiptoed to the closet. Instead of on a high shelf, her gun safe was on the floor, tucked in a corner near Fletch's boots.

Careful to not make a noise, she opened the small

safe and removed her Sig Sauer. She checked the magazine. It was already loaded. Unfastening the safety, she waited.

Would whoever was out in the rest of the apartment come looking for her?

Or she wondered if it would be better for her to find them.

Taking a deep, cleansing breath, Michelle made the decision that she had survived the scene she just wrote. She survived more than the initial trauma. She wasn't going to get taken out in her sleep.

Step by step, she moved toward the bedroom door. The Sig Sauer was lighter than Fletch's Glock. Her earlier trembling was gone, replaced with determination. Light spilled from below the door to Fletch's office. Michelle was certain it wasn't on when she went to bed.

"It's just Fletch," she told herself on repeat. The gun was still in her grasp, her finger on the trigger guard. She pushed open the door to his office.

"Shelly."

Michelle lowered the gun at the familiar light-green stare. "What are you doing in here?"

"I didn't realize you were living with Arrow," Peterson said, sitting behind the computer she used in this room.

She kept the gun at her side. He was lying. "You came here to see me after the press conference in Indianapolis."

Peterson stood. His smile seemed forced. "You're right. I must have forgotten. I apologize if I woke you. I obviously wasn't thinking. You see, I was looking for the hard drive you've been working on."

"Why?"

He motioned to the living room. "We should talk."

There was that same tone, the one that expected obedience.

Michelle was done with loyal obedience. "It's the middle of the night. We can talk tomorrow."

"I can't wait until tomorrow."

"Does this have anything to do with Fletch and Leo's mission?" she asked.

"It does." Peterson looked around the room. "If you will give me the hard drive, I'll be on my way."

"Fletch had it."

Peterson's voice hardened. "He didn't have it. Leo didn't have it. It's not in the complex computer lab. That only leaves here."

This wasn't right. The small hairs on the back of Michelle's neck stood to attention. She took a step backward. "I think you should leave."

"Shelly, Arrow and Leo encountered a problem."

Her breathing hitched. "Are they all right?"

He shook his head. "They encountered security at the target's residence. There was an exchange of gunfire."

"At Arron Nelson's house? Was Fletch shot?" She could hardly form the words.

Peterson's smile disintegrated as he pulled a gun from behind his back. "I wish you didn't know that name, Shelly." He took a step closer. "Give me your gun."

"You're telling me Fletch is dead?" In her heart of hearts, Michelle knew that wasn't true. They were connected, bonded in flames. If he were dead, she'd know it. She would feel it, the way she felt the loss when her father died.

"Give me your gun."

"You're working for Arron Nelson," she said. It was the perfect plot twist, one she wished she'd have realized a minute earlier.

Peterson took another step toward her.

Michelle lifted her gun. "That's how Arron Nelson avoided arrest during the takedown of Crossroads. You're on his payroll. You allow the little people to be found to make the agency appear effective."

"We do good work. Your father and mother did good work."

Peterson's finger moved, but Michelle's finger was already on the trigger.

He cursed, his shot whizzing by Michelle's body, striking, and splintering the door.

Her blast sent Peterson backward. He tripped and fell over a desk chair as the bangs ricocheted throughout the apartment. She ran forward and kicked his gun out of his reach. Her shot hit his right shoulder in time to throw off his shot.

"Fucking bitch," he screamed, his hand covering the bleeding wound.

Her gun was pointed at his chest. "Where's Fletch?"

"I told you. Now get help."

Michelle's voice calmed, too calm. "Tell me where the hell Fletch is, and I won't shoot you again."

"I haven't heard from them."

"You alerted Nelson that they were on their way." When he didn't answer, she moved her finger from the guard to the trigger.

"Yes. Nelson's people were waiting for them."

Peterson hadn't heard from Fletch or Leo.

That meant that maybe things didn't go down the way he planned.

Michelle could kill Peterson, but if she did that, he wouldn't pay for his traitorous acts. Instead, she searched him for more weapons, removing belongings from his pockets. He squirmed but was obviously feeling the loss of blood. She pulled an extension cord from an outlet and disconnected the plug on the other end. He continued to curse and fight, as she secured his hands together. A length of duct tape shut lips and quieted his threats so she could think.

Who could she call?

Who else in the agency was dirty?

She only knew one other person.

FORTY-FIVE

With Peterson secured and his gun on the kitchen counter, Michelle went in search of her phone. It was still the one Fletch purchased at the truck stop. She called Fletch. The call immediately went to voicemail. Thankfully, after the day in the computer lab, Olivia and Michelle exchanged numbers. At nearly three in the morning, Olivia answered on the second ring.

"Shelly, is everything all right?"

"No. Do you live far?"

"Are you at Arrow's place?" Olivia asked, sounding more awake.

"Yes. I'm worried about Arrow. Do you know how to reach him?"

"I'll be there in a few minutes."

Michelle disconnected the call and checked on Peterson. He was still fighting the extension cord. She wished she had whatever the deputy tried to inject her with. That would keep Peterson in his place. She opened a drawer at Fletch's main desk and removed the hard drive.

Peterson made noise behind the tape.

Michelle took the hard drive to the closet in the bedroom and locked it in her gun safe. Next, she took off her pajama shorts and slipped into a pair of blue jeans. She was about to put on a bra when the doorbell rang.

Through the peephole Michelle saw Olivia. She opened the door. Olivia's hazel eyes shone in the cold air. She was wearing a heavy coat over pajama pants. "That was fast."

"We only have two apartment buildings. I live that way" —she gestured with a shake of her head— "on the second floor. What's wrong?"

Michelle let her inside and closed the door.

Olivia looked around. "Arrow has a nice place. I always wondered what it was like."

This wasn't the time to discuss the condition of the apartment when Michelle arrived. "You said you've been with the agency for ten years."

"Shelly, are you all right?"

"Peterson broke into this apartment and threatened me."

"What the fuck?" She opened her coat, revealing a holster. "Where is he?"

"I thought you said you were brain not brawn."

Olivia removed the gun from the holster. "You don't spend ten years in the agency without learning a trick or two." Her hazel stare met Michelle's. "Where did he go?"

"He's in there." Michelle pointed. "He's not going anywhere. I shot him."

"Damn, you do belong here. Tell me everything."

"I need to get ahold of Arrow. Peterson sent Leo and him into a trap."

Olivia's eyes widened. "You're serious."

Michelle nodded. "How do you reach agents on missions?"

"Usually, you wait for them to contact you. But I know the pilot who flew them out. Let me try to reach him."

Michelle took a ragged breath. The adrenaline racing through her circulation was morphing to fear, fear for Fletch.

Olivia removed her phone from her coat pocket and hit a contact. "It went to voicemail," she said to Michelle.

"Shit. It's what my call to Fletch did."

Olivia spoke, "Pete, it's Liv. I know where you went. Tell me if Leo and Arrow have returned."

When she disconnected the call, she looked at Michelle. "What are you going to do about Peterson?"

"No idea. He's not the top, is he?"

"No. Top here, but here is only one place. I say we contact *the* top. His name is Grant, Graham Grant."

"How do we reach him?"

Olivia's eyebrows arched. "We need to get into Peterson's office."

Michelle grinned. "Hold on for a minute." She went into the bedroom and came out with the items she'd found when searching Peterson's pockets including his ID card. "This should help."

Olivia reached for the card. "Maybe you should stay here and make sure he doesn't get loose."

Michelle tugged on her lip and sighed. "I want to trust you."

"Oh, you can trust me. I've had a feeling about Peterson ever since he arrived. I gave up my life for the agency. We don't tolerate traitors."

"Okay."

"Keep your gun close. If you have to shoot, hit center mass."

"I'd rather he be punished for his crimes."

Olivia winked. "The knee. It hurts like hell, and he won't be able to walk."

"Good advice."

Michelle paced the living room to the kitchen and back, time and time again. While she'd been willing her phone to ring and to hear Fletch's voice, it remained silent. She'd about worn a hole in the flooring when the doorbell rang again.

Olivia was outside with two large men, reminding Michelle of Fletch and Leo.

Michelle reached for her gun, unlocked the safety, and opened the door.

"I got ahold of Grant." Olivia tipped her head from side to side. "This is Rock and Colt. Top gave the order for Peterson to be held in the brig until things get sorted out."

Michelle sighed. "What about Fle—Arrow?"

"Top said he'd investigate."

Michelle nodded nervously as she let the three inside. "Peterson is in there." She pointed to the office.

"Is it locked?" asked either Colt or Rock.

"No, it locks from the inside."

Both men removed guns from their back holsters. The one with facial hair opened the door. "Ma'am?"

Michelle and Olivia walked toward the door. Cold air met them. Blood smudged the floor next to the extension cord Michelle had used. The window was opened.

"Shit. I was in the other room. I didn't hear a thing."

The two men looked at one another. "Lock that window," said the one Michelle thought was Colt. "We'll find him. No one's getting away from here on foot."

"Liv," the other man said, "can you take Shelly to your place?"

"Of course."

Michelle turned, seeing the bedroom in disarray. "He was in my bedroom."

The men again lifted their guns and entered the bedroom as Michelle held her breath and reached for Olivia's hand. They stood perfectly still until...

"Clear," one of the men yelled.

Michelle rushed past them and into her closet. She let out a sigh. Her gun safe was where she'd hidden it, and it was still locked.

"What's that?" Olivia asked.

"It's what Peterson wanted. It's the hard drive with my father's files."

"Bring that with you."

Michelle nodded.

After securing the apartment, Michelle donned boots and her coat, and with her gun, phone, and the gun safe in tow, she accompanied Olivia into an elevator she'd never before seen and up to the second floor.

FORTY-SIX

ichelle sent Fletch a text.

"I'M at Olivia's place. Please call. I'll explain when we are together."

As SHE HIT SEND, she said a prayer that they'd be together again. Looking around, she found Olivia's apartment was the same basic floor plan as Fletch's. Her furnishings were more feminine, colorful, and bright.

"Coffee?" Olivia asked after she'd shed her coat and holster.

It wasn't yet four in the morning, but sleep seemed impossible. "Thank you. Cream and sugar."

"I have milk."

Michelle nodded. It wasn't the same, but it would do. "I like how colorful your place is."

"Thanks. It's my safe place. I wanted to brighten it up."

"What's it like," Michelle asked, "living here for so long?"

Olivia shrugged as she handed Michelle a steaming mug. "I'm used to it. There are some fun bars and restaurants in a few of the nearby towns."

"One day, maybe, I'll be able to leave the complex."

"Do you know when that's going to happen?"

Michelle shook her head. She looked up, fighting tears. "Peterson said he called Nelson and warned him that Leo and Fletch were coming. What if...?"

Olivia tapped the sofa beside her and sat with her feet beneath her. She held her own mug of coffee. "Arrow showed up a few years after I got here. We don't talk about particulars of missions, but he's been on his share. Leo too. And I believe they've survived much more dangerous situations then a setup at a mansion."

Michelle inhaled. "I think I care about him." She shook her head. "It's probably PTSD or maybe I have hero complex and Arrow's my hero. I can't imagine being here and working for the agency without him."

Olivia's phone rang. Her eyes grew wide at the name. "It's Grant."

"Calling a private phone?"

Olivia nodded and hit the green icon. "Top." Her lips came together. "I understand." A long fissure formed between her eyebrows. "Oh. You're welcome." Her gaze met Michelle's. "Holdcraft, yes. The same." Finally, a smile curled her lips. "I'll tell her. Thank you." She disconnected the call.

"What?"

"I'm sure Arrow will want to explain it all to you."

Tears spilled from Michelle's eyes. "He's alive."

"Yes. Leo too. They were ambushed, but I told you, Arrow and Leo have encountered worse. They reported directly to Top, suspicious that their mission had been compromised."

"It's all true. Peterson set them up."

"It appears that way."

Michelle let out a long breath and laid her head back against the sofa. "I'm suddenly exhausted."

"I don't have a guest room, because as you can imagine, I don't get many guests. But you're welcome to lie on the sofa. I can get you a blanket and pillow."

"Are Arrow and Leo on their way back?"

"They are."

"I'll wait."

Michelle didn't intend to fall asleep, but she did, because she woke as she was being lifted. This time she didn't fight off her attacker. Instead, she inhaled the familiar scent of soap and danger and lifted her arms around his neck. "I love you."

"I fucking love you, too."

It was then she realized she and Fletch were in Olivia's apartment and had an audience. Michelle's cheeks filled with warmth as she saw Olivia and Leo. "Oh, I'm embarrassed."

"Don't be," Olivia said. "I love happy endings."

Fletch lowered Michelle's feet to the floor. "Not all happy."

"What?"

"Colt and Rock found Peterson."

"Good," Olivia said.

"I hope they throw the book at him."

Leo replied, "The agency is a one-way ride. Peterson knew that and thought he could play the system. Apparently, Top has been monitoring Peterson for the last few months."

"He's guilty," Michelle said. "Does the agency have trials?"

Everyone but Michelle shook their heads.

Her eyes widened. "Oh my God, is he? Will they?"

"He is," Fletch said. "A single bullet to the head. He knew he wouldn't survive if he didn't end it himself." Fletch's smile widened. "And here Leo and I thought we had an exciting mission." He laid his hand on Michelle's shoulder. "I've got myself a super spy."

"Natasha Romanoff," Olivia said.

"Who?" Michelle asked.

"Wait, you're not a Marvel fan?"

Michelle shook her head. "I've always been more of a DC fan. Love me some Batman."

Fletch put his arm around Michelle. "We've got forever to show you the wrong of your ways."

"And once you can leave the complex," Olivia added, "there's a nearby theater that shows Marvel marathons once a month."

Michelle looked up at Fletch. "Will that day come?"

"It will. First, we need to prove Perkins's connection to Nelson and that he killed Denny."

"It's in the works," Leo said. "We told Top how you helped find the file that nails Nelson's coffin. He also heard about your takedown of Peterson. When you make an impression on Top in your first week, the agency will make sure things happen."

FORTY-SEVEN

"Hi, I'm Kenzi."

"And I'm Ali."

"Welcome back. We hope everyone had a nice Labor Day weekend."

"I'm not ready for summer to end," Ali said.

"It sure was nicer in Iron Falls without all the snow."

"You're right. We told you last week that Sheriff McBride invited us back to Iron Falls, Massachusetts, for the grand opening of the Holdcraft Refuge. It seems that Dennis Holdcraft, the man murdered last January, left his estate to his daughter."

"However, we know that sadly, Michelle Holdcraft also tragically perished, following her father's murder. A car accident on a deserted highway in North Dakota."

"We talked about that last spring," Ali said. "I hate

that she never knew she was completely exonerated for her part in her father's death, the blowing up of the house in Indianapolis, and her mother's demise."

"Thankfully, IMPD uncovered doorbell footage from one of Ms. Holdcraft's neighbors showing Matt Wilcox breaking into Michelle's home before the explosion. No doubt, she was scared for her life when she ran off the road."

"Back in Iron Falls," Ali said. "Matt Wilcox was one of Sheriff Perkins's deputies. Thanks to hard work from all, he's now awaiting trial for his part in the explosion of Ms. Holdcraft's home."

"Yeah," Kenzi said, "we didn't have time to visit him during our trip. As we said, Dennis Holdcraft's estate was supposed to go to his daughter. His will stipulated that if for any reason it couldn't, he wanted the money donated to Exodus Lane, an organization that focuses on rescuing victims of trafficking and on training local authorities. With the generous donation, Exodus Lane opened a new center in Massachusetts called the Holdcraft Refuge."

"It gave me chills to see what this organization does. We often talk about human trafficking and to see the staff and volunteers who want to help victims was heartwarming."

"I couldn't agree more. And the best part of our weekend, we were able to meet Timothy Wells and his parents. He's such a strong little boy."

"This story is almost as twisted as one of D. Valentine's books," Ali said. "I've read all four, and I wish another one would come out."

"Oh, I read the other day that she had a manuscript ready before she died. She'd sent it to her editor at Broadway Publishing. It's set to come out after the first of the year."

"I'm going to one-click that pre-order today. It's on Amazon. The title is *The Fire Within*."

"Check it out," Kenzi said. "And now a word from our sponsor."

FORTY-EIGHT

Sarah, Michelle's new name, was working in the complex computer lab when the door opened. "You're home." She jumped up from her chair and met Fletch halfway across the room, throwing her arms around his neck.

Their lips met. Fletch pushed her back, keeping her at arm's length as his dark stare devoured Sarah, warming her skin beneath her clothes. "I couldn't stay away."

"Are you going to tell me where you went?"

His sexy lips quirked. "We can work out a deal of some sort."

Sarah grinned. "I love working out deals with you."

"First," Fletch said, "I brought a few guests with me. As you know, I had a meeting with Top."

"Don't tell me Mr. Grant is sending you away

again." She couldn't hide the disappointment in her voice.

"No, Chell" —some habits die hard— "he wants to meet you in person—the famous Michelle Holdcraft."

"Shh," she hushed. "I heard she died. Tragic end. Her car caught on fire."

"The ultimate eraser."

"Shit." Her blue eyes opened wide. "Top is here." She looked down at her blue jeans.

"Stop, you're gorgeous."

Sarah grinned. "I'm glad you think so. Where is he?"

"He's in Applegate's office. He said he'd come here next." Fletch cocked his head to the side. "I couldn't wait to see you."

Applegate was the new Peterson, and over the last seven months, she'd righted the ship that Peterson had almost sunk.

The door behind Fletch opened. A distinguished gentleman with white hair, reminding Sarah of Bradley Whitford, entered.

"Mr. Grant," Sarah said, offering her hand.

His handshake was firm.

"Sarah." He paused. "I believe that's the name Arrow told me."

"Yes, sir. Sarah Louise."

"Sarah, I've wanted to make this trip since you first joined us. How are you adjusting?"

She looked at Fletch who was at her side. "Arrow has helped me."

"And you've helped the agency. I thought it was time for you to be introduced to our director of research" —he chuckled— "if we had titles, that is. Michelle," he called.

When the door opened, Sarah's knees weakened as she reached for Fletch's strong arm with one hand and clenched the locket with the other. The woman before her was the image of what Sarah would look like in thirty years.

"Shelly, I've missed you. I'm so proud of the choices you've made."

"Mom?"

Thank you for reading FEAR OF FLAMES, a romantic thriller.

COMING SOON:

NAUGHTY AND NICE - A Brutal Vows Holiday Novella

November 2025

STANDALONE ROMANTIC SUSPENSE:

DEFENDING LOVE

June 2025

BRUTAL VOWS:

NOW AND FOREVER

May 2024

TILL DEATH DO US PART

June 2024

BOUND BY A PROMISE

October 2024

QUEENS AND MONSTERS

January 2025

TO HAVE AND TO HOLD

March 2025

~

SINCLAIR DUET:

REMEMBERING PASSION

September 2023

REKINDLING DESIRE

October 2023

~

ROYAL REFLECTIONS SERIES:

RUTHLESS REIGN

November 2022

RESILIENT REIGN

January 2023

RAVISHING REIGN

April 2023

RELEVANT REIGN

June 2023

~

SIN SERIES:

RED SIN

October 2021

GREEN ENVY

January 2022

GOLD LUST

April 2022

BLACK KNIGHT

June 2022

STAND-ALONE ROMANTIC SUSPENSE:

LIGHT DARK

Republished 2024

Previously: INTO THE LIGHT and AWAY FROM THE DARK

SILVER LINING

October 2022

KINGDOM COME

November 2021

DEVIL'S SERIES (Duet):

DEVIL'S DEAL

May 2021

ANGEL'S PROMISE

June 2021

SPARROW WEBS

WEB OF SIN:

SECRETS

October 2018

LIES

December 2018

PROMISES

January 2019

TANGLED WEB:

TWISTED

May 2019

OBSESSED

July 2019

BOUND

August 2019

WEB OF DESIRE:

SPARK

Jan. 14, 2020

FLAME

February 25, 2020

ASHES

April 7, 2020

DANGEROUS WEB:

Prequel: "Danger's First Kiss"

DUSK

November 2020

DARK

January 2021

DAWN

February 2021

THE INFIDELITY SERIES:

BETRAYAL

Book #1

October 2015

CUNNING

Book #2

January 2016

DECEPTION

Book #3

May 2016

ENTRAPMENT

Book #4

September 2016

FIDELITY

Book #5

January 2017

THE CONSEQUENCES SERIES:

CONSEQUENCES

(Book #1)

August 2011

TRUTH

(Book #2)

October 2012

CONVICTED

(Book #3)

October 2013

REVEALED

(Book #4)

Previously titled: Behind His Eyes Convicted: The Missing
Years

June 2014

BEYOND THE CONSEQUENCES

(Book #5)

January 2015

RIPPLES **(Consequences stand-alone)**

October 2017

CONSEQUENCES COMPANION READS:

BEHIND HIS EYES-CONSEQUENCES

January 2014

BEHIND HIS EYES-TRUTH

March 2014

STAND ALONE MAFIA THRILLER:

PRICE OF HONOR

Available Now

STAND-ALONE YA ROMANTIC THRILLER:

ON THE EDGE

May 2022

TALES FROM THE DARK SIDE SERIES:

INSIDIOUS

(All books in this series are stand-alone erotic thrillers)

Released October 2014

ALEATHA'S LIGHTER ONES:

PLUS ONE

Stand-alone fun, sexy romance

May 2017

ANOTHER ONE

Stand-alone fun, sexy romance

May 2018

ONE NIGHT

Stand-alone, sexy contemporary romance

September 2017

A SECRET ONE

Prequel to MY ALWAYS ONE

April 2018

MY ALWAYS ONE

Stand-Alone, sexy friends to lovers contemporary romance

July 2021

*QUINTESSENTIALLY THE ONE

Stand-alone, small-town, second-chance, secret baby
contemporary romance

July 2022

*ONE KISS

Stand-alone, small-town, best friend's sister,
grump/sunshine contemporary romance.

July 2023

*ONE STRING

Second-chance, enemies-to-lovers, fake-date, little-sister's-
best-friend, forbidden, stand-alone contemporary romance

July 2024

*All Riverbend interconnected stories

$\sim$

INDULGENCE SERIES:

UNEXPECTED

August 2018

UNCONVENTIONAL

January 2018

UNFORGETTABLE

October 2019

UNDENIABLE

August 2020

ABOUT THE AUTHOR

Aleatha Romig is a New York Times, Wall Street Journal, and USA Today bestselling author who lives in Indiana, USA. She has raised three children with her high school sweetheart and husband of over thirty years. Before she became a full-time author, she worked days as a dental hygienist and spent her nights writing. Now, when she's not imagining mind-blowing twists and turns, she likes to spend her time with her family and friends. Her other pastimes include reading and creating heroes/anti-heroes who haunt your dreams!

Aleatha impresses with her versatility in writing. She released her first novel, CONSEQUENCES, in August of 2011. CONSEQUENCES, a dark romance, became a bestselling series with five novels and two compan-ions released from 2011 through 2015. The compelling and epic story of Anthony and Claire Rawlings has graced more than half a million e-readers. Her first stand-alone smart, sexy thriller INSIDIOUS was next. Then Aleatha released the five-novel INFIDELITY series, a romantic suspense saga, that took the reading world by storm, the final book landing on three of the top bestseller lists. She ventured into traditional publishing with Thomas and Mercer. Her books INTO

THE LIGHT and AWAY FROM THE DARK were published through this mystery/thriller publisher in 2016.

In the spring of 2017, Aleatha again ventured into a different genre with her first fun and sexy stand-alone romantic comedy with the USA Today bestseller PLUS ONE. She continued the "Ones" series with additional standalones, ONE NIGHT, ANOTHER ONE, MY ALWAYS ONE, and QUINTESSENTIALLY THE ONE. If you like fun, sexy, novellas that make your heart pound, try her "Indulgence series" with UNCONVEN-TIONAL. UNEXPECTED, UNFORGETTABLE, and UNDENIABLE.

In 2018 Aleatha returned to her dark romance roots with SPARROW WEBS. And continued with the mafia romance DEVIL'S DUET, and most recently her SINCLAIR DUET.

You may find all Aleatha's titles on her website.

Aleatha is a "Published Author's Network" member of the Romance Writers of America and PEN America. She is represented by SBR Media and Dani Sanchez with Wildfire Marketing.

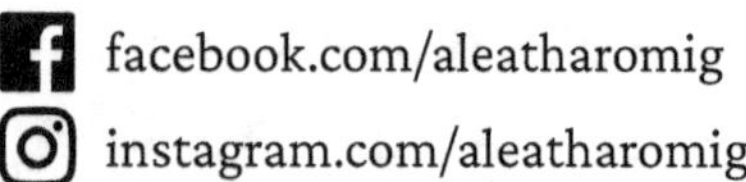